PENGUIN METRO READS
LOSING MY VIRGINITY AND OTHER DUMB IDEAS

Madhuri is the director of a creative production house that can do almost anything in the media from making brochures to producing TV shows. She is a complete media professional, having worked in all forms of the visual medium—TV, advertisements, documentaries. She has worked as a senior assistant director for film-makers like Subhash Ghai, Kaizad Gustad and Rohan Sippy, and music director Anu Malik.

Madhuri has an MA in Communication and Films from Jamia Millia Islamia—her thesis film, *Between Dualities*, won her the National Award for best documentary on women's issues in 1999. Besides media, she is passionate about travelling, yoga and reading. She is currently working on commercial film scripts and her next book. She is active on Twitter, Facebook and writes a blog (http://madhuribanerjee.blogspot.com/).

PRAISE FOR THE BOOK

'Two spiritual beliefs that work magically to live fully in every aspect of daily life . . . including losing your virginity . . . are . . . A. Everything is a choice B. Once the choice is made . . . let go . . .! More power to Madhuri for recognizing both in this book . . .!'

—Sushmita Sen

'Madhuri's spunky, vivid take on negotiating sexual space in today's insane social environment has won her several fans across gender divide!'

—Shobhaa Dé

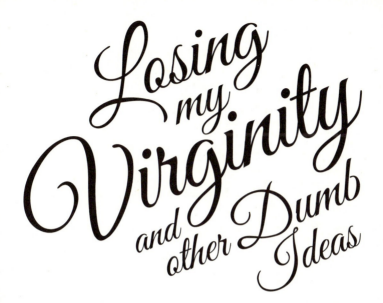

Losing my Virginity and other Dumb Ideas

MADHURI BANERJEE

Penguin
metro reads

PENGUIN METRO READS
Published by the Penguin Group
Penguin Books India Pvt. Ltd, 11 Community Centre, Panchsheel Park,
New Delhi 110 017, India
Penguin Group (USA) Inc., 375 Hudson Street, New York, New York 10014, USA
Penguin Group (Canada), 90 Eglinton Avenue East, Suite 700, Toronto,
Ontario, M4P 2Y3, Canada (a division of Pearson Penguin Canada Inc.)
Penguin Books Ltd, 80 Strand, London WC2R 0RL, England
Penguin Ireland, 25 St Stephen's Green, Dublin 2, Ireland
(a division of Penguin Books Ltd)
Penguin Group (Australia), 250 Camberwell Road, Camberwell,
Victoria 3124, Australia (a division of Pearson Australia Group Pty Ltd)
Penguin Group (NZ), 67 Apollo Drive, Rosedale, Auckland 0632,
New Zealand (a division of Pearson New Zealand Ltd)
Penguin Group (South Africa) (Pty) Ltd, 24 Sturdee Avenue, Rosebank,
Johannesburg 2196, South Africa

Penguin Books Ltd, Registered Offices: 80 Strand, London WC2R 0RL, England

First published in Penguin Metro Reads by Penguin Books India 2011

Copyright © Madhuri Banerjee 2011

All rights reserved

10 9 8 7 6 5 4 3

This is a work of fiction. Names, characters, places and incidents are either the product of the author's imagination or are used fictitiously and any resemblance to any actual person, living or dead, events or locales is entirely coincidental.

ISBN 9780143415121

Typeset in Bembo Roman by SŪRYA, New Delhi
Printed at Manipal Technologies Ltd, Manipal

This book is sold subject to the condition that it shall not, by way of trade or otherwise, be lent, resold, hired out, or otherwise circulated without the publisher's prior written consent in any form of binding or cover other than that in which it is published and without a similar condition including this condition being imposed on the subsequent purchaser and without limiting the rights under copyright reserved above, no part of this publication may be reproduced, stored in or introduced into a retrieval system, or transmitted in any form or by any means (electronic, mechanical, photocopying, recording or otherwise), without the prior written permission of both the copyright owner and the above-mentioned publisher of this book.

To all my girlfriends, far and near; over the years, you've inspired me with many stories. I admire all of you for your strength, willpower and humour. Each and every one of you is unique and special in my life. Without you, my life is bland and boring.

... As long as I know how to love, I know I'll stay alive

I will survive—Gloria Gaynor

One

I looked across at the other table and saw a couple kissing passionately.

'Great,' I thought, 'even girls half my age are getting laid!'

I went back to sipping my coffee and reading the papers.

1 April—my birthday—I had turned thirty.

The cruel irony of being born on April Fool's Day had haunted me all my life. But today, I really felt like a fool.

I was alone in my favourite coffee shop, Coffee De, which had these lovely, bright, mismatched chairs, sofas and cushions. And yes, it served the best coffee and no one disturbed me. I was there almost everyday, having my muffin and cappuccino, reading the papers, or a book, or just working on my laptop on some new assignment. The great thing about this café was that it was open from five in the morning to late at night. So I could be here from dawn to midnight, as I generally was most days of the week.

And today was my birthday. It was seven in the morning. I ran down here to have a pick-me-up before the calls would start coming and I would need to sound cheery. Only to find a couple already making out. Jesus! Couldn't I have some alone-time on my birthday at least?

Thoughts ran through my head. 'You're old now,' said the little voice, '. . . you're ALL alone. And everyone needs someone to love, someone to share their lives with, someone to grow old with, someone to . . . HAVE SEX with.'

Sex. Sex. Sex. It all came down to that. Here I was, thirty years old, and still a virgin.

Unmarried. Single. Alone. A virgin. A virgin. Yes, it resonated in my head. Nope, I couldn't get away from that word. For so long I had thought it was okay to be one. A virgin, I mean. I believed that I would find the right man who would cherish me and I would treasure him. The 'One Great Love' that would blind me into losing my virginity after we got married. But that was the spiel I had given myself for over fifteen years. And my mother, even though we never spoke about sex, because God knows that's just a taboo topic, would have been proud of me.

But today I felt old. And that theory didn't work.

On the brighter side though, I didn't look my age. I did have a few layers of fat around my belly, but nothing a good shirt couldn't camouflage. The extent of my exercising was a Jane Fonda DVD I had acquired a decade ago, which I would put on and jump around to for forty-five minutes every week. I had shoulder length, black hair and olive skin. And I had beautiful eyes. They came from my grandmother. It was a lovely shade of grey, and because of them people could never figure out if I was an Indian or a South American. But despite my hair, skin and eyes, I had never had a real date in my life. So here's the thing, men elude me. I've read all the books about men and how to get a date but I've never really had a steady boyfriend. After the first five minutes I feel the man is really stupid, extremely juvenile or highly pretentious. I have an IQ that's, mildly putting it, above average. It might have given me the title of 'over achiever' in school, but never gave me a boyfriend. Frankly, I did not think I even needed one. I was too busy achieving things in life to have a man ruin it.

I played the piano, I learnt animation and I studied modern art for fun in my spare time. I knew seven different languages, which brings me to what I do. I'm a freelance interpreter. What that actually means is that I translate languages for people, for example from French to Hindi, or Spanish to English, or

Russian to French. The embassies call me to help them translate important documents from their native language to ours, to 'Indianize' it. Or when they hold a conference, I am the one the Indians would hear on their headphones translating a particular speaker's speech. Or when delegates from different countries come, I help translate talks between dignitaries. Like when Lalu Prasad Yadav had to meet the railway minister of Russia, I was called to help translate their conversation. It was another matter that I could barely understand what Mr Yadav was saying and probably translated what *I thought* he should have said.

Most times, I'm a guide for important delegates' wives or families. I love my job even though it can become very erratic. It pays well and I get to meet some interesting people from around the globe. And it helps that I live in the melting pot of India, Mumbai.

My parents currently live in Bangalore. My dad's in the foreign service and we've moved around a lot. That's why I know seven languages, because of the different countries I grew up in. Finally, when I was old enough to say I'm done with moving, I left them in Moscow and moved to Mumbai.

It was strange at first, trying to find a footing in this city. Mumbai was definitely a harder place to be in than Russia, America or France put together. But it gave me so much more than all the other countries. And that's why I decided to stay here and make it my home eight years ago.

I stay in a rented, one-bedroom apartment in Bandra. It's grossly overpriced and there's no view, but I completely love it. I've done it the way I see art through the ages, from Renaissance to Cubism, with colours and images jumping out from every corner. Something like this café. And that's why I was sitting here to collect my thoughts on my birthday; it felt like an extension of home.

Which is why I was irritated that a couple of teenagers had decided to meet here before going off to college and were sucking on each other's pimples.

The topic of my virginity came back again. I had always been a social recluse. I didn't have many friends and the only people I spoke to, outside my close circle, were clients. I always had a hard time opening up to strangers. I seldom found a deep connection with anyone and that is why I was still to lose my virginity. And if that wasn't enough reason, I was mortified about getting pregnant or ending up with a life threatening disease. Protection wasn't always hundred per cent foolproof and I wasn't willing to take any chances!

But today I felt it was Time. The time had come to change. I could feel a wave of a revolution coming over me. Sex and relationships could be two different things. I should forget about understanding men and just have sex with them. That's what my head was saying. Who said age doesn't play with one's hormones? Today, mine were raging like the blazing dry lands in Wisconsin.

The phone rang. It was my best friend Aditi.

'Happy April Fool's Day, babe. What you doing?'

Aditi had been my friend for the last eight years. She was the first friend I had in Mumbai. And it was the most awesome meeting ever. I had taken the First Lady of France to see a film shoot and help her interpret Hindi and Bollywood better. Aditi was the assistant director running around trying to get a particular hat for the lead actress. While the director was screaming his head off, she noticed the First Lady's hat and quickly came over and asked her to take it off and hand it to her. I was appalled and didn't know how to translate this galling request.

But Aditi said very firmly, 'I don't care who you are, but I'm part of a mega-crore industry and will lose my job if I don't get that hat now!'

So the First Lady took it off (after I translated what Aditi had said, a toned down version, of course) and gave it to her. We got an umbrella to shield us from the sun, and Aditi returned the hat after the shot. Later, Aditi took us around the set and introduced us to the Superstar of Bollywood. The First Lady said she had never had so much fun and Aditi and I exchanged numbers and have been friends ever since.

'Having coffee,' I replied to her blandly.

'Intravenously?'

'No, re! At CD's. Sipping the usual strong cappuccino,' I said.

'What plans for today? Anyone plan a surprise thirtieth birthday party for you?' she mocked knowing that I had very few friends.

'Nothing much. No delegates in April. So I'm broke.'

'You poor thing. That is a terrible April Fool's joke that God is playing on you! So let me treat you tonight. What say?' Aditi asked.

'Okay.' I replied, and then as an afterthought, 'I also have some news!' I said enthusiastically. 'I have finally made up my mind about the "problem" I have had.'

'What problem?' Aditi asked.

'My virginity,' I whispered, cupping the mobile phone so no one would hear me.

'Ah, that problem! If you remember, I've been telling you since the last century that you should do something about that,' she said laughing at her own joke.

'I'm serious. Really, I need help.'

'Okay, we should not waste any more time then. I mean, it's already been three decades!' And she laughed again while I cringed. 'Let's make it happen tonight. Let's de-virginize you! See you at the bar at 8, okay?' she said authoritatively and hung up.

I smiled. I could always count on Adu.

I hung up the phone with supreme confidence. It was going to happen tonight. And then I could shake this monkey off my back and get on with my life. I planned to have a great thirtieth birthday.

Two

I went back home from the coffee shop with a happy heart. I had woken up that morning feeling old, fat and very alone. Now I had a plan. I entered my one bedroom apartment and saw that there were books all over the place. It was generally a very neat and tidy place, thanks to my maid, who I noticed had not yet arrived. I surveyed the place. My bookshelf was in a mess and my cushions were all over the floor. The hall, or the living room, was spacious with wooden flooring. Yes, that was where the extra three grand a month from my rent was going, but I loved the flooring. I had a large, white sofa against one wall that I had got painted Prussian blue, a bookshelf against another and bright cushions from Fab India all over the place. There was a cuckoo clock that I had kept even though it had gone dead from too much cuckooing and now only showed the time. The walls were decked with several framed paintings of artists that I loved. One wall had ten miniatures of Salvador Dali's works. And another, Monet's lilies from across his lifespan. My bed was large with bright sheets and mismatched pillows that had faded over the years. A bright red chair rested against the window where I sat and looked outside at the row of shops downstairs. This was my home. And I loved it. And right now, it was a mess. Where was my maid?

Just then the doorbell rang and I went to answer it muttering to myself, please let it be her, I don't want to clean today. Not that I would have cleaned any other day because I'm just not into cleaning. I don't know how people love to keep scrubbing away and tidying up when there are so many far more important things to do. It wasn't the maid. It was a large bouquet of flowers from the only man in my life. The only man who had been there for the last thirty years. My dad. I called him up immediately. He was out on his morning jog. I admired the old man for his enthusiasm for sports. If I had his genes, I would have been a model instead of working so hard at being an intellectual.

'Pops! What's happening?' I asked.

'Koko. Happy birthday!' he said, panting while breaking into a fast walk rather than stop his exercise totally.

'Thanks for the flowers. They're gorgeous!' I looked at them and they really were gorgeous. I loved flowers. I thought they brightened up the place. But I would never buy any myself because, for me, they were a waste of money. And also I would have to trim them, put them in a vase, maintain them. I didn't have the patience for all that domesticity.

'I'm glad you like them. I hope they gave thirty lilies to signify your age? And not less than that?' he checked. He was always checking things. So what if they had not. How did it matter? But to him, it did and he would call up and reprimand people and tell the entire florist service to be better Indians!

'Yes, they have, Pops,' I said exasperatedly and then asked, 'Where's Mom?'

'Oh, she decided to skip the walk today. Her back was hurting from sleeping in a wrong posture last night,' he answered. I had inherited my mother's excuses. She was always pretending to fall ill to get out of exercising and, as a result, had wide hips that she was forever complaining about. It was a vicious cycle that she had not got out of for the last twenty-five years.

'Okay. Anyway, bye Dad. Will call Mom now,' I said, since there was never anything much I could share with my father except my love.

'Koko! Remember that you're thirty now,' he started his lecture. 'And it's time you decided what you want to do with your life. Remember, it's the last year to sit for the services. So think about it!' My father had always wanted me to sit for the services because there was 'nothing better than serving the country' as he put it. He still hadn't realized that I had left them eight years ago and had found a career I liked. He just thought it was a hobby and I would eventually become, like him, a 'servant' for the government.

I hung up just as the bell rang again. It was my maid. Before I could reprimand her for being late I saw that she had got me a present.

'What's this?' I asked, taking the box from her hand.

'For your birthday,' she said, as she went to keep her polythene bag of a purse in the kitchen and start cleaning my house.

'You know, I was going to scream at you for being late,' I told her and then asked, 'Can I open it now?'

'If you wish.' Then she said as an afterthought, 'You know, you've never screamed at me in the last eight years I've been working for you!'

That was true. I just couldn't. She did not turn up a number of days and was late most of the time, but she kept my house spotlessly clean, looked after me when I was sick or down with a cold and was completely trustworthy with all my belongings.

I opened the present. It was a candle from Mount Mary church. It was a lovely thought. 'I prayed for you this morning that you would find a good husband. And you have to light this candle at home to make the wish come true.' She was in my room, putting a new pillow cover on my pillow. I went over and hugged her. 'Thank you,' I said. She smiled.

Then she went back to business and I got a few phone calls from some friends from the animation class and some from a few clients who remembered. I didn't have too many friends, unlike Aditi, who was always the toast of the town. I kept mostly to myself with my nose buried in some book and with 'Wi-fi' entering my life and apartment, the Internet would keep me busy for many hours on some new online course. I was a geek.

I looked around my apartment and realized that even my TV was broken and I hadn't got it fixed. I did not need to.

I went into the kitchen to make myself some tea. I was out of tea. So I thought I would make myself some coffee. I was out of coffee. I shouted out to my maid, 'Martha, where is the tea and coffee?' I asked.

'Top shelf, above washing machine,' she replied.

Now why would she keep it there, I thought.

She entered the kitchen and explained as if she had read my mind, 'I cleaned the whole kitchen yesterday. It was quite a mess from when you last tried to cook on Friday.'

'I was hungry. I made daal,' I replied.

'Oh, that's what it was on the ceiling!' she mocked. 'And for future reference, the tea is on the shelf next to the stove since you have a lot of chai and the coffee is next to your coffee machine.'

'Yes, but I never use it.'

'Because you're too lazy to learn. And I make it for you.' Oh, she knew me so well.

Martha was always right. I didn't know how to cook. Of all the things I had learnt in my life, cooking was not one of them. I hated cooking. I saw it as a part of being domestic, which I was not. My parents had often wondered how I would manage alone in Mumbai seeing that I didn't cook, clean, shop for the house and barely knew some groceries and chemists' numbers. But I told them the trick in running a successful house was to have a great manager. What Mom was to Dad, Martha was to me. My domestic manager. Which reminded me that I needed to call Mom. I dialled her number as I went in to my clean bedroom that smelt like lavender.

'Many happy returns of the day, darling,' said my mom on the other end.

'Thank you, Ma,' I replied, sitting on the bright blue couch.

'Tell me, what's new?' she asked, stereotypically, hoping I would say there is a man in my life and give her hope that she might have grandchildren one day.

'I've started a new diet with my new dietician,' I said, full of excitement that was immediately punctured by my mother heaving a long sigh and saying, 'Why?'

'Because Mom,' I said slowly as if I was trying to explain Quantum Physics to a five-year-old, 'I need to be on a diet! I want to lose some weight. My jeans are not fitting me anymore. I've put on three kilos.'

'Kaveri,' my mother said sternly. She had named me Kaveri and decided that all short forms were an affront to the beauty of the name, and hence would not call me anything but that. 'All you need to do is go for a walk once in a while and stop eating muffins. You'll automatically lose weight. I don't know why you spend so much money on all these people. You've been to some seven dieticians now.'

'Five,' I immediately corrected her. She was right as usual, but I didn't want to let on and give her the power to be right. 'But I need someone who can understand my lifestyle and yet give me a balanced and healthy diet.'

'What healthy?' my mom argued. 'Eat an apple when hungry. There. Now give me ten thousand rupees for that information since you're spending that much on someone telling you the same thing!'

I had actually spent tens of thousands of rupees on different slimming centres and dieticians to curb the expanding waist that I had inherited from my mother. But I would always fall off the bandwagon when I became bored and would go off to have muffins at Coffee De. That made me feel better, but it put all the weight back on.

'I have to go, Ma. I'll talk to you later.'

'You have a lovely day and remember I wish that you get married this year.'

'Great. That at least gives me 365 days to find a man,' I said cheekily and hung up.

But I had decided, marriage or no marriage, tonight at least, I would get a man!

Three

Aditi and I generally met at the same bar whenever we needed a drink. It was called 'Float My Boat' and it had all these little boats as tables and everything nautical attached to it. But the reason why we liked this place wasn't the ambience, which was strictly okay; it was because of the amazing cocktails the bartender could make for an extremely reasonable price. We never got bored of trying as many as we could till we were buzzed enough to take a cab back home.

On my birthday, the bartender sent us a complimentary long, ice filled, pink drink. We toasted.

'Cheers!' I said.

'To your resolve,' Aditi replied.

Aditi was a conventionally good looking woman. She had long brown hair, a slim figure and dark eyes. She could have passed off as a model if it hadn't been for her very bad skin—she had pockmarks left from a severe case of chicken pox in childhood that no amount of make-up could conceal.

We looked around and saw a few men at the bar and a couple sitting at a table. The men didn't look interesting at all. They were the corporate types in plain blue shirts of various shades and grey trousers. A few even had laptop bags on the floor.

'Well we can't start with anyone here,' I said breaking the silence.

'Clearly not!' she agreed. 'What we need is a list of things that you do *not* want in a man,' she said. I looked at her questioningly while she continued. 'See everyone is going to say sense of humour and rich. But what you need to know is that every man does have a sense of humour and most men can fend for themselves at our age. So what is it exactly that you do not want and then eliminate those types of men. Otherwise we'll end up like them,' she said and pointed to the couple at the table that had, already bored with each other, started text messaging other people.

I nodded to the group at the bar, '*That* for starters,' I said with a grin.

'No! Please!' She stretched her words for effect. 'No one wants that for starters. Maybe for dessert . . .' she punned.

'You know what I mean. I'm not like you. I can't do with just anybody,' I laughed.

Aditi had a history. She had slept with some forty-two men and then lost count. She believed that men were only supposed to be used. They were good for only one thing and so she wanted to use that thing well.

'Hey!' she exclaimed. 'That hurts!'

'You know what I mean. I didn't mean it in a bad way. I admire you for it. That's why I've come to you for help.'

I didn't really admire Aditi for all the men she had slept with. I believed that there needed to be a better way to vent your day's frustration than to pick up just any guy you knew. I mean, go to the gym, or get a massage or something. But Aditi had a different viewpoint. She believed that one day she would get married, and then she would be faithful to her husband forever. That meant at least thirty to forty years of being with only one man. So she thought she might as well have as many before she hooked up with the one. But by the looks of it, Aditi wasn't planning to get married till she was fifty.

My philosophy was different. I didn't believe in infatuation. Infatuation, guised as love, made people lose focus. There are so many things one needs to achieve and one has got very little time to do so before old age creeps in.

When you get involved with a man, half of your life is wasted in waiting for his call, then asking him to propose, then waiting for him to come home, and then wishing he was away. By the time you realize that love and men make you weak, you want to be single again, but by then you're already in your early forties and have done nothing to show for in your life.

For me, I had to be married to have sex. And marriage meant finding the One Great Love. I had always assumed that I would get into an arranged marriage, then fall in love with my husband and then be with him for the rest of my life. No infatuation involved! And in the meantime, be as much as I can be, and do as much as I can do. And even though Aditi had found the idea boring, she had admired me for my resolve.

All until now.

My thirtieth birthday. I was not married. I didn't have a guy whom I loved or was even remotely interested in, and all the suitors my parents had set me up with didn't match up to the definition of a man, much less the One Great Love. I was slowly beginning to see myself as Mrs Haversham from a Dickens novel, who was alone and senile.

I knew that Aditi was secretly very happy that I was leaning towards her philosophy, albeit a little late in the day.

'Oh, hot guy, three o' clock, entered,' she said all of a sudden. And indeed there was a nice, clean shaven man in light blue jeans and a white shirt who had just walked into the bar. And right behind him was his friend, a nerdy guy in glasses, short and very unassuming. I immediately picked 'the nerd'. He seemed as unsure as I was. Maybe we would have a conversation and be friends before we venture down the dark alley . . .

However, Aditi had a different plan. 'Go ask that white shirt guy out,' she prodded me.

'Are you crazy? He's way out of my league!' I screamed incredulously.

'If you don't aim for the stars, you'll always remain a virgin,' Aditi screamed back.

'That doesn't even make sense Adu,' I said, laughing. 'And besides, I think I would be better off with the nerd.'

'The ugly boy there?' she asked, shrugging her shoulders. I nodded. 'Damn, girl, he's a three pinter!' Three pinter, of course, means you would need to be down with 3 pints of beer and buzzed in order to like the guy.

'I see potential,' I added my two bits confidently.

'Okay, then go ahead. Make your move!' She encouraged me as if she had just given me permission to marry her dog.

At precisely that moment, my courage deserted me.

I looked pleadingly at Aditi, 'As you might have noticed over the past eight years that we have known each other, I don't have a move!'

'Fine, I'll show you.' She got up, straightened out her dress, picked up her clutch purse and walked to the bar, right next to where the boys were standing. Then she leaned over ever so slightly to call for the bartender while giving the men a glimpse of her cleavage. I watched the Master Flirt in action with a smile on my lips. I had seen this before, but never for a date for me.

'Hi,' she said to the bartender who knew us really well and was aware of her tactics. 'It's my friend's birthday today and I want to give her something special. Could you please see if there is anything back there that could surprise her?' The bartender nodded. 'And I'll have a whisky and soda please!'

This time, the bartender raised his eyebrow. Adu gave him one of her famous stares. Then she turned towards the boy and said, 'Nice shirt.' And walked away.

Back at the table, amply swaying her hips and crossing her legs when she sat down for the boys to see her long legs, she said, 'Five minutes, and they'll be here.'

And they were. With the two drinks that she'd ordered. Aditi knew men as if she had studied the science.

'Happy birthday!' said the nerd holding out a drink for me. Aditi waved them to sit and the white shirt sat next to her putting her whisky in front of her.

'That's pretty hard liquor for a lady,' he said.

'I'm celebrating and need a buzz faster than these colourful drinks are giving me,' she said flirtatiously.

They introduced themselves and started telling us about their professions. It turned out that the nerd was from IIT. He was a computer code programmer or something like that. He said he loved retro music and kept giving me information about the bands as each song played through the evening. Aditi, meanwhile, and as expected, had hit it off with the white shirt. He was an RJ on a popular radio channel and was telling her about all the celebrities he had interviewed. They had a lot in common. I could see him as another potential number on her list.

As for me, I didn't feel the chemistry. The man was a bore. I felt I would just explode if I heard another fact about Duran Duran or Wham. And my morals came flooding back. I thought I would have been ready to give my virginity to just anybody. But that little voice in my head said that if I had waited this long, I could afford to wait a little longer.

When the nerd tried to put his arm around me, I moved away slightly and picked up my drink and looked in the other direction. But men never give up, so he tried again. This time, I was clear in my communication, 'Look, I can't be touched. You see, I have a heat rash all over my body and my skin is extremely sensitive right now.' From there the conversation took a downturn. Not that it was going anywhere anyway. All I wanted to do was get out of that place. I could see Aditi was having a good time. So I excused myself and told her to join me in the ladies room.

'What's up with you?' she asked, as soon as we got in.

'Adu, I've got a headache from all that drinking,' I lied. 'And that guy has a bad case of body odour. I'm just going to go home. But you chill.'

'No, no, I'll come home with you. It's your birthday,' she insisted.

'No, seriously. I'm going to go home and sleep immediately.

What's the point of you coming with me then? We'll catch up later this week.'

'What about the mission?' she asked with a twinkle in her eye.

'Let's work on that again soon, huh?' I assured her with a smile.

'Are you sure?' she asked apprehensively.

'Yah. Now go have fun. Call me later!' I walked out towards the front door and she went back to the bar.

As I walked back home, I realized that maybe giving up one's philosophy wasn't that easy. I was a traditional girl living in a modern system. I should have been proud of myself for sticking to my beliefs. I had seen how much trouble a man could bring to a woman's life. Women had been trying to understand the opposite sex while pouring over girly magazines, having long discussions with each other in office loos, writing to agony aunts in magazine columns and even Googling on the subject—all the while pumping each other's egos about the fact that they were far better and deserved much more. Why would I want to be like them now? I had always been unique and proud.

But I knew the answer to that one already. Because no matter how much you achieved in life, a day would come when you would feel all alone in this world. And today was just that day for me.

Four

The next morning my dietician reprimanded me for having alcohol, muffins and coffee. 'Coffee?' I asked, and was told that it was a terrible addiction and if I wanted to lose any weight and make progress, I would have to stick to green tea. After taking my measurements and other indicators establishing that I was very fat, the dietician gave me a strict exercise schedule and a near starvation diet that I had to adhere to before reporting back in two weeks' time.

I've always had a love–hate relationship with my body. I've tried to love it enough to look like the model of a Cosmo cover, but ended up hating that it didn't adhere to any of my diets or workout regimes. But I hadn't given up yet. I still believed that if I needed to lose my virginity, I might need to lose my weight first.

My mother's words came back to me. I had been to five dieticians so far. From eating every two hours to having soy milk when I was hungry to only drinking lime water through the day and, the worst, to having juice made from vegetables thrown in a blender that would make my skin glow, I had tried it all. And no matter how hard I tried to hold up a diet, at the end of a gruelling week of starvation and workout, I would fall back on my wayward eating habits by taking a trip down to Coffee De.

Then, as I walked back home after my appointment, I realized that if I walked all over Bandra everyday, I would get forty-five minutes of exercise and would save money from travelling in an auto.

That little voice spoke again and I knew that wouldn't happen for too long since most of my 'resolves' were broken in a few days. I recognized that the decisions I made myself were trashed as soon as I understood another viewpoint. I had lived life on the bench most of the time and I was happy about it.

Suddenly, my phone rang. It was the Italian Embassy. I was told they wanted me to do some work for them and I had to go to their office immediately. I took an appointment to reach in about an hour's time so that I could go home, change and make it there before they closed for lunch.

Back at home I scavenged for my grey business suit, the one I always wore for interviews and the one that I noticed had now faded at the back. I pulled it out, rejected it, and for the next twenty minutes I took out every piece of clothing from my wardrobe to find the appropriate outfit to make a good impression.

I have always been indecisive about clothes. Most of the time I was trying to hide my ungainly hips, so everything was oversized in my closet except for a few nice things that Aditi had picked out for me.

I somehow fitted myself into a full sleeved, white shirt and black trousers and added small pearl earrings to complete the no-nonsense look. Then I marched right out and caught an autorickshaw. Half way to the embassy, I realized that the buttons on my white shirt were popping open and there was no time to go back and change! I desperately needed this assignment since I had no other way to pay my rent. So I bought a bunch of safety pins from a lady at one of the traffic signals and tried to put a few on my blouse but it ended up looking all lopsided while the driver had a field day watching me in his rearview mirror. When I got to the embassy, it had closed for lunch but I was shown into a room where there were some people waiting for me. I was sure it would be another brochure translating assignment and wanted to take their work and leave quickly.

'Kaveri, please come in,' said the man I generally interact with at the embassy. He was a typical, aged Italian—wrinkled skin, blue eyes, and a smile that must have made hearts melt in the old days.

I went and sat down and said yes to a cup of coffee. I loved the lavazza they served and, being the caffeine addict I was, I never missed an opportunity to have several cups while I was there.

'Kaveri, these are the new documents that have just come from the High Commissioner. It's a new brochure they plan on printing in Hindi to encourage more Hindi-speaking people to travel to Italy. Can you please translate them?'

'Sure,' I said. 'But why didn't you just have it couriered to me?'

He looked thoughtful for a moment and then gave the most genuine answer, 'I forgot!' Then he smiled and my heart melted. Of course I would do it! The man still had enough charm in him to persuade women like me!

When I got home I quickly got to work on the project. I was one of those people who didn't wait till the last minute to finish things. I wanted to be ready well before. That's why I always met deadlines and I was always called back by the embassies. They knew that what a normal interpreter would take two weeks to deliver, I would finish in three days.

But just when I got to understand the subject, random thoughts flooded my head.

I realized that my resolve to lose my morals was coming from a feeling of deep dissatisfaction in my life. Maybe if I wasn't pursuing all those interests and making deadlines, I would have been with a man. Maybe my idea of love and arranged marriage was all wrong. I had presumed that there would be a sign somewhere telling me when I should fall in love and when to get married.

But there had been no sign.

So maybe, there would never be a sign.

And it was that thought, right there, that just scared me. I'd waited my whole life for something that was never going to show up. Maybe I wasn't one of those people who deserved love, or maybe Aditi had it right all along.

But that couldn't be correct. Because I've seen Aditi completely messed up after dumping men. No matter how much she says she has the power, a part of her *has* emotionally died. And one night when she became completely drunk, to the point of passing out, she blurted out that it was becoming harder to find 'good' men.

Work had always been worship. I couldn't stand being dependent on anyone. Maybe my strong sense of economic security scared men off, because I wasn't the type who would want a *man* to look after me. I would want a man as an intellectual partner. So I couldn't do the whole serve coffee thing in arranged situations and was a flop with my parents in the marriage department. But I still believed someone would find me. I didn't have to go look.

These thoughts were making my head hurt. They were making me confused.

I had never been the romantic type. But I wasn't completely against the idea. So was I repelling the men? Was I just being a prig when I met a new man and asked him about his favourite opera?

I didn't have the answers. And the questions kept coming.

For the first time, I wondered, Who am I?

Five

Aditi and I didn't meet till two weeks later. Her job was such that if she got stuck in a shoot, she would have to finish the schedule before she could even breathe again. She had often told me that it was a thankless, harrowing job with little pay, but I knew she loved it because she was just that bit closer to the film stars, which was like a six-degree separation from fame itself. I had a feeling that Aditi wanted to be in front of the camera someday but she had never had the chance. So she wanted to be as close to it as possible.

We were at the See Vu bakery shop for a quick snack when Aditi started making a list. Her list of men that she thought I could go out with. Aditi was a few years older than me and so she thought she knew all about men. She had been giving me advice for the past eight years. But I had seen her have many heartbreaks as well. They would crush her spirit for a long time and maybe that was the reason for her promiscuity. So I had decided that I wouldn't get involved with a man. I didn't need the heartbreak, or the advice. Thinking these lofty, but foolish, thoughts I had reached the ripe old age of thirty and finally I was ready for both.

'Darling,' she started sincerely, 'I can't believe you've never been on a real date. I mean, I've been on hundreds and it's really very simple.' She seemed so proud of being wanton. Instead of berating her for lack of better judgment, I felt morose. I envied her sense of gay abandon.

Even though I had never been with a man, I realized that if I had, it would have been disastrous. With my confused, convent educated upbringing, I would feel Jesus Christ was glaring down at me every time I kissed a man. When my Hindu upbringing kicked in, I would be Sita who needed only to be with her Ram. And when I became an atheist, instead of the gods, I would feel the men were judging me.

'That's all very well for you. But honestly, going by my expectations, I think I'll remain a virgin till I get married,' I proclaimed, stuffing a lemon tart down my throat.

'By the way,' she said as an afterthought, completely ignoring my statement, 'what were you doing when you were in all those countries? Reading books?'

'I was too young . . . and I was with my parents!' I swallowed and continued, 'Besides, I had Dad's escorts wherever I went, which kind of threatened the boys, and you could not blame them, they were only sixteen. But hello! You're not listening! I'm saying this is not going to work so let's just go shopping instead, huh?'

'Shut up. Now tell me what are the things you want in a man,' she asked.

'Oh, you know, the usual: good looks, extreme intelligence, well read, loves art, understands . . .' I started on my list.

Aditi cut me short, 'Boring! Boring! Boring! Are you looking for someone our age or your dad's friend who is a seventy-year-old professor? Let's do this again. I'll make the list this time. First of all, he has to be good in bed, handsome, rich . . .'

I was about to protest when the bearer came over and smiled down at Aditi, asking what more could he bring her, and she flirted back for a bit. Despite her bad skin, she always had an effect on men. I guess that's why all forty-two of them looked beyond her face and down to her cleavage, which, I might also add, was fabulous.

Plus Aditi always had plans. She never sat around wallowing in self-pity, like I did. I suppose, because of her cheerful attitude, her count was as high as it was and mine zero.

'First of all,' she started, after the waiter had left, 'we need to get your hair straightened or coloured or something that makes it less blah.'

'Thanks,' I added sarcastically. I was now stuffing my face with jam droplets that were in the flavours of raspberry and blueberry mini pastries. Pure heaven! She continued pointing her pen at me, 'Nobody likes to screw a frizzy-haired chick. A new hairstyle is what you need. Then we need to get a better wardrobe. Something more revealing. All these kurtas make you look too intellectual.' Here, she looked me up and down and frowned disdainfully at my attire.

'But I am!' I protested. I thought I had done okay with a long, pink kurta and jeans and some lovely accessories, but Aditi didn't seem to approve.

'Yes, honey, but men don't see intellectual. They see cleavage! Men need something for their imagination. And you becoming a borderline nun doesn't help.'

The stress was making me reach for another chocolate tart and I silently nodded my head, going along with the idea until a thought struck me, 'How much is this going to cost? It seems like my bank balance is depleting already. Don't you remember I was broke a few weeks ago? I thought we could just buy a nice black dress and I could laid!'

'You can't get something if you don't sacrifice something in return,' Aditi said authoritatively, as if she was a guru giving advice to a disciple.

'Why can't I just work on my personality? It's a lot cheaper and I have heard that men really dig women with a sense of humour. Can't I learn some new jokes or something? Here's one,' I immediately started before she could butt in, 'What is the thinnest book in the world?' I waited for the standard two seconds to reply, 'What Men Know About Women!' And I grinned at my own stupid joke.

Aditi looked at me as if I was an alien. 'Ya. That went very far, didn't it? Leave this to me. And don't be cheap. You won't regret it . . . And please stop eating these calorific things! Men don't like fat women.'

'You're no fun,' I grumbled while picking up my bag and following Aditi out of the bakery.

So started my Mission. Mission De-virginization.

We left the patisserie and headed to the parlour to get a new look.

At the parlour, we flipped through some magazines and argued on what would look good on me. Then we argued with the stylist on what he should do. Then we argued about how much it would cost, then we argued some more on whether we should order lunch since this was going to take the entire day. Mostly it was Aditi arguing with herself on what would look good on me while I kept shut and went along with whatever she said. By the end of it, her arguing had given me a headache.

But being a determined woman, I was ready to go the whole hog with this project and soon enough, I was in the zone of washing, drying, ironing, colouring, washing, and it went on.

Aditi got a phone call from her boyfriend, or whom she called the 'flavour of the month'. She went off to chat with him while I sat and flipped through some more magazines in an awkward, 'don't move your head' position. A woman came and sat next to me. Just then my cell phone fell on the floor and very sheepishly I requested her, 'Please can you pick up my cell phone. I don't think I'm allowed to move with this cardboard stuck to my hair.'

She smiled and picked it up.

'Thanks,' I said.

'Is this your first time?'

I looked at her strangely.

'Getting your hair done, I mean?' she said, clarifying.

'Oh yes!' I beamed, ready to give her the dirty details. 'I've had straight but frizzy hair all my life. I guess I've never maintained it too well. All those split ends and what not,' I smiled and continued, 'I just wanted a change. Actually my friend thought I needed a change since it was getting me nowhere in life!'

The woman laughed, 'I know what you mean. I got my hair straightened some four times before I realized I was just happy with myself and didn't care about the men.'

How did she know it was about a man? But then I thought she had entered into a personal space and my shyness took over. I wasn't too comfortable talking to or about men. So I nodded but kept quiet and went back to flipping through my magazine. I also wasn't one of those people who could chat up with anyone and everyone. If it was for work, my other, 'business', personality came out and I could go on, but on a personal level, I was a timid sheep.

The lady caught on. 'I'm sorry. I didn't mean to offend you. I think you'll look lovely. If a change is what you need, then by all means go for it. But remember, no man is ever worth it.'

She dipped into her purse and took out her card and reached over to give it to me. 'Here's my card. Call me if you want to show me your new look!' Then she left, joining her friend who had just finished a pedicure.

I looked at the card. It said:

Deepa M.

TV & Film Director.

I had been sitting next to a film director and I didn't even know it! What I also didn't know then was that this card was going to save my life when I least expected it.

Before I had a chance to think over the whole thing, Aditi came back. 'Loser!' she almost barked on her phone and then plonked herself on the seat next to mine.

'What happened?' I asked, deciding not to tell her about my encounter and instead focusing on her. In any case, Aditi was so self-obsessed that if the topic didn't go back to her in someway, she would run out of conversation.

'I had to dump this guy,' she said nonchalantly. 'And he was being such a pain and a cling on—like most men are. I mean, why can't they ever get a hint?'

'Why did you dump him?' I asked.

'Because a way to a woman's heart is directly proportional to a man's . . .'

'Stop!' I put my hands over my ears and shook my head in disgust. Trust Aditi to have dumped a man for the 'smallest' of reasons. For me, dumping was out of the question. I believed I would fall in love just once and marry him, not necessarily in that order.

Aditi was a 'man magnate', attracting men within the first five minutes. I needed to have an intellectual conversation with a man. I needed him to enlighten me, inspire me, teach me! He needed to be interested in learning, growing, and have a thirst for knowledge in art and travel. All Aditi wanted was a six pack. And that's why she could have as many men as she wanted, whereas I, being picky and choosy, had none.

After four and a half hours of sitting to get my hair done, I finally swivelled around in my chair to look at the new me. I did look different. Lighter. Shinier. Glossier. Broke-er!

It had also made me a pauper.

Aditi loved it. She thought it was a glam look that would make film stars envious. Everything for her was comparable with films. She decided to take me shopping, but I said I had a huge crick in my shoulder from sitting still in a chair for hours and was going home. In any case, I had blown way too much money in one month to go shopping. So I went home and stood in front of the mirror and looked at myself for a long time. I started liking the new look. I felt confident. Thinner even! Maybe this wasn't such a bad idea. I was ready to go out and meet some new men! The new me was going to wow them. All I had to do was change my philosophy and I would be de-virginized. The mission was on its way!

Six

<u>Date No. 1</u>

It is said that when you ask the Universe for something, you generally get it. But you've got to be careful about the details, because most of the time, it can just belt out any old trash. So even though my heart said, 'give men a shot', most of the men that came my way made me think, 'just shoot him'!

For example, there was this banquet manager at a posh hotel whom I used to meet quite often, since most of our international conferences were held there. He would discuss the arrangements of food, beverage, layout of chairs and stage with me. Not once did he try to ask me to have lunch with him. Then, just as I told the Universe I was ready, he asked me out to lunch. We were going through the layout when he casually dropped it, 'Do you want to continue this over lunch?' And I said, 'Okay,' even more casually. But honestly, I was quite excited! I noticed him a little better. Brown eyes, rugged jawline, tall, bespectacled, bony fingers, and a very impish smile. All in all—a cute package! I could see myself liking him. We had, in fact, shared a lot of conferences together and we knew what we both thought about the flower arrangement and menus. See, I needed to feel that I had something in common with a guy. Otherwise I could never go out with him. I had to believe that somewhere we connected, even if it was over something small.

So we went to the coffee shop, where we had a lovely lunch and went through the plans for the conference. After that, he asked me out for a drink, but I said I would be too busy with work over the next couple of days. Then I hinted that I was always free for breakfast. He caught on and asked what time would I be here in the mornings. I said eight because the conference would start by ten. So he said he would see me the next day for breakfast at eight. I believed that my romance had begun. Before I could call Aditi and tell her she need not bother about finding a man for me, I figured that I should go on at least one date first.

When I reached the lobby the next day, he was nowhere to be found. So I called him up in his room.

'Hello,' he spoke in a sleepy voice. I could make out that he had not woken up.

'Hi. Did I wake you up?' I asked tentatively, not knowing what to say.

'Ya. I'm so sorry. Let's catch up tomorrow, okay?'

'Okay,' I said, a bit disappointed, and hung up. If he had *really* been interested, he would have been here. I didn't want to be a Betty in someone's life. I wanted to be a Veronica. So I went off grumpily to the conference room, and just as I got into the lift, I saw him. He was there holding a daisy.

'A rose is too corny,' he said, as he gave me the flower. I smiled and walked with him to an empty banquet room where a single table had been set for us. We sat down and then the most unexpected romantic surprise awaited me. A host of bearers entered with every form of food that was available for breakfast and dessert from all the restaurants. It was absolutely lovely and I gorged out. My dietician would have killed me but she would have understood that it was for gaining the love of a man!

I looked at him and told him, 'You know I'm most happy when I'm fully fed.'

'Most people are,' he said, sipping coffee. His eyes were dreamy. I felt we could have a real connection. But there I went again thinking long term when the focus was to keep it to the 'current mission'.

'And this coffee is absolutely delicious!' I said holding up my empty cup. 'I'm so used to making rubbish, packet coffee that this decoction is heavenly.' He nodded and poured me some more, lightly resting his hand on mine.

'You smell great,' he whispered. I felt all shy. Wasn't this too forward for a first date? And that too in front of so many people? But I didn't stop him. I looked back and smiled my most charming smile and lightly kept my hand over his, resting on the table. I hadn't had romance in years. I needed this. But instead of going with the flow, I went the other way and made a complete blunder in changing the topic. In my defence, I wanted to get to know him better.

'So you've done hotel management?'

'Yup.'

'And where did you go to college?' I inquired.

Then the bomb dropped.

'Oh I didn't. I went straight for hotel management after my twelfth standard.'

'Oh,' I said, a bit disappointed. I shifted back my hand and body. I suppose it was too harsh a gesture from a moment ago. He picked up on it.

He tried to cover up, 'Well, I think higher education in this country is a joke. We spend three years learning a subject we'll never use like history or English and then another two years doing an MBA or some other post graduate degree. But after all that education, we're still unsure if we'll get a job. You know what I mean?'

I did know what he meant. That was a reason for not studying. But I came from a family that believed that knowledge was power. And I studied for fun. How could I possibly be with a man who had just passed his twelfth grade and had not even done a BA? What could I have possibly talked about after a few more meetings? He was definitely not my Great Love nor good enough for a first date.

It ended then and there.

I got back into the conference and over the next few days I didn't reply to any of his SMSes, even though it killed me to correct his spellings. *They're means they are, not there are!*

Date No. 2

My 'close friend' Aditi, who knew me so well, fixed the next date. I say this sarcastically because it was a complete disaster. Her co-assistant director had been single for a long time. I could figure out the reason as soon as I saw him. But she had taken pity on him and me and fixed us up. He came to pick me up an hour late because he had got caught in a traffic jam from Andheri to Bandra, which was most likely, but shouldn't he have at least figured that out? That he could not have, struck me later when we began to chat. He revealed that he rarely moved out of Planet Lokhandwala! All the shooting was done outdoors or in Film City or Filmistan, which was further away from Andheri, in the opposite direction of Bandra, and all the recording, editing and dubbing studios were in Andheri anyway. So why should he ever move the other way, he asked me defiantly? Because there is life outside your little bubble! I wanted to scream.

Anyway, Raj Malhotra (ya even his name was 'filmy') picked me up and I noticed that he was only five feet four inches tall and he wore glasses, which were designer trash. But the most prominent trademark was the overpowering scent, or rather stink, of his perfume that reached me before the lift did to my floor!

'You did say you wanted him to smell nice,' Aditi would remind me later and I would reply, 'Ya but not as if he has walked through the ground floor of Lifestyle mall with everyone giving him a free sample!'

'Opium,' he said very confidently half way through our meal when I asked him what the smell was.

'It's really pungent,' I tried to cough. He shrugged it off and went back to chomping down his noodles. We had gone for Chinese food and he had ordered the regular three of his favourite dishes—hakka noodles, chilli chicken and shredded lamb in hot garlic sauce—and then turned to me and asked, 'Do you want anything else?'

So I had said, 'Yah. Mughlai, but thanks for asking!' He guffawed loudly but I knew he hadn't got it. I just ordered a soup and let the food be his decision.

When we started talking, the conversation never went beyond him and his industry.

'You haven't seen the new *Don*?' he asked incredulously.

'No. I haven't even seen the old one.' He almost choked on his noodles, which might have been a good thing, but he washed it down with his second glass of ice tea.

'Okay. What about Karan Johar's films? Kkho, kank, k3g?' He used the acronyms as if I would naturally understand what the full forms were.

'Are these sci-fi thrillers?' I asked.

He almost fell off the table. I had heard about them vaguely and I had seen each of them in parts on cable during a boring night alone. But I didn't remember the full forms or recollect too clearly since all Hindi films seemed the same to me. I had never eagerly awaited for a film, to watch it first day of the weekend, or what he called, 'first day, first show'. No, I had not done that for Bollywood films. So I told him.

'Which planet do you live on?' he asked.

Okay, so I knew I was a freak living in the supposed oasis of Hindi cinema, but honestly, I had never got a chance to love Bollywood with so much passion because I had lived abroad most of my life and had grown up on world cinema. I would watch films to deconstruct them rather than enjoy them and I could never enjoy the songs that came in vital places of the plot in Hindi films. I was more of a *Breakfast at Tiffany's* kind of gal rather than a *Break ke Baad* one.

'Well, I know the different aspects of the evolution of women in Hindi films,' I spoke in my defence. 'I had even done a paper on it for fun, for an online univ course I'd joined. I've also been on every set with Aditi, so I know all about film making, not to mention the types of cameras, lenses and Foley sound. So ya, I know films!' I said gleefully, hoping to find some connection with this man.

'And yet, you don't go watch films?' he asked incredulously with noodles stuck between his front teeth.

'No, not really. I have sometimes . . . and I watch a lot of it on TV since all the channels play it within six months of its release. I think it's a waste of time and money to go to watch it in a multiplex where you end up blowing 500 bucks or more every weekend on tickets, popcorn, Coke and post-movie dinner. It's all a big gimmick that I'm not buying!'

He then went on to name some twenty more films of the last few years, still hoping I had seen at least some of them. Didn't I just get through to him? Did my words fall on deaf ears?

So I asked him about world cinema. I named a few directors from across the globe who were famous and had won awards for their films. Raj knew of none.

I suppose since all these films were in black and white, he had never seen any. He claimed that he didn't get them at his local DVD store and, in any case, if he couldn't adapt it into a Hindi film, there was no use watching it.

I decided then that I would have to stop Aditi from fixing me up if this was the priceless piece she was dishing out.

But the climax of the night was when I said I would take an auto back home and he said, 'Okay! But can I call you some time?'

The date could not have gone worse. And yet the man wanted to meet again? Why is it that men feel the need to keep pursuing in the hope that a woman might start liking them? Here's a hint, if she doesn't ask you to call her, she hopes you never will.

Date No. 3

I finally met an interesting man who was a politician. I thought we would have a lot in common. I even started dreaming that we would grow old together, debating intellectual topics that would stimulate our brains and bodies. But when I met him, after accepting him as a friend on Facebook, I realized that intellectualism was as far from him as virginity was from Aditi.

Manoj was a people's person. What that means is that there were people who were continuously around him. He seemed as if he was forty years old even though he claimed to be only thirty-three. And like all politicians, he wore khadi. I am not sure whether politicians are not allowed to flash Reid & Taylor or if they are genuinely fond of the handspun cloth. But beige was blah.

Anyway, he picked me up in his Ambassador with two other cars following us.

'Hi,' I said, as soon as I got into the car. 'Who are all these people?'

'Oh, this is the driver, this is my bodyguard,' he said pointing at each person individually. 'This is my secretary. And this is my brother-in-law's nephew, who is training to be a politician. He will contest in the next elections.'

I looked over at a very sullen, acne-faced boy who could not have been more than sixteen years old and I'm sure he would have rather played video games than contest any elections. When we got to the restaurant, a few more people came out of the other two cars, but he waved his hand aside and they all got back in. If it hadn't been so menacing, it would have been ridiculously funny. We sat down for dinner, with his bodyguard standing behind us and his secretary and the sullen boy at the adjacent table. The food came without us ordering. And the bill never did.

Manoj washed his hands in the finger bowl and wiped it on the tablecloth. When I asked what happened to the bill, as I wanted to split it, he laughed, 'Women don't pay. Even I don't pay. When you're a politician, people respect you.'

'By not giving you a bill?' I asked.

'Well, yes. It has become the norm. Because you have endorsed their restaurant, you have graced their presence.'

'But you've eaten their food!' I insisted.

'Enough!' he raised his voice and suddenly, I was a little scared. And then he softened his tone and said, 'How does it matter? Leave it. Let's discuss your parents and family.' He asked this all the while looking down my shirt, which I immediately corrected so that absolutely no cleavage would show.

Damn Aditi and her revealing clothes!

But I was quite done. When I tried to initiate a discussion on politics it left me thinking that he was a thug. He had got his way by terrorizing people and forcing them to vote for him. When I discussed his family, he mentioned he only had a mother who was also in politics. And when I tried to ask him about his educational credentials, he laughed so heartily that chicken came out of his nose. All his 'credentials' had been purchased.

I quickly ran back home and deleted him from my Facebook. I decided never to go into politics or date men who were available through social sites again.

Date No. 4

After having failed miserably to find a man for myself in all these years, my parents took it upon themselves to find one for me. I think there must be a code somewhere for all parents to get interfering and annoying once their child hits twenty-eight. From then on, their only topic of conversation with their child, who has been successful, independent and brilliant so far, is when and whether she will get hitched to the bandwagon called marriage. Suddenly all the talk about how they want you to be famous, strong and proud dissipates into 'when should we call the pundit, dear?'—so insensitive to people who might not have found their life partner by then. And I have a feeling most marriages in today's society happen because of the pressure parents put on their children to give them grandchildren, rather than for reasons mutual to the couple. But in any case, my mother set me up to meet a man. 'He's a lovely boy (somehow she could never say the word 'man'). He has come highly recommended (which meant someone from her kitty party knew of him vaguely) and he's doing very well for himself (meaning working in a boring bank).' To keep her happy, I agreed to meet Sanjay.

She was right. He was 'lovely' and 'stable' and knew my aunt really well. He, however, turned out to be my distant cousin! My vague mother, in her overexcited state had not checked how we knew him. It turned out that he was my second cousin's cousin. Okay, so not completely related, but it still freaked me out. At first sight he was nothing much to look at—slightly large, tall, fair, simple. But then when we started talking, I was totally lost in him. He could draw cartoons on paper napkins and he did my portrait on a piece of paper. He understood art better than I could have, and he pointed out that I had made an error about van Gogh, which I was sure I hadn't. But he whipped out his Blackberry, Googled it and, lo and behold, he was right. Impressive!

But instead of embarrassing me for my mistake, he apologized and secretly told the bearer to buy me flowers from the gift shop of the hotel and presented it to me. He also sang Sinatra and didn't like Bollywood movies. His voice was deep and when he sang, I could imagine myself in a concert hall applauding him. We were just so alike. And the best part was he was born the same day as I was.

'Shut up!' I exclaimed, after he told me.

'I can't believe you were born on 1 April!' he laughed. 'We'll have to share our birthdays together then.'

I was transfixed. I had found the perfect man! I was even willing to let go of the fact that we were distantly related, I'd enjoyed his company so much! He had rejuvenated my brain cells. He didn't have body odour or smell like the Garden of Eden. What more could I ask for? But there was a problem. And I knew it as soon as we went from chatting like friends to being romantic.

'You know, when I saw you at Nitya's wedding, you looked absolutely ravishing,' he said. I smiled and he continued, 'I knew then that you were the one for me.'

'The one?' I laughed. 'We didn't even know each other then!'

'But Kaveri, haven't you felt sometimes it takes only one meeting to know a person for a lifetime, and sometimes it takes a lifetime to know a person?' I nodded vaguely. I'd never had that connection with anyone but I didn't want to seem like a novice in front of this worldly wise man.

'I feel as if I know you already. Let me take you on a real date.'

'A *real* date? Like where?' I asked. I thought we were on a date.

'Well, I would whisk you away to Paris,' he said excitedly. I raised an eyebrow. I knew he would say Paris since we had been discussing how it was such a beautiful city some time back. 'Then from there we would go on a wine tasting trail across France. Bordeaux, Chablis, blah blah . . . We would go in the Eurorail, staying as long as we want in the area of the wine we liked. We would lodge in small bed-and-breakfasts, waking up next to each other, taking showers together and I would get you tea to remove the hangover we would have from too much wine and sex the previous night.' I sat transfixed and listened as he continued with great enthusiasm.

'Oh yes. Our sex would be wonderful. It would be a mutual bonding of our bodies, pleasuring each other at regular intervals till we need to complete the act. We would wake each other in the middle of the night and sneak out to the lawn and make mad, passionate love, hoping no one saw us, but secretly relishing the fact that we were being dangerous, risqué, different!

We would sit by the river and see the beautiful French countryside and have cups of espresso and pastries. Our lives would be so perfect! We would have wine, see works of art and make love till we were exhausted, and then have some more.'

He looked at me now and said, 'That's what I would do with you. Is that more than one date? I'm sorry!'

I looked at him and smiled. That would have been so perfect and I told him that. It would have been a lovely life, not to mention an awesome date. There was only problem. I wasn't attracted to him. And really, wasn't that just too mushy for the first date? I mean, get a grip. You are, after all, a man!

We must have spent several hours together and yet I couldn't feel the 'spark'. I only started feeling icky from all that sweetness. I didn't know love at all but I knew one thing: there needed to be some sort of chemistry, some sort of balance. And even if we were completely alike, I couldn't feel it. It was uncanny.

I could see my life flash in front of my eyes. If we got married, we would do the same things together. We would complete each other's sentences and we would never differ on vacations, children, art. We would be One—in the truest sense of the word. And after a while, we would get bored. We would *need* the difference. We would long for the new, the exciting, and the passion.

So I decided that we could be friends. And I left him with tears in his eyes and a broken dream of a forever with me. I also left him with a fake number in case he got psycho and started sending me more flowers to woo me back. I decided never to let my parents interfere with my love life again.

Seven

After going on a few dates I realized that even though I had opened myself up to the Universe, I hadn't opened up to men. The men, to me, were useless. They didn't contribute anything to me to allow myself to sleep with them, much less be my Great Love. After all, I was giving them a really precious part of myself. My heart. That had to be worth something, and for me, the memory of 'the first time' had to be special. So if no one fit the bill after two months of looking around, I didn't think they ever would. And this was precisely what I was trying to explain to Aditi at Stop n Shop while returning gifts.

Aditi got gifts from her rich boyfriends that she seldom liked. So she would always go back to the store and plead with the manager to exchange the gifts she didn't want to keep. So far, we had gone return-gift-shopping rather than actually shopping for something we wanted.

'Please, sir, I can't stand this gold chain. It's just bad luck for me. Even more, after the man broke up with me.' Slow tears started trickling down as Aditi continued to plead, 'I need to move on and buy myself something nice in exchange for this.'

'Fine. Just pick up anything of the same value,' said the large, dark, bushy uni-browed, old storekeeper looking at it and then referring to the computer in front of him, 'it's for four thousand rupees.'

'Four grand?' Aditi exclaimed, her tears suddenly drying up. 'Only?' she said with disbelief. 'What a cheapskate dude!'

I looked away and walked to the sunglasses section. She soon followed me there with her refund coupon muttering to herself, 'The men of today are passing off cheap items to woo women. If only I'd known better, I would have dumped him a week earlier.'

'Oh come on!' I said exasperated. 'Four grand is not cheap!'

'Oh ya? For what I gave him, it should have been a car!'

'Well at least you're getting some. The only contact I've had with any man has been with my dentist,' I grumbled.

And since I didn't want to hear the details of her sex life, I turned to the lady at the counter with a pair of sunglasses in my hand and asked, 'How much are these?'

'Rs 1,500,' she replied.

Aditi in a grand gesture told her, 'We'll take them,' then looked at me and said, 'On me!' I smiled and thanked her while she continued saying, 'Don't worry about it. If men are good for money and sex, at least we should use it for our happiness. Speaking of which, have you got any lately? Money or sex?' and she laughed at her own joke.

'No,' I said, walking up the stairs to the women's clothing section. 'I think all men are useless. They don't stimulate me intellectually at all.'

She stopped mid track. 'Honey!' she drawled, 'they're not supposed to stimulate your brain. They're supposed to stimulate your clit!'

'Shhhhhh . . . There are kids in here,' I said, looking around and blushing.

Seriously, sometimes hanging out with Aditi was more an embarrassing experience than a pleasant one. But then she would do these nice things like buy me sunglasses without a thought and one couldn't help but love her. She went hunting for a decent pair of jeans and I looked through the racks, following her.

I started off on a theory that had been brewing for the past few months in my mind, 'Men are a complete waste of time. Look at what you are doing. First you have to shop for new clothes, new shoes and new accessories to impress a guy. Then you have to play dumb to get down to his level, then you wait for *him* to call, then you have a fight, which leads to a heartbreak, and then you start the process all over again. What's the use, dude?' I exclaimed in one breath.

Aditi took five pairs of designer jeans and a few tops and walked into the dressing room. The lady didn't say anything to her, so I did, 'You know you're only allowed three pieces of clothing in there, right?'

'Ya,' she said. 'But I've come here so many times that the dressing room lady knows me by now and figures it's easier if I take all of them in at one go rather than be here for hours chewing her head.'

Point! So I kept quiet.

She came out parading a few jeans and decided to pick one. Half her budget was blown on that.

'Isn't it better to keep a gold necklace for later when you really need the money than blow it on a pair of jeans that you don't need now?' I asked prudently.

She looked at me as if I was a moron.

'Later, I'll be dead. Right now,' she paused for dramatic effect, 'I need to look good for the men who will buy me stuff for later anyway.'

One could never beat Aditi's logic, and I had to admit she did look good. Her long, chestnut hair, carefully retouched in the L'Oreal salon every two months and a lean body that was worked out at the gym at least thrice a week made her look like a model in her size 28 jeans. Instead of being an assistant director in Bollywood, she should have been a heroine.

But today her logic about men was all warped for me.

'Men,' I started, 'need to intellectually stimulate me for me to go anywhere with them . . . No! I don't like that colour. It's hideous!' I said in between, referring to a pink paisley top she had chosen. 'The men I've met are mentally vapid and physically challenged.' Aditi and I had the kind of conversation most outsiders wouldn't get. We could have one main topic and several side stories and never lose track of any of them. We multi-tasked with our discussions!

She poked her head out of the dressing room and asked startled, 'You mean they have a small willy?'

'Shhhhh . . .' I said, for the second time that day. Then I looked around and added, 'No, I mean they're all average looking and short anyway.'

Aditi liked shocking people. That was her thing. She spoke loudly and laughed even louder so people would notice her and be scandalized. I had become so used to her that I knew when she would take off on something. But it still made me cringe sometimes when she couldn't act normal, always wanting attention from everyone wherever we went. But I kept quiet. Aditi was a good friend and I really didn't need to annoy her to prove a point.

She came out of the dressing room, carrying the clothes she wanted to buy on her arm. She signalled to me to go towards the cashier with her while she commented, 'Look at the statistics. 60 per cent of our male population is below the poverty line and ugly. 10 per cent is rich and ugly. 10 per cent is old and ugly. 10 per cent is adolescents and ugly. That just leaves 10 per cent who are good looking. Now these men might be around our age, they might be married and they might even be too full of themselves to notice you. But to find someone who is intellectually stimulating *and* good looking, well the statistics are completely against you!'

I couldn't believe she had thought so long and hard about that answer. Or maybe she was just bullshitting me. But I began to wonder. If you went by that logic, every single woman had compromised in her relationship. And that no woman was completely happy.

So I replied to Aditi, 'We never compromise when we take up a job. We don't compromise when we buy new jeans. So why should we compromise on relationships that are supposed to be the most important aspect of our lives? When I go to buy something and it doesn't fit I don't say, "at least" the colour is right, or if we have to buy a house, we don't give a crore and say "at least" it's in a nice locality even if it is too small. We don't take anything in our lives we're not completely satisfied and happy with. So why do we take crap from men? Or for that matter, crappy men? Why are we saying "at least" he is funny, or "at least" he is rich? Why do women compromise on the biggest thing of all? The men!'

Aditi didn't reply. Instead, she changed the topic, which was so typical of her. She could never be wrong. And when she didn't have an answer or was uncomfortable with a question, she would change the topic completely and pretend as if the earlier conversation was over with her last statement. It was a very ostrich way of living life, but she had mastered it.

'Now we need to pick out some new clothes for you. With your new haircut your old clothes are not making you look glam enough.' Aditi went on to pick some brightly coloured, shiny shirts and some short skirts.

'I'm never going to wear these short, overly revealing things!' I exclaimed in exasperation since I was feeling too lazy to even try them out.

'Trust me. You might not wear them now, but when you do find a man, you'll want to.' She shoved me into the dressing rooms and I went off muttering something.

I was so glad that she had forced me, because when I emerged, I looked amazing! She was right—as usual. So I went and spent a small fortune on new clothes to wear and no one to wear them for. But at least I was ready!

I was ready to fall in love and get married. Oh sorry, lose my virginity! Did I just mix the two? Maybe the lines were getting blurred after all.

Eight

I met *him* in Goa.

I was actually there on work, chaperoning the Princess of Finland, along with her many bodyguards. It was extremely hot in the afternoon on the second day of her visit and the Princess couldn't take the heat—coming from a land of icebergs. So she decided to stay in the hotel and go for a spa. She gave me the rest of the day off.

I quickly changed into a red off-shoulder blouse and white mini skirt that Aditi had picked up for me and went off by myself to find a shack and drink away the afternoon and most of the night. After walking on the beach to find just the correct shack to sack in for the next twelve hours, I came across Sunny's. The shack was closer to the rocky edge than the beach and there weren't too many people at two in the afternoon. So I got myself a table overlooking the sea and ordered a beer. Surprisingly, the shack was cool despite having no air conditioning and just an air cooler blowing at the tables. And since it was secluded, I didn't have to deal with pesky couples, kids or rowdy office parties.

I started humming to the music playing in the background. This was the life! Soothing retro music, cool breeze, a beer and solitude. These were the times I loved my job as a freelancer. Just as I was about to call out to the waiter for some fried calamari, a man walked in and sat at the table next to me. Madonna's *Like a virgin* faded in. *Irony* was my aunt.

The man was gorgeous.

No, that's an understatement. He was a Greek God personified. Everything about him screamed, 'Model'. He was tall, with dark, wavy hair, light brown eyes and a body that could pass off as one of the bodyguards from Finland. He was wearing a white linen shirt and khaki shorts and sunglasses. He sat down at the table next to me and placed an order. I was trying hard not to stare, but it was difficult.

After some time, the waiter appeared with a plate of fried calamari and put it on my table. I said flummoxed, 'I didn't order this.'

The Greek God spoke, 'No, I did.'

'Sorry,' said the waiter and switched the plate to his table and left.

His voice was melodious. Not the waiter's, the Greek God's. A lovely deep baritone. I nodded towards the plate and then looked around for the waiter, 'That actually looks good,' I said, 'I'm going to order one myself.' The waiter was already on it. He knew anyone who came to Goa could never resist a plate of fried calamari especially on a hot afternoon with a chilled beer already in place.

'Here, I'll lend you some till you get a plate.' The Greek God said unexpectedly.

'No, it's okay,' I blushed. I took off my sunglasses and pushed them to the top of my head so he could notice my eyes, the only good feature about me apart from my wrists, but that hardly counted.

'I'm serious. Here, grab one.' He handed the plate to me and I took one piece and put it in my mouth. Then he took a fork and picked a calamari with it. I was mortified. Why hadn't I thought of using a fork? I had unceremoniously touched his plate. I didn't know what to say. I began to blush again. But he seemed nonplussed and introduced himself.

'Hi, I'm Arjun.' The Greek God had a name, a name that was eulogized in Indian mythology. I was swooning. I needed to get a hold of myself. Maybe it was because I had too many drinks on an empty stomach, or maybe because he oozed sex. I felt as if I was swirling.

I took my hand out to shake his and found the courage, 'I'm Kaveri.'

After what seemed a long time but was actually a few seconds, he asked, 'Like the river?' I nodded. He continued, 'So you're south Indian?' I nodded again and added, 'Partly. And partly . . .'

'Beautiful,' he said without missing a beat. I smiled. I might have been looking like a tomato. Suddenly hiding my big stomach and small cleavage was the top most priority on my mind. So I leaned forward and sat up a little as close to the table so he couldn't see too much of my body.

'What about you?' I asked, sipping on my beer and all the while thinking that it would be so wonderful if we got married and had sex!

He took a long gulp of his beer and said, 'Partly not beautiful and partly from here.'

'Ohh but you are . . .' I mumbled. Oh god, I wish I could have kissed him. I was going mad.

'What?' he smiled and asked.

'Um . . . I mean, you're from Goa?' I corrected myself.

He nodded. He stopped drinking, eating, being. He just kept looking at me. In a deep, intense way and his eyes said a lot more. But I didn't want to misread them. That was it. I knew then that what we had was chemistry.

'Yup, from Ponda,' he said, finally looking away and then asked looking back at me, 'What brings you to my land?'

'Work,' I replied and smiled. I tried to sound normal. Instead a squeaky girlish voice came out and he smiled. I had not done this in a long time. Flirting didn't come easily and my back up called Aditi wasn't around to make me look good.

'Oh, you look like you're doing a lot of work!' he smirked.

I smiled, 'I have an afternoon off.' I ran my fingers through my hair, desperately wanting him to fall in love with me.

'Let me guess, you're an agent to a Bollywood star?'
'No,' I laughed softly, trying to be coquettish.
'You're a model in search of real food?'
I laughed out loud, secretly happy he thought of me as a *model*. 'No! I'm a freelance interpreter.'
'What's an interpreter?'
'A person who translates languages for delegates coming from different countries.'
'Oh, there's a job like that? Wow. That must be cool.'
'Ya. Sometimes. And sometimes it can be extremely taxing,' I said nonchalantly. 'What do you do?' I asked politely.
'I'm in TV.'
'Are you an actor?' I asked.
'No,' he said very seriously, knowing how good looking he was, 'I work in syndication for the media.'
'Wow, that's exciting,' I said, not knowing what it really meant but wanting to impress him.
'Hardly exciting. Makes you travel a lot and you get to drink a lot of airport coffee.' He left it at that and looked away. And I didn't pursue it. I guess he didn't want to talk about work. We sat there for a while not talking and just looking at the sea.
'I love this place,' he mumbled after some time.
'Hmmm,' I agreed.
'It's so much better than beaches across the world that are more famous.'
I looked at him stunned and asked, 'Like?'
'Miami, Hawaii, Mexico, France.'
'You've been to all these places?' I asked.
He turned to me and said, 'Oh ya. My work made me travel to all these places. I hate travelling though. If I have to do so, I will, but otherwise my idea of a perfect vacation is right here.'
'Home, you mean?' I said. He nodded. I didn't want to tell him about my world travels. I loved travelling. I thought it enhanced you as a person. And I didn't want to tell him that I would rather be travelling than be home with my parents. Just

then, there was a strong gust of wind and the ketchup that was on the table fell on my lap. My white skirt was completely stained.

'Shit!' I cried out.

He got up immediately and poured water all over it and I was shocked. We both just stood there with our mouths open for a while till I started giggling.

'I'm so sorry,' he said, smiling a bit. 'I thought that would help!'

I started wiping the sauce and my wet skirt with some napkins. It became worse. We both began to laugh and I gently held his arm pretending not to fall over with laughter. 'I'm such a klutz,' I proclaimed, all my coyness coming to naught.

'Oh, join the club,' he said.

'You? No!' I said, feigning shock and laughing some more.

'Ya, why do you think I'm all about the cutlery?'

'Oh really,' I said and squealed with more laughter. 'I was wondering why a guy would pick a fried calamari with a fork when it's easier with two fingers!' I teased. He laughed some more.

'I wasn't the one who ordered ketchup.'

'Hey. Ketchup tastes good with everything!'

'Ya, I'll bet you have it for breakfast with toast,' he said while nudging me gently.

'How did you know?' Laughter followed. All our pretenses of trying to be cool for each other had gone out of the window.

'I think I should go change or something,' I said.

'Oh don't go. Just put my shirt around your waist and it'll soak up most of the water.'

He took off his shirt and handed it to me and said with a twinkle in his eye, 'I'll buy you as many beers as you want ... if you stay,' and then suddenly, he quoted a famous painter, 'You can drink to me, drink to my health, you know I can't drink any more than that.' He finished with a flourish.

I quickly looked away suddenly conscious once again and

trying not to stare at his hard body. My mind was whirling with thoughts about how I could just rub my hands all over his perfect 'pecs'. I started feeling hot and said shyly, 'No don't worry about it. I'll just put some napkins on it.' We sat down again and he looked at me and said, 'You're really stunning, you know that?' My body started tingling. But my mind gave me the logic that I barely knew him.

So I tried to change the subject. 'Hey, you know what you just said? Those were Picasso's last words.'

'Really? I read it on a t-shirt somewhere yesterday,' he exclaimed, ordering more beer for us.

'Really?' I asked, scarcely believing that the famous painter's quotes could be put on t-shirts that are sold in Goa. 'I thought only the Rolling Stones got onto t-shirts.'

He laughed. 'Okay, you're right. I didn't. I was just trying to impress you with some quotes by famous guys.'

'You mean a famous painter!'

'Well, I was in Paris a few times and visited the Louvre. It was then that I became fascinated with art. I've never said that to anyone. Everyone will think I'm just a pansy!'

'No you're not! How could you be? You look . . .' and then I stopped myself. I was smitten by a stranger. A stranger who looked like a Greek God and knew my favourite subject. 'J'taime Paris,' I said.

And he replied back, 'I still think the French are really foo foo though.'

'Foo foo?' I asked, sipping my beer.

'You know, uppity, pretentious, wannabe. Foo foo.'

I laughed till there were tears rolling down my cheeks. 'There's no such term, Arjun! But it makes so much sense!' I said and then when I collected my thoughts, 'But I still think the French language is very beautiful.'

'It's hardly a language. Most of the time the French are saying 'aaah', 'oh' and 'um'. They gesticulate with their hands and you understand the gestures, not because they complete the sentence.'

'But look at English as a language. The phonetics alone is a nightmare for students. Which should we follow, the British or the American system?' I contested. I was actually having a debate with a stranger who had made me open up to him.

'Personally, I think language is a manifestation of the behavioural pattern of a race,' he said, while ordering yet more beer for us.

'Meaning?' I asked, interested that a man that good looking could arouse me intellectually as well. Ahem!

'Well look at Bengali. It is a slowish language with a lot of emphasis on "o" and when do you say "oh"? When you are stretching lazily. Hence, the race itself is a lazy lot made to work hard, but the language is reflective of their nature. Look at Tamil. Tamil is spoken very fast; it's not a languid language. That's because Tamilians are always in a hurry to achieve something. They need a language to be curt and crisp and to the point so they can speak it fast. Phonetics is completely different. Get what I mean?'

I nodded, but said, 'That's a very general statement to make though. I'm sure neither a Bengali nor a Tamilian would like to hear that! I mean, I know so many hard-working Bengalis and an equal number of languid Tamilians. Okay, what do you think about Hindi or Punjabi?' I asked. And he told me some more theories he had. And I refuted him some more.

Our conversation lasted for hours into the sunset and we were wonderfully buzzed with beer and each other. He was amazingly cool without trying to be so. He had impeccable manners and made me look like I had grown up in a village, even though I had travelled the world. He was undoubtedly the most interesting man I had ever met. We chatted about art, films, books and the French Riviera. But what was most astonishing was that he made me see life through his eyes. Even though I might have known the subjects better, he gave me a new perspective to them. I knew this man had many more tricks up his sleeve and I wanted to wait and watch!

I was having such a good time that I didn't realize I needed to get back to my job or I would be fired. So I thought I should go check on the Princess and wash away my beer buzz and sandy hair.

We decided to meet later for dinner. I don't know what it was, but somewhere in my heart I felt I had known him forever already. It was a strange feeling, one I had never had before. Oh my god, was this my first infatuation? Did I just have a 'love at first sight' day? I needed to call Aditi and tell her that just a week after giving up on men, I had found one. But then again, I knew this was something I didn't want to share immediately. I felt that by talking about it, I might jinx it. And I did not want to jinx the only connection I'd ever felt with a man in thirty years!

I went back to the hotel feeling like a teenager. Maybe this is what people meant all along. A feeling that makes you *want* to wait for a man. The feeling called Love.

Nine

We not only had dinner that night, we ended up having a snack somewhere at two and breakfast at dawn by the beach. It was truly magical. The evening went something like this.

8.30—Lobby hotel

Greek God looked wonderful in a pair of dark blue jeans and a black shirt. He was casually smart. I went over and air kissed him on the cheek as if I'd known him forever. He smelt of Acqua di Gio, a light smelling but expensive cologne. Thank god I had showered well and washed the smell of beer and sand off my hair. I could see him checking me out in my blue chiffon top, black skirt and high heels that I'd kept only for special occasions. Just when I thought he was going to compliment my look, he turned around and said, 'Would you be comfortable in that on a bike?' Then I saw the Yamaha behind him.

'I would be uncomfortable in a skirt if we were going on that. I'll just go and change,' I said and he nodded, 'I'll wait here.'

So I came down wearing my jeans and an emerald blue, sleeveless top with a white shrug, losing the heels for silver flip-flops. He saw me and smiled.

'Ready,' I said.

And this time he made no bones about checking me out while saying, 'Perfect!'

Greek God seemed to know all the by-lanes of Goa really

well. So I asked him the obvious question, 'How do you know Goa so well?'

He clarified, 'I used to live here. I was born and brought up here.'

I nodded my helmet head. He insisted I wear a half helmet even if I was pillion.

Cruising along the streets of Goa for about an hour, he had shown me all the tourist spots that I had not seen. Goa looked glamorous by moonlight. It reverted to the quaint town it used to be with small bars, music and merriment spilling on to the streets. The world seemed to stop while people stepped out of their mundane lives and enjoyed themselves. The energy in this city was infectious. Unlike Bombay or Delhi, or any other city in India, the people of Goa were warm and friendly and partied every day of the year. So whenever you were there you would feel like partying as well.

We slowly took a turn about an hour into the drive and he pointed to a small red and white bungalow with porch lights and a lovely manicured green lawn in front. He had stopped and we were looking in from across the street into the house. He took off his helmet and said, 'That's my house.'

'You're serious?' I asked incredulously. He nodded and smiled. I felt all tingly.

Here was a stranger who was sharing a little bit of his private life with me, as if he wanted me to be a part of it. And then he said, 'We can leave the helmets now. We're going for dinner to a place close by.'

10.15

We were sitting at an Italian bistro, a five-minute drive from his house and looking at our menus when one of the waiters came over with a bottle of wine and poured it in the glasses. I looked confused and was going to say, we didn't order yet, but Arjun smiled at me and said, 'I've already ordered for the night. I didn't want to waste a minute with you.'

I felt that tingly sensation again. I put down my menu and gave it back to the waiter.

'Why didn't you take me to a Goan eating joint?' I asked.

'Well, we had so much calamari and sausages and fish as snacks in the afternoon that I felt a change would do you good,' he said. He seemed very sure of himself. It was as if he had taken the reigns of the date and he would woo me in style. 'So, tell me more about your job. Do you need a degree for it?'

I picked up my glass of wine and clinked it with his, 'Cheers!' I said and continued, 'Yes. I learnt all these languages but my degree was from a university in the USA that specializes in how to translate languages.'

'Oh, you've studied in the USA?'

'Yes, for a short bit and then I did the rest online . . . because I went back to staying with my parents who were missing me too much.'

'Only child?' he asked, sipping his wine while the waiter came with a basket of hot, soft, garlic bread.

'Yes,' I said, stuffing my face with a garlic bread. He, however, took it from the basket with tongs and then ate it with a fork and knife. I thought for a man to have such table manners was quite extraordinary. I wondered, however, what he would have done if the bread was crisp. But I found out soon enough when a large, thin crusted, crisp, cheesy pizza with Goan sausages came in front of us. This too, he had with a fork and knife while I dug into it with my hands, folding the pizza and putting it in my eager mouth.

He continued with the questions, 'So, do you meet a lot of interesting people?'

'Yes, sometimes. I've met the Princess of Monaco, the German Chancellor and the Russian President. But most of the times I'm editing journals, books and other such boring stuff.'

'No, no. It's not boring!' he said.

'Actually, it's a misconception that translation simply implies a word by word interpretation of the text. It involves moving the soul of a text into a different body. And not just anybody can do it. It requires a lot of patience and soft skills like being a people person or staying curious about current affairs and which delegates do what,' I rambled on, trying to sound intelligent for this man.

He stayed interested through the evening and dinner, which was absolutely scrumptious with a spicy pesto-crab fussili that followed the pizza and a tiramisu to end the meal. I went on talking about my life and the places I had visited. I suppose the roles had reversed in a few hours. Instead of him wanting me to sit with him a little longer, I wanted to make the date go on.

I thought that he would drop me back since it was already midnight and we had finished an entire bottle of wine but Greek God just turned to me and said, 'Come, we need to go to our next destination.'

12.45 a.m.

We were on a private yacht sailing down the Mapusa River. This was the best date ever! The yacht was a dream. It had rooms that would make the presidential suite in a hotel seem inadequate. And here we were, sitting on the deck with another bottle of wine and a personal butler while watching Goa bathed in moonlight. Greek God pointed out all the spots again as we passed through the Salim Ali Bird Sanctuary at Chorao Island, and the villages of Salvador Do Mundo and Brittona. The cruise also took us down the Mandovi River, past the bright night lamps of Panaji–Miramar on one side and the gorgeous Reis Magoa and Aguada Fort on the other. It was really magical.

Another bottle of wine followed and our conversation became sporadic as we just enjoyed each other's company and the lovely night. I rested my head on his shoulders, surprised at myself for becoming this comfortable with a stranger so quickly. So unlike me, who had always been stand-offish with my earlier dates.

It was around four in the morning when I decided to take a

short nap and check out the bed in one of the luxurious rooms. I was fast asleep before we hit the docks and I slept right through till about seven in the morning when I woke with a start.

7.00 a.m.

I felt disoriented and didn't know where I was for a few minutes and thought I should scream out for help. But then I saw Greek God sleeping in his clothes on a sofa close by and smiled. Then I gasped with fright. I was still on a 'date' and my morning breath and morning hair together was more frightening than hurricane Katrina. So I quietly got up and went to the toilet where I freshened up as best as I could. I decided the no make-up, wet-ponytail look would be much better than the grizzly, smeared-mascara one.

When I came out, Greek God had gone and I panicked a little. What if he realized I was a terrible date and had left me to fend for myself?

I walked out slowly to the deck and our personal butler told me to wait till he came out. Apparently he had gone to freshen up as well. It wasn't like the movies where both parties woke up smelling like roses and looking like daisies. Real people needed to use the toilet early in the morning!

Greek God came out looking fresh as if he was prepared for this, with a new shirt and a day old stubble that made him even yummier than the night before.

He smiled and said, 'Hey, you! Slept okay?'

'Amazingly well for an unfamiliar place,' I said running my hand through my hair. God, why didn't I have nice hair, I thought. Then I remembered I had spent a fortune on my hair only a few months back and was pretty proud of it then. Why was I feeling so conscious now?

'Ready for breakfast?' he asked. I nodded in anticipation. 'This way,' he said.

Then he helped me get off the yacht and led me to the beach.

I saw a mat laid out on the beach with a basket on the side as I got off.

'What's all this?' I asked.

'An authentic Portuguese breakfast,' he replied.

And so I dug into the meal and kept praising his ingenuity for making a woman happy.

'Oh, you have no idea how I can make a woman happy,' he said, his eyes twinkling.

Just then I realized, damn, I'm not getting this for free. He wants 'more' from me than just scintillating conversation! Obviously my face had revealed my chain of thoughts and he quickly added, 'Relax. I'm not that kind of guy.'

I had no idea what kind of guy he was! I had been talking about my work, my family, my life, Aditi and I barely knew anything about him.

'Arjun,' I started, 'I know nothing abut you! I've been going on about myself for the last twelve hours! I must have sounded like a self-obsessed bimbette.'

He laughed. A deep, throaty laugh that I had become used to by now since he had been pulling my leg with his wicked sense of humour all night.

'Well, if you spend the next two days with me, you'll get to know everything you want,' he said that as a challenge.

But then a thought came to my head—the Princess! I was here on work. I needed to get back.

'Arjun,' I said apologetically, 'I can't. I have work. And then I'm leaving tonight. I'm sorry. Oh God! I so want to though . . .'

'It's okay,' he said, getting up. I followed. We really hadn't finished, but I presumed he was ready for me to leave, so I got up and looked at him expectantly. But he took his card from his wallet and gave it to me. 'My cell phone number is on that. You call me if you get free anytime. Otherwise, I'll hope to see you in Mumbai, okay?'

'Okay,' I said sadly. This date was ending on a bad note

because of me. He had given me his business card. As if what we had last night was a business meeting! I wanted to change his mind about me, us, last night. So I leaned over and kissed him. It was an impulsive gesture and he didn't protest. In fact, he was quite shocked, but he reciprocated! And the kiss we shared after that was absolutely delicious. It smelt of cologne, Palmolive soap and coffee. It was sweet, not mushy or slimy or like any of the other kisses I had had with those vague men in my life. It felt like 'the kiss'. The one I would remember for the rest of my life. All girls have had that. It's the only one you remember every time you think of the kiss that changed your life.

'I'm going to take my bike back home now. There's a car that will take you back to the hotel,' he looked the other way and continued, 'which is not far from here.' He said smiling down at me, still holding my waist.

I nodded dumbly.

'Bye, babes,' he said, and started walking towards his bike, which was parked on the other side of the road.

'Arjun,' I called after him stupidly, 'thanks.'

And then he was gone. And I didn't know if I would ever see my Great Love again.

Ten

When I went back to the hotel, I was feeling horrible that I had to leave Greek God. I knew he had given me his number but do people actually end up meeting in Mumbai? With everyone having such busy lives and lazy weekends, it seemed impossible to keep the friends you did have, not to mention, take the effort to add new ones.

And the kiss ... I just could not get over that kiss. I was hooked. I wanted more. I didn't know if it was a dream I had or if I really met the love of my life. I had to find out.

I reached the hotel at around 8.30 in the morning and quickly took a shower and wore my business suit so I could be ready for work by 9, as the Princess had asked. But I waited and waited for her to call me, all the while sipping on cappuccino and day dreaming about Greek God. It soon started raining. The monsoon was here. I wanted to jump in joy and run to Greek God. But I had to run to the Princess's room instead. She finally buzzed me at 10 and I went to her suite on the top floor of the hotel. I waved to the bodyguards on the way and tried to get away from a few photographers who were shooting anything going in and out of her room, looking for a story.

'Good morning, Your Highness,' I said upon entering, not sounding like my usual cheerful self. But she didn't seem to notice.

'Darling! You know what has happened?' she said effusively.

I shook my head but she didn't wait for a response as she

stood in front of the mirror holding her hair, 'I've got sunburn.' She did look a little red but I had just assumed that that was her natural colour. Her make-up artist, sitting on a chair nearby, spoke to me, 'It's true. I'm trying to find a foundation to cover it up, but I'm afraid all I can do is cover her with this fake tan gel for now. It will hardly last till she showers again, which I presume would be by this afternoon and then what will we do?' The make-up artist was speaking in a state of panic.

This was the problem? Lack of fake tan gel. I was going to laugh. Real people had more serious issues. But obviously in the land of the royalty, these were classified as problems.

I tried to keep a straight face and said, 'Do not panic, Your Highness.' But Her Highness was already rambling about how she would look to the press and she wasn't so worried about the Indian photojournalists but the international paparazzi that would splash her photos all around in *People* magazine and call her family poor since she could not afford sun block or fake tan gel. I offered to get her some, but obviously the *only* one that she used was available only in Europe.

'So the local grocer won't have it?' I muttered cheekily under my breath.

I ordered her some breakfast through room service, but she insisted on only having black coffee once all the food came in.

'There is only one solution,' the Princess said. The hairdresser and I looked at her as if the 'Oracle' would now speak.

'I need to use that last bit of gel and leave Goa immediately to go to Mumbai, where, hopefully, Roberta, my secretary, will be able to find it or have it flown in by tonight for the dinner party I have to attend.'

The two attendants nodded their heads in solemn agreement and the translator spoke, 'I think that might be the best, given the circumstances.'

'I think it's a shame though that you didn't get to see the whole of Goa. Such a pretty land,' I said.

And then she said something that made me want to get up and

kiss her which would have meant the bodyguard would have slammed me down and made me into mince meat. 'Why don't I relieve you of your duties once you see us off at the airport? You can call the embassy for another interpreter to meet us at the airport and take over when we land in Mumbai. You can finish seeing the land of Goa and come back, on your own money, of course. I won't be paying for this.'

I didn't care if she never paid me for anything but she had just given me my life back, so I gave a little yelp that sounded like her dog Fee Fee. Miss Foo Foo's dog was named Fee Fee! I had to tell Arjun.

'Yes, Your Highness,' I ended up saying. 'Whatever you say.' And I bowed and exited the room. I was already running back to my room dialling his number in my head.

Eleven

I dropped the Princess off through a mad rush of paparazzi, a slew of cars and a host of bodyguards. Then after bowing to the Princess one last time, I kissed the ground of the airport and made my way back to the shack where it had all begun.

Greek God was sitting there looking amazing in his stubble and a dark green t-shirt over a light blue pair of jeans, sipping a cup of coffee, which he gulped down as soon as he saw me. Suddenly I felt shy as I approached him. What if I had been thinking about this the wrong way? What if he was here to tell me he was busy?

But soon my fears were quelled as he got up and pulled me closer to him and gave me a long, hard kiss—one that reminded me of the first time and I was tingling all over once again. It had not been a dream after all.

'We don't have time,' he said as he took my hand and led me away from Sunny's. 'We'll sit and drink beer later. Now, I have to show you more of Goa!'

So I let him lead the way for most of the day. And I had a blast. We went straight away to the spice plantation in the town of Savoi Verum, which is ten kilometers north of the city of Ponda and about a half hour taxi ride from Margao. We had lunch and took a tour of the plantation, all the while sneaking away into bushes to steal quick kisses.

At one point, he just took me in his arms and held me real tight. I knew he wanted me because I saw the way he was looking at me. He brushed his hand against my back, sometimes softly letting his palm linger on my arm. When he wanted to comment on something, he would come real close to my ear and whisper, while taking in the smell of my hair. My heart was racing. I wanted so desperately to take him back to the hotel. But I was too shy to say so.

We skipped the 'Indian Elephant Experience' and headed out again by early evening to Anjuna beach. The flee market was on and I shopped and bargained to my heart's content while he stood by holding the many bags and muttering that I was never going to use any of this stuff when I got back to Mumbai. The rain clouds came and went and we had brief showers in between, which made the whole day even more romantic.

We got wet in the rain and found a secluded spot to dry off. The rain seeped through my light shimmer shirt and I saw him noticing my breasts. He caught my arm and pulled me towards him and kissed me deeply. We had a soul connection. I knew it. He tried to put his hand beneath my shirt and I shied away. 'Please,' he murmured and I gave in. I was new to this. I wanted his appreciation. I let my hands move across his chest. God he had a perfect body! He kissed me softly. Lightly. On my eyes, my lips, my neck and moved down. Clothes were still on but the tingling had started. I could see he was ready for something more. But I didn't know if I was. Someone somewhere laughed. He became conscious and the moment was lost.

He smiled and smoothed my hair. Then said, 'Devons-nous aller?' (Shall we go?)

And I said most reluctantly and sadly, 'Sure.'

By dusk we were exhausted since we hadn't slept the previous night as well. But so much adrenaline was pumping through my chest that I felt by sleeping, I would miss out on the most fun day of my life. We finally sat down at Pattiez for some delicious coffee and cake. We saw the sun set from there and I wondered whether this was just a holiday romance or would we have a longer relationship once we got back to Mumbai. So I decided to ask him some pertinent questions.

'Arjun,' I started in my 'we-need-to-talk' voice, 'I've had an amazing time. Of all the places I've travelled, and all the people I went around with, these two days with you, have been the best vacation ever.'

He smiled and sipped his coffee. I wanted to continue but didn't know how to.

Maybe I was just jumping the gun. Maybe I should play it cool and not sound clingy and needy like most women. So instead of continuing, I just said, 'Thank you.'

'What's with all the thanks Kaveri? I'm having a great time too, you know.'

Well, that was a relief. I didn't want to be the bore in the man's time off in Goa. But suddenly he became quiet. 'But there is something I need to tell you,' he said seriously.

You know when you have this intuition that if everything is so good, something must be wrong? Well as soon as he said that, I could sense something was wrong. And then suddenly, my world was torn apart. Right there, I would know what a broken heart felt like for the very first time in my life.

'I'm having this great feeling about us. I know we can have something special ...' he said and I felt relieved for a moment. But then he continued, 'I don't actually live full time in Goa, you know. I live in Mumbai. That's where I'm working. As I told you earlier, in a channel?' he asked if I remembered and I nodded yes.

'Well, I live in Mumbai with my wife.' He paused for a second, while looking at the flower vase in front of us real earnestly as if he was trying to convince it that it was an okay thing to say. I thought I hadn't heard right but he continued really quickly, 'I've been working in Mumbai ever since I finished my studies here because I really wanted to do something better ...'

'Go back to the earlier part ...' I cut him off. He sighed and reluctantly started with the details. He looked as if he was defeated. As if he knew that by telling me he was hurting me, while talking he laid his hand on my hand and even moved towards my space. 'We met when I had just started working. She had joined the same company as a marketing intern and I was trying to find my footing. Then I got a great offer in Delhi and she gave up her job to be with me. We decided to get married then. When I got this position, we came back to Mumbai.' He paused, since, by now, the expression on my face was of pure confusion. I felt my face dropping and my heart wilting.

Again he moved closer but I quickly moved away. He had already moved into my heart. I wasn't going to let him move into my side of the sofa. I know I sounded ridiculous but I was determined he sit exactly where he was, opposite me.

'My marriage is on the rocks. It's only a matter of time before it's over. We just need to settle the . . .' he was mumbling away and all I could think of was what a fool I had been to fall for the basic charms in a man—humour, intelligence and an amazing body. I had never done that before! I had scrutinized every man in every way possible. Even in the last two months, I had given up on men on flimsy grounds because I had thought they weren't worthy of my love. And here, in a matter of minutes, I was throwing myself at this man.

'I haven't even seen her for so long. After we came back from Paris . . .' he was mumbling, but I was already analyzing the situation. You had always been practical about men, so what was it about him, Kaveri, that made you go all wrong, that little voice asked. And a feeble answer came back, maybe it was the exotic location, a vacation after a long time, a departure from the normal, a lot of alcohol and a free day from daily domesticity.

I looked up and he was waiting for my response. I had blanked out. I had been pretending to listen. 'You just committed adultery. With me. That makes me an accomplice in a crime!' I completed softly. Instead of being shocked at this statement, he suppressed a smile and said, 'A very beautiful accomplice. In a crime of passion!' I looked at him wryly.

There was no more hope in this. I needed this infatuation to die, but all I could do was say, 'This is an affair. And it's wrong. And we're hurting an innocent person.'

'No. It's not like that.' He tried to reassure me, though I had no idea why. 'This is the first time I've ever felt this way about anybody. I'm sorry, but I'm a very faithful husband and have been for eleven years. It's just that . . .'

'Stop!' I didn't want to hear anymore. It felt like all my dreams were collapsing. But my logical side was already taking over and saying, he was just a great fling in Goa. And if I stayed on he would convince me otherwise. So I got up and said, 'Thank you for everything, but we need to stop now before we go any further and hurt a lot of people. I must go . . .' I choked on the last few words. I knew that I wanted something more but I would never forgive myself for getting involved with a married man.

'Kaveri!' he held my hand, stopping me. 'Please just hear me out and then leave.'

So I sat back down. I don't know why. Maybe I felt I owed the guy that, after all that he had done for me the last two days. And he wasn't the one who initiated the first kiss. I had. So I heard him out sincerely instead of being uncomprehending and vacant.

'I've learnt the hard way that you shouldn't marry your best friend. Marriage should mean more than that. She started resenting all the sacrifices she made for me and I started resenting how our lives had turned out. We stopped giving each other space to grow. And then we started giving each other too much space not to even bother. It was a dichotomy that loosened all the threads of our marriage. I'm sorry. I shouldn't even tell you what the problems are. But all I can tell you is that I swear on my parents that this is the first time I have kissed a woman besides my wife.'

I could only nod. Aditi would have screamed and shouted and slapped him right there. But all I could do was agree with him and feel sad for myself. So I just repeated myself, 'Arjun, I think I should go now.' And then I kept sitting . . .

He looked at me while I was looking down at the table. I blinked back my tears. I didn't want to go. I didn't want him to be married either. I have no idea why I stayed put. But I did.

I guess that was the first of my dumb ideas.

He sighed a long deep breath of relief and motioned for the waiter to fill our glasses with water.

After taking a sip he continued, 'You know, on a funny note, marriage really kills conversation and you're the only person I've talked to the most in these last few months ... on a personal level.' He tried to break the ice. I tried not to feel sorry for him. 'My wife and I are no longer in a loving marriage. She wanted to try and make the marriage work a few months ago by taking us on a four-day trip to Paris ... I spent most of my time in museums and she went shopping ... We didn't even connect in the most romantic city. Since then, we've been living separate lives ... I mean, she came back and a few weeks later, left to be with her parents. She needed to tell them we weren't working out. And I could no longer hide it from my parents, so I came here to break it to them ... And then I met you ... I met you and felt like there was a breath of fresh air in my life. After so long.'

'And how do you think I should fit into this life of yours?' I asked with hope and trepidation that he wouldn't brush me off. My parents would be mortified if they came to know that I was having an affair with a married man. I would be mentioned in hushed conversations in the cocktail parties they go to, and their friends would smile at them apologetically, blaming my behaviour on modern day evils and influence of the bad Bollywood culture of Mumbai, which I am not even a part of. Oh, how cruel life was!

'I don't know ... I know that's too much to ask for anyway,' he mumbled in the background, but my mind was already trying to plot as to how this could work.

'Hmm. What? So what are you asking for?' I said, still praying silently.

'I'm asking for your friendship. No strings attached. You can lead your life any way you want . . . I just want to be part of it somehow . . . because I can't lose you.'

'You can't lose me?' I asked tentatively it's crossing my arms and sitting back, keen to look more fierce than I felt. 'What does that even mean? We've known each other just two days. It's okay if we never see each other again, na?' I asked trying to sound cool and undemonstrative, but my high-pitched voice, that came out whenever I was nervous, made my words squeaky and shaky. I kept playing his words in my head over and over again, now and for many months to come. *I don't want to lose you.* Something that a man in love generally says. Or so I believed.

'Kaveri, please. You yourself admitted that you had a great time with me and I can see that we're both very attracted to each other, so why are you hesitating so much? I'm just asking to be your friend.' I must admit I was a little foxed at this point. I was the one who had fallen for him! He had never shown any signs of reciprocation except for the stolen kisses I had pulled him into. Man, I had been a slut and was paying deeply for it!

'. . . So why can't we just continue to have a great time?' he was saying, 'Look you're leaving tomorrow morning. Let's just enjoy the rest of the evening together and then I leave it completely up to you. If you want to stay in touch—great for me! If you don't . . .' he hesitated and added, 'I don't even want to think about it.'

I began thinking about it. It was true that we'd had a great time together. Even in that short span of two days, he'd come closer to me than any man ever. In fact, he'd been the one and only real date I'd ever had. That itself was nice. Who says women can't be friends with married men, I questioned. People don't make friends by asking 'are you married', do they? They become friends for so many other qualities—and I liked the qualities in Arjun. He was fun to be around. He had a wicked sense of humour, and, for the first time, I had felt comfortable around a man. I wanted to do better, think harder, love deeper around him. I didn't really want to give that up!

When I finally came out of my reverie and looked up, he was watching my face intently—his eyes hopeful, pleading, even, and full of dread for my decision.

Maybe we would not have a forever. But I suppose I could have a few more hours with this great man I'd found. A thought that would become my biggest blunder later. But for now, I didn't want to give up on this. I wanted someone who understood me as well as he did and make me laugh and live spontaneously as much as he did. Once my decision was made, I didn't for a second think that I should have gone with my earlier logic instead of my heart, a decision that would wrench me in deep sorrow subsequently.

Twelve

I had made up my mind.

I wanted to remain friends with this man and I told him so. But we didn't know what to do with each other any more. After nearly two hours passed we planned to have dinner at a shack close by.

We exited the hotel on his bike and drove to a beach. As we were walking on the beach he took my hand. That's when I started getting emotional. On hindsight, that was not a good thing to do with a stranger, but I had had a pretty hectic, tiring and heartbreaking day. He took me in his arms and assured me, 'Kaveri, please don't cry. I'm so emotionally attached to you already. I don't want to lose you. I promise we can work this out. I promise,' he said sincerely.

So I dried my tears and felt better. He took my hand and we started walking towards the shack. How fickle a woman's mind is when she's in love. She oscillates between confusion and logic—all the while trying to find scraps of hope and reassurance. The unspoken truth is that a woman always knows that her first instinct is right. Not the one that her heart led her towards, but the one that told her to be cautious.

We sat at the shack and he broke the ice by talking about my favourite subject, art. We were chatting about our favourite painters when he suddenly said, 'You know I've always wanted a tattoo.'

'Really? Why?' I asked, sipping on my third glass of wine

hoping I would get drunk enough quickly to obliterate the last few hours.

'Because I think a tattoo is an expression of something that is inherently you, and is a permanent piece of art.'

I smiled and said wryly, 'Ya, till you're about sixty with shriveled skin.'

Then he leaned over and caressed my arm and said tenderly, 'You'll *never* have shriveled skin.'

I looked at him warmly, but shook my head and became all prim again, 'Okay, so here's a question! Since we are all changing as human beings, what if who we are today, is not what we will be at sixty? Do you still want that permanent piece of art on you?'

He looked thoughtful and rubbed his stubble chin. The one that I had become so used to kissing some four hours ago but was deliberately trying not to maul right now. 'I think most people get tattoos because it's cool or funky or some such shit. They don't realize that it's not like a new pair of jeans that you can throw away after a year. A tattoo has to be symbolic as well as be aesthetically pleasing. Like people who get "Om" tattoos because they believe in its philosophy. But if you get something dumb like an ancient Egyptian sign that means nothing to you, just looks very good, all over your backside, well . . .' He shrugged his shoulders and continued, 'I have nothing to say about that.'

I smiled again. It was so easy to be with him. He could pull me into a conversation on any topic and we would be laughing and debating in no time. But the nagging feeling of him being married just wouldn't go away. I didn't know how I was doing this. A few hours ago, I had wanted to take him back to my hotel, and now we were discussing some lame tattoos. What was happening to me? Why didn't I just leave and go back to Mumbai and forget about this man? But since I had made up my mind to be his friend at least, I thought I should be chummy and nice. In any case, this was the last evening we would have together before I flew off to reality. I should make the most of our last supper. But I fell silent. I couldn't go on talking about random things. It became tougher as the night wore on. My mind was conflicted for the first time and I didn't have control of the situation at hand.

God, we had got along so well! Is this what a real relationship would be like? I thought.

We had had a great time together, pulled each other's leg and we could talk about anything under the sun. And to feel all this for a man in just forty-eight hours was so unexpected and pleasant. It was then that I thought of Aditi again. I hadn't spoken to her in the past week. What would she say about this new development in my life? Would she tell me to just go with my heart or slap my face and tell me that I can do better with my life?

But where was the 'better'? I was thirty years old. I had dated men in my twenties and even recently, I had gone out with a few people. My parents had given me full freedom to choose my life partner. But where was he?

'Hello!' Arjun snapped his fingers and broke my chain of thought. His smile made me blush. He had probably guessed what I had been thinking about and looked at me romantically. Really, his eyes could not have shown more expression of what he wanted right there.

He continued on the same topic. 'You know, the tattoo I would get is of the sun. Gaudi's Sun.'

'What?' I asked, suddenly inquisitive.

'In Barcelona, there is this famous artist, Antoni Gaudi. Now, he depicted the sun in this most unusual way. It's a mosaic. It's vibrant with all these colours and layers. It's not just a sun, it's a symbol. It's a discourse on the real and the imagination.'

I looked at him, trying to understand what he was saying. But he tried to impress me some more and continued, 'Kaveri, Gaudi is more than just a painter, an artist or an architect. His work carries meaning to different realms. He uses nature to depict something larger. It's actually quite fantastic!' he said, smiling to himself.

I looked at him then. A part of me wanted to hear more about this, to listen to this man talk forever. He inspired me. He motivated me. He understood me. Wasn't that what a perfect man was supposed to be?

But that voice of Reason came back and my headache returned.

'Please, Arjun. Stop. I can't talk about random stuff anymore. I don't care about the tattoo. I care about us. Will this end as soon as we finish dinner? Will we have nothing more to go on with?' I rambled. I sounded foolish even to myself. But I was a little lost girl in this forest of love.

He took my hand and looked into my eyes, 'Not if you don't want to.'

He had really opened up to me. If he was truthfully saying his marriage was over, then why shouldn't he move on? After all, a man also needs some fun in his life and he needs to have friends. What was the harm in me giving him that fun, and being a friend? This relationship was becoming more and more acceptable to me as we chatted. But a part of me was still angry and hurting. I blurted out, 'You should have told me you were married. I could have had the choice then to remain friends before ...' I caught myself from saying 'falling for you'. I stopped mid sentence.

'I'm sorry I led you on. But please give me a chance!'

'But you're married Arjun,' I said softly shaking my head. 'I can't be ... I've never been ... my morals ... I'm ...' I struggled to get the correct words.

He took my hand and put both of his over it and held it tight for a long time. Then he looked at me and brushed my hair away from my face. 'Please. Stop saying that. It doesn't matter. Sometimes you find your soul mate after your marriage ... You're so beautiful,' he whispered. 'Just give me a chance.'

Was he my soul mate? Was he supposed to be anything? But

my brain told me to get over the married part and look at him more clearly. Was he what I had wanted if he was single? And the answer was right there in front of me. I knew then what I had to do.

'Arjun,' I said softly. 'How about you come back to my room and we chat there for a bit? The music is too loud here,' I said trying not to sound desperate.

He looked at me as if it was a test. 'Are you sure, Kaveri? I don't want you to regret anything later and blame me for it.'

'I'm a grown woman. I know what I'm doing,' I said with more stubbornness than confidence. I was actually a little tipsy and didn't really know what I was doing. But you only live once, I thought. Maybe I'll never find the right man. Maybe, when I told the Universe I wanted to lose my virginity, it didn't answer back with, 'Here's the perfect *single* guy who wants to spend the rest of your life with you, Kaveri.'

I didn't want to wait till the perfect single guy came along. I might have to wait for years, and by then I would be old and haggard. I mean, look at Aditi who has been sleeping with all the wrong men and she still hasn't come across the one person she loves and is willing to marry. Arjun was my Great Love. There, I said it. I had found him. The man I was looking for, to give me what I needed, yearned for and desired all my life. My Great Love. Who cared if he was married? He was there. And he wanted me.

I could either take that chance now, or wait till I got married to someone else. Besides I had promised myself that I would be true to my 'values'. The conflict had been killing me all day. It had to stop now. He paid up and we went to my hotel room.

Yes. I had made up my mind.

Thirteen

Hotel room. This is not how I imagined it. He draws the curtains. Lights switched off. A warm glow comes from a corner. I look around and see it. Lavender scented candles. How? Hotel gift shop, he says. I'm so scared. And yet eager. He approaches me. I'm shy. He kisses me. Confidently. Deeply. Gently. He pulls my hands over my head to take off my shirt. Not yet, I whisper. He holds me tight. Gently. I ramble incoherently. He holds my chin up. You don't need to, he says, it's okay. I confess, this is new. He hesitates. I draw him in. I want it. I take off my shirt. I'm self-conscious. Gasp. You're gorgeous! he mumbles. I fumble with the buttons of his shirt. He looks deep into my eyes. Not judging. Just wanting. Hoping. I see him. Striking body. Stunning bronze skin. He moves his hands down my back and draws me closer. He nuzzles my neck. I run my fingers through his hair. I'm so unsure. Maybe I should stop. I try and speak. Unsuccessfully. He smothers any words that may emanate from me. Sure movements of the tongue. Deft. I sigh. I stumble back, and we land on the bed. He swivels me around and kisses my back. His hands tenderly move to my breasts. I want more. He gently lays me down. I quiver with anticipation. He kisses my navel. Glides down. I stop him. Too soon. Silence. He continues. Oh God! What have I been missing! It's so wrong. He's not mine. He finds me with his mouth. I moan. He breathes me in. Don't stop, I beg. He smiles. Are you ready, he asks? No. Yes. Now. He pulls me down, holds my leg and begins to slide into me. I groan. Should I stop, he asks afraid to hurt me. Yes, no, don't stop, I beg. He moves in deeper. It burns. Long, slow strokes.

Softly. Surely. Gently. So good, I murmur. Faster, harder, rougher. Pain. Pleasure. Oh, I know now. My back arches. He holds me tighter, breathing heavily. My nails dig into his back. He smiles at me as he moves. A half-smile. Eyes locked with mine. Not flinching. The room smells of us. Of love. Of lust. Of sweat. Sigh. Minutes become hours, night becomes day. Our bodies still entwined. Am I doing this correctly, I think. And then, right there, I know. I let go. He unwinds. We smile. I say with my eyes—I'm a woman. I'm Yours. I'm Whole. He knows.

Coffee. That was my first thought. I have no idea why but I guess since I've never been too much into alcohol, the first comfort, warm feeling I wanted was from a hot cup of coffee.

So I got up and made myself a cup of coffee. It was almost dawn now. The most beautiful sky I've ever seen lay before me as I sat on a chair near a window overlooking the sea. My body trembled from all the action of the last few hours. My skin couldn't stop tingling. My heart was overwhelmed with the feeling of being loved and my body was exhausted from being appreciated. It had been fantastic and I had no more words left.

He got up and sat on the other chair by the window. In my hotel room. With his cup of tea. The sun was hitting him from behind the large windows. God, he was good looking! If he hadn't been, it wouldn't have been worth it. Really, that was shallow, but it was true. The fact that his amazing smile and personality added to his looks helped. But no, I was digressing from the fact: HE WAS MARRIED!

Shit. That made me The Other Woman, I never thought I would be! Especially, when I'd been a virgin till only a few hours ago. But I didn't want to think about that. The more I tried to shut my mind to that fact, the more it kept coming back.

I remembered that Alanis Morissette song, *Ironic*. The one thing you really want from life and when you get it, it turns out to be at the wrong time. So we sat in silence and finished our coffee and tea. It was my turn to speak and he respected that. So I made him wait. I didn't know what to say anyway. I should have asked him to leave, and told him that I never want to see him again.

But then, I was in love. In love with a married man.

Love.

One word.

So many questions and never any right answers. A word that makes people do extraordinary things—in my case, extraordinarily stupid things. My senses had deserted me. A word that is most clichéd and yet most potent. I knew now what I had been missing. But I also knew that it couldn't have been with any of those men that I had met earlier. No. This was destiny. Fate had brought us together at this stage to share our bodies and our lives and know that it didn't take a lifetime to get to know a person. Sometimes it took seconds.

And let's not forget the Love-Making. I thought it would be awkward but it was not. It was tender and gentle. Yes, it hurt, but it was this lovely feeling, like when you jump into a blue, inviting, cold sea on a hot day, it stings at first but the feeling when you're in that water with the sun on your back, it was like that. It was exhilarating. It felt like I was finally free.

The memory would not be bitter if we had to part now forever. But, oh god, would we have to part forever? I felt guilty and yet so happy. I smiled at him. I had got into this knowingly, from the beginning. But I was beginning to feel crummy about what we had to do now.

'So what should we do now?' I asked, hoping for some answer that would make me happy without the guilt pangs.

He looked at me, shrugged his shoulders and said, 'Take a shower?'

I smiled. 'You know what I mean.'

He took a sip of his drink and said, 'This is nice and hot. You know how to make it exactly as I like it.' He was moving away from the topic. I felt uncomfortable. I had led him on. I had made him sin. Adultery. I felt ashamed. 'Thank you. I have a knack,' I said nonchalantly to his compliment on the tea. I think he guessed my tone.

Unsure.

He nodded and continued, 'I think you're the most beautiful, intelligent, enigmatic woman I've met. And I have no idea what to do from here. So, what you want to do is completely up to you.'

I stayed quiet, thinking this over. I finished my coffee and kept it back on the table in front of us. I wanted to ask him if he loved me the way I loved him. But I knew that was a stupid question. Because I think only women are capable of feeling such strong emotions within such a short span of time.

'I want us to remain friends,' I said finally.

'Just friends?' he asked, too quickly and eagerly. Thankfully.

'I'm not so sure that this relationship can be any more than that,' I replied. I wanted it to be more and yet I had all these conflicting emotions. What would my parents have thought of me if they knew the truth?

'Kaveri,' he said, putting his cup down firmly, 'I want more than a friendship. What we had . . .' he stopped and took a deep breath and continued, 'You know what . . . whatever you say is okay with me.' And that's all he said. And then he got up and went to take a shower.

Did he want a relationship or a commitment or a fling? What exactly did he mean, I wanted to ask? But I just stayed quiet, happy in the thought he wanted something at least. But we had a whole lot of issues to clear up. So I asked after him, 'Arjun, you're married. How do we take this further anyway?'

'Arjun!' I asked again, hesitantly.

He came out of the shower after five minutes with a towel wrapped around him and said dispassionately, 'You know, we'll just have to be careful. I don't want us to be seen by anyone where the news might go back to her. I want to break it to her once she's back from her mom's place in Assam.'

So I nodded and agreed. It would hurt his wife. He was right in being cautious.

'And,' he continued, as he gelled his thick black hair, 'we'll have to see how we feel about each other and take our relationship forward.'

See how we feel? I'm already in love with you, I wanted to say. But he didn't feel it. He wanted to test the waters, which I suppose was a logical thing to do. Maybe I could show him how much he could be in love with me. I thought I would prove what an indispensable, desirable, devoted girlfriend I could be and then he would realize that he was in love and marry me.

'Sure,' I said nonchalantly and headed to the bathroom. But he pulled me closer to him and held me tight.

'I want whatever you want. I'll spend as much time with you as I can and we'll see where this goes once we go back to our daily lives, okay?' I nodded and before I could say anything, he pulled me down on the bed and moved his head towards my neck again. He started kissing me softly on my ear.

'I have a whole lot of tricks that you haven't seen yet,' he said in a naughty tone and I smiled and said, 'Show me.'

Later when I was in the shower, I stared at my reflection in the mirror. I knew I had changed in the last three days. I had gone from being a woman who didn't know anything about men to one desperate to hold on to the man she had just slept with. So what if he was married? I had taken on challenges in my life and this was just another one. He himself had said his marriage was on the decline. I just needed to push it down the drain. And then I would be Mrs Arjun D'Souza. I didn't want to wash away this smell of him that was on me now. I didn't want to dissolve the feeling on my body of sweet surrender. I didn't want Greek God to be a fling. I wanted permanence. My plan was already hatching in my head when he entered the bathroom and kissed me. He dragged me back outside and we went back to a routine we became familiar with only a few hours ago.

Then after taking a shower and making love for the third time that morning, we quickly packed and he drove me to the airport. We parted like lovers and promised we would meet during the week once he came back to Mumbai. I was looking forward to meeting Aditi, and telling her about my plan. Oh, she would be so proud of me!

Fourteen

Once I was back in Mumbai, the first person I wanted to call was Aditi. I really didn't know how she would react to me seeing a married man, and to top that, sleeping with him. I decided to go over to her place since she text messaged that she was at home, cleaning her cupboards.

Aditi had taken the decision to live in Lokhandwala all her life. When I had first come to Mumbai, she had just moved into a two-bedroom apartment away from her parents' in Pune. She wanted a roommate. And so I had become her first roommate. And we loved each other's company, not to mention the apartment itself. It was on the fifth floor overlooking a mangrove, which was so rare for an area like Andheri. It had two small bedrooms with attached bathrooms, but the living room was large and extended out to a balcony. We had bought colourful throw cushions for one corner and a low divan as a sofa for the other wall. We used to sit most evenings contemplating life over cups of Irish coffee. Sure, we could barely afford it but, as she said, if it wasn't a nice space, it wouldn't have been so much fun.

Then her parents visited us and soon enough, started regularly occupying her room while she slept on the divan outside. Feeling it was much too crowded for me, I moved out and found a place in Bandra while her parents permanently settled into 'our' apartment. By now they had presumed it was their place, too, and Aditi occupied my old room.

I felt awkward about talking to her in front of her parents

about this new development in my life, but since she had insisted that I come over, I had no option. I greeted her parents and sat with them in the living room and answered politely all their queries about work and laughed appreciatively about becoming grey before a man came into my life, as her mother fondly gave me tea and glucose biscuits.

Then Aditi said she had to finish cleaning her wardrobe and we were excused while her parents went back to watching TV, which was on mute even when they were conversing with me.

'So how was your vacation?' Aditi asked, as she opened her light brown cupboard door and threw out some clothes from the bottom shelf on to the bed.

'Good,' I said casually, going towards the window to look at the mangrove below. I missed seeing it every morning. Over a period of time, Bandra had become one concrete jungle and trees were a rare sight.

'Don't give me that. I know something is up. Tell, na,' she said, as she sat down on the bed folding the clothes into piles.

'Okay,' I sat down on the chair next to the window, still holding my cup of tea that had become cold. It was much too sweet for my liking anyway. 'Can I please have some coffee, with sugar separately?' I asked.

'Nandu!' she bellowed, in the direction of the kitchen to their full-time servant, 'Ek pheta hua coffee, cheeni alag se. Jaldi! (One brewed coffee with sugar served separately, and make it quick!)' Then she turned towards me and raised her eyebrows in question again, all the while sorting out her clothes.

'I met someone . . .' I said quietly so that her parents wouldn't hear.

She almost squealed till I raised my finger to my lips and pointed to the door reminding her of her parents. I couldn't imagine how Aditi, being so outgoing, lived with her parents, especially since she had come to Mumbai to find her freedom.

'They can't hear, yaar! They're too obsessed with watching the new Sony serials on full blast. So tell me, who is this gem you've managed to find . . .'

I was careful as I spoke, 'He works in Mumbai. He's from Goa, though. And I think I'm in love with him!'

'What?' she asked incredulously, 'How long were you in Goa? A year? How can you be in love so fast?'

So I went on to describe the first date and Aditi listened in rapt attention with 'oohs' and 'aahs' at the same places where, a few days ago, I had been thinking the same thoughts. When I finished, I had omitted the part that was most important.

But she jumped up and came to me and gave me a big hug and said, 'I'm so happy for you, Kavu! Tell me all about it? How was the first time?'

'Well it hurt pretty badly but he went slowly over a long period of time and we did a whole lot of other things that made it really comfortable.' She waited for me to continue, but I didn't want to elucidate, all of a sudden. I felt that this was really private and it should be so. It should not be discussed in detail with even your best friend. I wanted it to be a memory I would cherish and not something that Aditi could take apart for her pleasure. So I shrugged my shoulders and said, 'That's it.'

'That's it?' she shrieked. 'Shut up! Tell me what he did and how you felt. I still can't believe *you* did it with a total stranger!'

I knew she would think that. That's why I didn't want to tell her that I did it with someone who was my 'soul mate'.

Explaining that to Aditi would have taken longer than describing the experience so I just threw my hands in the air and said, 'See, you're off the hook now! Mission De-virginization accomplished!'

She shrieked again and gave me another hug while her mother shouted out from the living room if everything was okay. Aditi assured her that all was in place, shouting back.

Honestly I didn't know how Aditi could have had so many men given her strict upbringing, the constant watch of her parents from a few feet away and a full time servant in the same house to boot!

I smiled.

Just then Nandu came in with my coffee and I started sipping it not knowing how to explain the part that I was deliberately leaving out. Aditi sensed something was up and asked then, 'So what's wrong? Why are you not telling me everything?'

I knew I would have to tell it all, so I took my time, 'I think he's great and all and I'm completely in love and he's also smitten, but . . .' I paused.

'But?' she prodded. I didn't want to ruin the moment but it would have haunted me if I didn't tell her right away. But the moment I said it, I knew that I would regret it for the rest of my life.

'He's married.'

'He's MARRIED?' she hollered, throwing her hands up in the air characteristically, the drama queen.

'Shhhhh. Please!' I said, hoping her mother wouldn't come rushing in now. I so wished we weren't having this conversation with her parents in the other room. Especially since I felt that I had sinned deeply in front of people who thought I was a 'great influence' on their daughter's life and let them down.

She looked at me and gave me a very disapproving look. She shook her head and said, 'Leave him now. Before you get hurt.'

I couldn't believe this! Here was my best friend who had slept with men indiscriminately, being completely unsupportive when it came to me. The least she could do was to have asked if he was getting a divorce—which he had promised me. Somewhat. So I told her about his situation and that he had promised to get a divorce and be with me, but since our relationship was very new, he was taking it slow with me but that he did see a future. Maybe he hadn't said divorce and future so explicitly but I could *feel* it from him and added it to Aditi to make a more solid argument for me being 'in love with a married man'.

'Kaveri,' she spoke, with authority and contempt, 'married men do not get a divorce. It's an urban myth.' She enunciated every word as if I needed to be taught this valuable lesson about life.

'That's not true! Some people do. But anyways, I know what I'm doing and I want you to be happy for me.'

She stuffed the rest of her clothes back in her wardrobe and shrugged her shoulders. I knew she was angry with me for going against her laws of finding men.

It was my turn to get annoyed. 'Okay, why do you say it's an urban myth?' I asked rather hurtfully.

'Because I've been there. I've been with a married man. Don't you remember Sanjay? That was precious time of my life that went to waste, Kaveri,' she shot back.

I had always been a little defensive around Aditi. Our relationship was one of mentor and student and there had been times when she had had her heart broken and I had made her rum cake with Irish coffee, but I had never doled out advice about men to her. I had always listened. Then again, what could you really tell someone who was inconsistent and erratic in relationships in any case?

But this was the first time that I didn't want to listen. I wanted her to be happy for me. Just because her love hadn't worked out didn't mean mine would not as well.

Besides, our 'mission' had been accomplished. She should have wanted to celebrate. But here she was, acting like an aggrieved parent whose star child had decided not to pursue the chosen path.

So I kept quiet. And looked away from her. I could not argue with her. I didn't have too many explanations myself, but I wanted her to be happy for me. I was crestfallen.

So all I could say was, 'Not all married men are the same.' And I prayed that she would believe me.

It was five minutes of awkward silence before Aditi softened up, 'I'm sorry. It's your life. I was just being protective. Of course, I'm happy for you. Just keep one thing in mind, treat an affair as it is—an affair. Have minimum expectations and do things according to your convenience, not his. Okay?' She asked, assuming the mentor's role again.

I nodded.

She came over and gave me another hug and we made up. But

deep down I could make out that she really hadn't forgiven me. I knew that maybe I should not tell her too much. I wanted to prove her wrong. Love did change people. Married men did divorce if the right person came along. It was no longer an ugly word, no longer a stigma in our society. I thought I would show her what a 'perfect relationship' could be by breaking her myth, or what she had termed as 'urban legend'.

Fifteen

Over the next few weeks, I met Arjun almost everyday. He would pick me up from home or a conference and we would go out for drinks and dinner. Then we would go back to my place and make love a few times before crashing out on either side of the bed, both of us needing our space in between. It was heavenly. We got to know each other so well that it felt like we were married. Maybe the reason for that was because he stayed over so often that he had become a part of my daily existence.

I knew what Aditi had been talking about now, when she'd said, 'You know when you really feel "love", all the clichés come true, the happiness and the pain, the longing and the celebration. Until you have that, you're not really in love.' I could now understand the people around me who spoke about love and relationships. Until now, it had remained an elusive figure from a distant land.

As I got to know Arjun better, I realized we had many differences. Sure, he liked art and was a klutz like me, but that's where the similarities ended. When he wanted Italian, I would have a craving for Mughlai. He loved the mountains, I loved the beach. He liked jazz, I liked Madonna. He wanted to watch TV, I wanted to read. He wanted to go out, I wanted to stay in and order food. It seemed at every stage we were finding new subjects to differ on. But it was a new experience to know someone so different from me, who I was so hypnotized by. We listened to each other explaining what we liked and why we liked them. It gave us a new perspective to things. Here was a man I could finally look up to. I admired his sure way of taking charge and giving me the peace of not arranging things that I had done all my life.

For so many years I was the one who had decided everything, my move to Mumbai, my translating projects, my apartment, my maid, my daily groceries, paying bills, taking broken things to repair shops. To make so many decisions on a regular basis at every minute of your life for someone as laid back as me had been taxing. I could finally surrender to someone who wanted the best for me. And Arjun did it so well. He made my home, his home. He would call the grocery man and have things delivered. He would order food when we had a hard day at work. He would tell the maid what to cook and Bharat Gas when to come. He took control. And he controlled my life.

The maid was a little flabbergasted at first seeing a man who had almost taken over the apartment with his clothes in the washing machine and his razor on the bathroom sink. But soon she warmed up to him and they would chat up. I did not mind this in the least, as I felt that the two most important people in my life right now were connecting somehow. It was a weird thought since Arjun and I had never met each other's families and they should have been the most important people judging us. But for now this felt right. He even bought her kids new uniforms for their schools and became a big hit in her circle of friends who came by with some home-made pickle or banana chips from time to time.

Then like all couples do, at times we would fight over small things. I would tell him to leave and go back to his own place. And it would be my maid who would say things like 'good men are hard to find'. And I would invariably call him back into my apartment and she would be happy since he would bring her gifts. It was a weird equation.

But there were days when he was not around that she would also mention things that I didn't want to hear. 'Baby,' that was what she called me, 'I hope you know that the people in this colony are talking about you.'

I was a little taken aback, 'What are they saying?' I asked. She shrugged her shoulders as she changed the faded blue sheets on my bed with bright paisley ones, 'Oh you know, the usual, like, "Has she got married?", "Who is he?", "Living in is illegal" . . .' she trailed off. I presumed she wanted to know more about the relationship than the nosy neighbours, but I wouldn't feed her with gossip.

'Who is asking?' I demanded to know.

'The lady in apartment 201. You know they all sit downstairs every evening discussing people in every apartment, na?' she said, while walking into the kitchen, knowing fully well that she had me deep into this conversation. 'I don't really care since I think Arjun baba is wonderful. But I thought you should know,' she said, while taking things out of the cupboards to make lunch.

'Well, I don't care!' I said indignantly, and she looked at me strangely. I did care. I always cared about what people said and thought about me. That's why I dressed conservatively when I walked out of the apartment, that's why I studied so much, so that people would not think I was a bimbette, and that's why I preferred art to movies, just so that 'society' would see me with respect. So that my parents would be proud of me. So that maybe I could be as accomplished as them. Maybe.

This conversation would plague me for a few days till Arjun came back. I invariably wanted to know why we couldn't hang out more at his place. I told him the dilemma I had about him living in with me. But he didn't seem to bother too much about gossip. He was adamant about us not going to his flat. The repeated arguments we had about the subject went something like this:

'Arjun, I think we should stay at your place for some time. I can work from there and you can come home to all your belongings. It would make us get away from Martha and this building for some time.'

'No. That's not a good idea. Kaveri, can you move while I see the highlights of this match? Sachin scored a century and I missed it!' he said, while craning to move me away from the television.

'Why not?' I asked while moving to a chair close by.

'Because, baby,' he also called me that, 'there are photos of my wife all over the place and it would make you uncomfortable.'

'Then put them away!' I would demand with my hands on my hips. But eventually he would pull me into his arms and say he would soon and if I could just please think of better things to talk about since he had had a hard day. And I would feel guilty and change the topic to his work.

The thing that kept us connected was the sex. That was the best part. Our sex was, to say the least, a white lightening, mind-blowing, and 'Jesus' invoking astounding piece of work. Let's put it this way, if I was a German, it would have been more exhilarating than the Berlin Wall coming down. If I was a basketball fan, it would have been like a day spent with Michael Jordan. If I were a nonstarter in the film industry it would have been like having a bigger hit than Shah Rukh's on an opening weekend. Every moment was amazing. And that's where our differences evaporated. We liked the same thing. We wanted it the same way. We wanted it always. And we were always satisfied.

After one particular fight we had, Arjun and I had incredible make-up sex. Now the thing is 'make-up sex' is always better than regular sex. It's probably because there's a sense that we could have broken up or it could have been our last time together. Hence, the passion was raw, deeply intimate and, bordering on violence, even. Completely invigorating!

But back to our conversation. We were lying in bed when I broached the topic of my virginity.

'You know Arjun, I was a virgin when I met you.'

Arjun was quiet for some time and then he said, 'Really?'

I turned over to look at him and said, 'Ya. You didn't know?'

He shook his head.

'That's ridiculous. How could you not have known?'

He shook his head and put his left palm on the back of his head and said, 'Okay, I figured.' And he smiled and I looked at him thinking a million thoughts. I was quiet. The notions of what a bride feels like on her wedding night came back to me. The night I was with Arjun in Goa for the first time was good, but painful. But after that, it unlocked the treasure chest of pleasure for me. I could never have enough. I was the one who always wanted more, even if he was tired. I was the one who 'kept count' and made him laugh in delight. Just because I hadn't ever done it didn't mean I hadn't ever read about it. And knowledge is a powerful weapon.

'What did you do before that?' he asked suddenly.

'What do you mean?'

'Well if you hadn't had sex, how did you know about it or feel it?' I thought about that. I had read about it and I had spoken about it with Aditi, but I had never really wanted to do something on my own. A solo plane ride was not fun for me. I needed to fly commercial.

'Nothing, really,' I replied.

He was shocked. 'What? You never pleasured yourself?' he asked with one eyebrow raised.

I shook my head. No.

He continued, 'But didn't you want to? Weren't you frustrated because you didn't?'

I said, 'Well, once or twice I tried it. But it did not work for me. Aditi told me to use the hand shower in the bathroom, but the water was too cold and it never did anything and I got bored.'

'But there are far more things to try out than a hand shower, aren't there?' he asked.

Yes, there were. There were dildos, your finger and bubble baths, candles and romantic music while lying on your bed, watching porn and imitating the women. There were hundreds of things that people did, but which did not give me pleasure. I didn't feel the need to. Maybe it was because of my conservative upbringing. As it was, I had too many things to deal with. On top of that, the one or two times I tried, I was too disgusted with the whole concept. And it never led anywhere in the time frame I gave it, which was five minutes, so I left it forever. I was impatient. It was something I didn't need to learn or master.

'I never felt like it,' I said plainly.

'You mean to tell me that for thirty years you never had sex and you never even masturbated?'

'Nope, and can we cut the topic please? It's making me uncomfortable,' I said, trying to busy myself with some papers.

'That's incredible.' He mumbled and went back to reading a book.

Suddenly I felt stupid. Maybe I shouldn't have brought up this topic. I was making myself vulnerable to him. I wanted to tell him I was a virgin so he would think this relationship was special. Like I did. But instead, he asked me about pleasure and passion. A topic that I had never confronted myself with. I wanted to put on my clothes and get away from him. I tried to get out of bed, so I and muttered, 'Do you want some coffee or ice cream . . .'

He pulled me back in, realizing my discomfort and said, 'All I meant was that for someone who never had too much sexual experience, you're quite good in bed!'

I smiled, 'Do you mean that?'

'Yes, baby. I do.'

Then I felt a little better and opened up a little more. 'I think that was the main reason why I wanted to get laid on my thirtieth birthday. I remember thinking that I was getting old and I didn't have a man in my life. But it was not only to fall in love, it was to have the sexual encounter that I hadn't been able to provide myself.' Then, after a pause, I added, 'Maybe if I had been satisfied with myself, I would not have felt so desperate.'

He put his arms around me and kissed my neck, 'Do you regret sleeping with me?'

'No, baby' I said, 'I'm in love with you. I'm happy I did it with you and not that random nerd at the bar.' He looked at me questioningly, and I shook my head trying to erase the memory of the double date with Aditi that night.

We cuddled for some time before he asked, 'So if you had to go back to being single, would you shag now or wait to be with a man again?'

I got up in shock.

'Are you planning to leave me?' I asked with fear.

'No, pumpkin,' he said, pulling me closer. 'I would rather die than leave you. All I'm asking is what would you do now say if I went on work for a month somewhere?'

I hadn't thought about that. Had my viewpoint changed? Not really. But would I want to just hold back and wait for him to come back or would I pleasure myself? I didn't know. It is said that once the orgasm is a part of you, you can't let it go and you need it like an addict.

But masturbation was not just about an orgasm for me. It was a feeling of an intimate moment with a deep part of you. And like I needed to fall in love with a man to sleep with him, I needed to fall in love with that part of myself to be able to be intimate with it. I know that's confusing, but think about it. If you were truly not happy with another person, would you go hug him? No. Would you strip bare in front of him? No. The same thing applies to our inner and outer selves. I was uncomfortable with my outer self. It was just skin. I did not fall in love with who I was. I just accepted the nicest part of me was my eyes. So why would I touch myself when it felt awkward even to me?

I looked at Arjun and deflected the topic by saying, 'I'm not letting you go anywhere!'

Arjun pulled me closer and started moving his hands down my back. I knew what was coming. He started murmuring softly the fantasy that was playing out in his head. And then he held my head with his right hand and kissed me passionately.

Why would I need anything more when I had him every night?

Sixteen

If we pay attention to the universe, there are always signs of what will happen in the future along the way. Women in love choose to ignore it because they don't want to bring in 'rational' into 'happy'. And that's the mistake. If I had seen the signs early on ... But for now, I was happy.

One evening, we were lying around on my bed, when a thought came to me. I knew it was soon, but I felt our relationship had gone from friends to lovers so fast that we were ready for another step. Some people might wait for years to decide what they need and how they feel, but we knew in a matter of weeks that we were so right for each other, that it didn't matter that he was married.

But a loving relationship is always a work in progress and I wanted to know deep down what he was willing to do for me, and how much he was willing to risk. So while we were watching *Indian Idol* one particular evening, I started the conversation. 'Arjun, can we please stop this stupid programme and talk?'

Arjun responded, 'Okay.' Then he put it on mute.

'I said off, not mute!' I knew I sounded like a wife.

He grumbled something and turned it off. We were lying around feeling really lazy after working the entire week on hectic projects.

I took a deep breath and started, 'Arjun, where are we going?'

Arjun said with a teasing smile, 'What do you mean? I thought we were going to couch out here tonight?'

I hit him lightly. God, I was already a 'wife' (Worries Invited For Ever). 'I mean with "us". Is there a future to this?' I asked.

This time, he was serious, 'Kaveri, think about this, when we have moments with people, we cherish them more. Haven't we had a blast since we've met? It's because we meet only a few days in a week at the most.'

I wanted to remind him that he had been sacking at my home for quite a number of days in a week and he went home only to collect his bills and get his maid to clean the cobwebs.

But he chose to continue his speech as if he had prepared for it, 'How many happy marriages do you see around you?' He paused here for dramatic effect and shook his head as if to prompt me to say 'none', but I sat stony-faced, not giving into his argument.

He shook his head for me and continued, 'Marriage is an institution. A *mental* institution. An institution in which you stop cherishing, stop loving, stop needing, stop desiring and stop feeling.' He said with dramatic effect and paused before he continued, 'If we only had a day or two with a person in a week, we would make every moment count.' Here he moved his hands around and fixed his gaze on the ceiling as if looking heavenwards for inspiration, 'Then you know you only need to live in that moment and that moment will remain perfect. That's how you make happy memories.' He concluded with a flourish and went back to switching on the TV and increasing the volume as if that was the end of discussion.

But I wasn't done. Did he just say that we would never get married? That was not a pleasant thought for someone in her thirties. And for someone who's biological clock was ticking. I took the remote from him and put it on mute and said, 'But no one can live like that forever.'

'Why not?' he asked, disinterested already.

'Well, because all relationships need to move to another level. Otherwise we would remain in a teenage-like frame of mind, flitting from one person to another. It needs to move to something more permanent.'

Arjun replied, 'The permanence is in the infrequency, the temporary. All relationships could be much happier if we don't own the person.' He was not even looking at me, but trying to shush me up to hear what Anu Malik had to say about a new contestant. 'Besides we *have* moved to another level in our relationship. We're practically living together. Isn't that enough for you?' he asked rhetorically.

I thought about it. We were living together. And the magic had faded a little I had to admit. Instead of having mad, passionate sex every night like we used to, here we were contented with watching a stupid TV show. And instead of having long debates about art and our travels, we argued about what food to eat. This felt like a marriage. But it wasn't *legal*.

'Don't you need a companion in your old age?' I asked the typical question my parents would have asked.

Arjun suddenly explained to no one in particular, 'There. I knew he was out of key!' he said completely ignoring me and probably hoping I would be distracted with what was on the screen. But I wasn't. So I nudged him and said, 'I asked you a question!'

'Hmm . . .? What? *Arrey baba*, let it go. Who do you think will win?' But I knew he had heard. I was way too smart for him to fool me and I raised my eyebrow in anticipation of an answer.

He succumbed and turned his body towards me and took a deep breath as if to explain one final time to a five-year-old what the algebra of relationships was all about. 'Okay! Who's to say the person you are with today will stick around till you're old anyway? There's no loyalty forever. Mammals are not meant to be faithful.'

I butted in immediately, 'Are you saying you're not faithful to me?' My voice was raised already. I had read somewhere that high-pitched voices come only from women who are threatened by the fact that their mates might be straying. My voice seemed to border between a squeal and a soprano.

'No, baby,' he said, taking me in his arms and kissing me

deeply. He wanted to divert the topic but I pushed him away, crossed my arms and said, 'Explain!'

And so he did. 'I'm saying that maybe in twenty years, you might not be faithful to *me*, or I might die or something. Do you want to give up what we have today for a marriage that ends in unhappiness? I've been there, done that. Not good, I say.'

'But I thought it was because you hadn't found the right person?' I asked, hoping for a correct answer. I looked around me. I had made so many adjustments for this man. My perfect house, with perfect white sheets and colourful pillows, was all gone. Instead, there was a mass of papers and junk that lay all over the place that belonged to him. My fridge that had mini tarts and apple juice and dal makhani was replaced with granola bars, orange juice and pasta. My life, that had no room for a second of wasteful TV watching, had been filled with endless hours of general random programming. I had made the changes. For him. Didn't he want to take that leap of faith?

He kept quiet for the longest time and then as an afterthought sighed and said, 'When did love become so conditional? If all relationships start with no strings attached, then why do they become so dependent half way through?' He continued even as he got up, went to the kitchen and brought back the tub of Ferrero Rocher gelato we had ordered with our dinner. 'Women should just be happy in the thought of love. He loves you, you love him, let it be. Why do women eventually always want more? And then the relationship becomes about the woman trying to dominate the man. Women can never let a man go out and smoke, or drink, or party with the boys. And if a woman goes out to do the same with girls, a man has to respect her "independence". Where is the equality in today's world? It's all in favour of women, really.'

Then he started feeding me the gelato with a spoon and all I said was, 'Please don't drop this on my bed. I've just changed the sheets this morning.' I heard him muttering, 'Nag!'

But I thought about what he just said. He did make sense. We all want to be free and independent. But we choose to find companions to change and then become dependent on them. Why do all relationships turn into a game of controlling each other, when, in the beginning, we're ready to give so much space to each other? But he hadn't answered my original question. And as I was soon to find out, he never would.

For now, I was too deep into him to realize what a great dodger he was. And with that, he shut off the TV, put the gelato on the side table, and took me in his arms and murmured about how I should show him he was not equal or worthy to be with me. I could not argue any more. He had decided what we should do for the rest of the night. And even though I wasn't pleased with his answers, I knew I shouldn't push him too hard or I would push him away forever.

Seventeen

But things started going wrong very quickly. I wanted more. And he was not ready. I gave in most of the time because the sex was so damn good! I wondered if all relationships headed in this direction. Soon, work became more important for him. Then there was always family who would pop out of nowhere. Family that he needed to take care of. A sick aunt, an old grand uncle, a cousin recovering from cancer. They popped out of the woodwork. And being the great family person he was, he could never say no to them. Which meant he had to say no to me. As an understanding girlfriend, I tried to act cool and let him do the things he needed to. But I secretly kept hoping he would ditch something, someone, sometime, and want to be with me. I hoped he needed me as much as I needed him. I hoped he wasn't with me only for the sex.

And then a thought hit me one fine day. *Where was I going in my life?* I knew what I wanted. But how come I wasn't getting it?

Then one day, it became a bit too much for my patience and I lost my cool. Once again, he had ditched me for something that he could 'just not get out of', as he put it, and I told him the words that men hate to hear and women hate to say, 'I think we should take a break.'

But, as usual, he wouldn't accept and convinced me to meet him at Coffee De to try and change my mind.

'Kaveri,' he started off, 'I'm so sorry. Please forgive me. I've been so stressed with work and my family is pulling me in all directions.'

'So stop!' I said, still in a grumpy mood.

'I can't. I'm so tied up! I know I've put our relationship on hold, but I thought we had reached a point where I could ... at least for some time ...'

He saw my face thinking about it and so he continued, 'I thought you would be more understanding towards my situation. You don't really have a full-time job. You can work as you please and you don't have responsibilities like I do! Please try and be more supportive. I promise I will do anything you ask once this bad phase is over.'

I know I didn't have a full-time job, but my commitments were important to me. I had given up a few projects so I could spend more time with *him*. I had responsibilities towards my maid, my clients and my parents. But I didn't tell him that. His obligations obviously seemed far more important.

'Okay,' I said, categorically, 'I want to know where we stand.' If I was going to be patient, I needed to know I was a priority.

'What do you mean?' he asked, seemingly annoyed with this topic again. He called for the waiter and frowned back at me.

'Well, where is this relationship going?' I demanded, with my arms folded over the table.

'When we met I thought you said you were on a road trip to discover life.' He tried to pawn off the responsibility on me.

'Well, yes. But ...' I said, trying to figure out my thoughts suddenly.

'So, fantastic! I want you to fulfill your dreams. We've always said we're such individual people who need space and freedom. So I'm giving you all the space you need, darling. You should do whatever makes you happy Kaveri.' The waiter brought over our regular orders. His was a black Americano. Mine was a cappuccino.

What would make me happy, I thought, is getting married to you. But had I said that, I would have sounded un-cool and clingy.

'With no strings attached ...' he was continuing in the background sipping his drink. But somewhere I had faded out his conversation. If he didn't love me enough to know what I wanted, why was I with this man?

'Arjun,' I heard myself saying, 'I think we need to give each other some space.'

'That's exactly what I'm saying ... No, wait a minute. That sounded ominous,' he said, quickly correcting his earlier statement.

'No. I mean, we need to break up. I really can't go on with this constant ditching. When am I going to be a priority for you?' I heard myself echoing Aditi's words.

'Baby, you're always my priority. Sometimes life gets in the way, but you are always my priority and I always want to do things with you. It's just that right now work is very tough. I need to prove myself in my company. And the competition is rough. People are breathing down my neck. If I don't deliver, I could lose my job! I hope you understand that?'

'Stop rambling, Arjun,' I said quietly. I had heard this before. 'I'm fed up. I'm sick and tired of being your last priority. I've had it,' I heard my voice rise for the first time.

He smiled and said, 'I can't stop you from thinking what you do. I can't stop you from doing what you want but just know, the mind calculates, the soul yearns, but what the heart knows, only the heart knows.' He tried to be philosophical to win my heart. And my heart was breaking in breaking up with him. But I knew it was the right thing to do. And my mind told me, 'you can't let go of something you don't have'.

'Kaveri, please give me one last chance. I know I've screwed up, but I promise I'll do better. And if I don't make it work, then I don't deserve you and you can dump me. But please, one last chance ...' he begged.

I kept quiet.

He became angry and said, 'Don't play by your rules all the time. Don't be an emotional fool. Don't think with your heart all the time. Don't over-analyse and emotionalize everything.

Go with the flow. Be mature. Be a grown-up. Be wise and ease up. How many shit fits have you thrown and how many have I? Your feelings of insecurity are your own imagination. Let them go. Be secure. Be patient. Don't make this a one-way street. You've got to see where I'm coming from!'

I raised my eyebrows. He thought I was immature? Well, I could prove him wrong. I would stick with him just to prove him wrong! What was I saying? What did I want?

'I made a mistake. Everyone does. No one is perfect, Kaveri. I still love you, irrespective of what happens,' he finished.

I responded, 'Every time I take two steps forward in "us", you say or do something that makes me feel insecure . . . and I'm still insecure about us. And can you stop ending sentences with "irrespective of what happens".' I wanted to clarify my point of view.

Arjun softened his stance, 'Okay, I apologize.'

'This whole relationship is an apology!' I ranted, trying to sound authoritative.

'I'm trying,' he pleaded, taking a different approach.

'You're the most trying man I know,' I said, almost in tears.

We were both quiet then. Maybe I'd hurt him. But I was hurt too. I wanted more. MORE. Marriage. Why couldn't he just give in and say he would give me that?

'Okay,' he said finally, 'If you can't let it be, then let it go.'

I was shocked. Was he trying to break up? I didn't want him to give up. I wanted him to agree and do as I wanted. 'What do you mean?'

'Why do good people fall for bad ones? Therein lies your answer.'

I wasn't getting it. Was this another mind game that he was playing?

'Arjun, do you want to break up?' I asked plainly.

'No. But apparently you do, so I'm giving you the easy way out.'

I relented immediately.

'Arjun, I want you to improve. I don't want us to break up,' I spoke resignedly, suddenly scared that all my ranting might make him leave.

'Kaveri, I don't know what you want. Your mind keeps changing. I'm so confused. Are you giving me a chance?'

'Yes, but this is the last chance you'll get. And on some conditions,' I said, wanting it to at least go somewhere in my favour.

'Whatever you want. Just spell it out clearly for me. I'm not a mind reader.'

So I listed things that I wanted from our relationship. And later I would know that all girls list the things they need. And the needs never end. Sometimes the needs would be simple like 'be more romantic', or 'spend time with me' and then there would be more complicated ones like 'when do we get married?' The needs go on. And soon enough, the men realize they can't match up to the needs and slowly start withdrawing to what they already have, a woman whose needs are already met, a woman who was their wife.

Eighteen

Slowly I realized that besides the great lovemaking, Arjun and I weren't really sharing anything else. He had stopped staying at my place and our meetings became rare. And Aditi had picked up on the situation during our various phone conversations. After one particularly depressing day, I called her and told her he wasn't around again. She told me to meet her immediately on her set where she was working a day and night shift. She wanted to hear in person what my feelings were and whether I was on the right track, according to her.

She gave me a tight hug when we met and sat me down on a comfortable, but expensive-looking, sofa in a corner of her film set. She sat on the large cushions in front of me and held my hand.

'Now tell me what's going on with you,' she asked.

When I told her that Arjun had gone out drinking instead of meeting me the previous night and then came home only to have sex and leave in the morning, Aditi completely blew her top. 'Really, babe, I don't get you!' She said with her hands flying all over the place. 'If this man loves you so much, why doesn't he take out all the time in the world for you?' she continued. 'Here, you made plans to meet him, and he doesn't even care? That's just not on!' She was furious. I didn't know whether at me or him.

'I know ... I know ... but maybe he was stressed,' I began timidly. 'He does take out time for me but he has a job, not to mention the mortgage on his old family home in Goa with old parents staying there.' I tried covering up for him. I don't know why I did that, but I suppose I felt if Aditi was right, my relationship would be in serious trouble. A fact I couldn't face at that moment.

'Stop making excuses for him, Kaveri. Till when will you keep doing that? Here is a man who doesn't make you his priority at all!' She was unforgiving and brutal. She made sense. She had experience on her side. But I was truly smitten. I didn't know what was happening to me. I didn't want to let him go. I wanted our relationship to work and I thought I could change him to be the person I needed and make him be a better man.

'I feel I'm the transition, the freedom that he doesn't get, the greener grass,' I tried to explain. I looked around to see who could hear us. There must have been 200 people on the set. Someone must have heard her ranting and my weak responses. But no one reacted. Everyone went about their busy ways.

Obviously it came out all wrong. Aditi retaliated, 'Kaveri. Seriously! Do you just want to be the greener grass? I mean, before he came along, you had made a list of the things you wanted in a man. He doesn't even fulfill half of them. So why do you *need* him so much?'

'He does fulfill some parts . . .' I trailed off, unable to defend him or myself any more.

'Okay, so he is intellectually stimulating and he is good in bed. What about the fact that he abuses you mentally? Don't shake your head. He does. He cancels on you at the last minute and expects you to be understanding about his life. But he expects you to drop your plans to be with him and will not understand if you cancel. He is manipulating you!'

'No!' I said vehemently, not really believing myself.

'This is not love. This is the death of love!' She proclaimed loudly and went off to shoot another scene.

I was left alone to think.

Can love die? Can love be like life where, with a death, there is a birth? So if I give up on one man, I'll get another one? I didn't think so. Arjun was my *one* 'Great Love' I believed. If I knew it would hurt to break up, why would I want to go through it? All men had flaws. All women knew that. The one thing I needed to do was to just take the most fatal flaw and turn it around to work in my favour. But there was a nagging feeling I couldn't get rid of. I felt something had changed within me too. I had started getting depressed. Depression is like a layer of dirt on your body that's invisible to everyone except yourself. And it doesn't go away no matter how hard you distract yourself. And the more you try and wash it away by doing things that supposedly make you feel better, the deeper it sets in, because all the other things are ephemeral.

Does depression go away on its own or manifest itself again when tragedy strikes? I didn't know the answer and I was too scared to tell either Arjun or Aditi. Both would react so differently. One would freak out and probably leave me and the other would make me leave him. I didn't want either. I was confused.

Aditi came back after shooting the scene and said that since the lighting was being put up in another part of the set, she could sit with me for a while longer. She had brought back the sticky sweet 'cutting' chai, that you get on shoots, along with a packet of biscuits. We sat there in silence for a while, eating and slurping hot tea. It was a cloudy day. I could hear people say that it was going to rain. In my heart too, I felt that it was going to rain.

Aditi broke our silence finally by saying, 'Are you *really* happy?'

'Yes. I've never felt this way about any man. And you told me that love is about compromise. Well, today I'm the one compromising, but tomorrow I know he will.' I had spoken a little too soon, probably because I had rehearsed it before she came back.

'If that's what you believe, then I'm happy for you,' she said, and looked away. 'This is a bad relationship that never ends.' She proclaimed and sighed at me.

I was getting a little annoyed. Maybe it was her self-righteous attitude towards me or the fact that she had hated him from the moment I had told her about him. Or maybe I was frustrated about her sarcasm and Arjun's involvement with me. But I snapped. What did she know anyway? Where was her perfect man and her ideal relationship? She was a grown woman who was still an Assistant Director. Shouldn't she have moved on to do something better with her life, her career, her marriage even? I spat back at her. She replied that she was looking to make a movie but needed to go through the grind of filmmaking like everyone else.

I brushed her aside. I said sarcastically, 'If that's what you believe, then I'm happy for you!'

She got up to say she was leaving since she had work to do. Then Aditi said something that really shook me, 'One day, you'll get tired of the roles you play and long for the life you deserve. Unless you choose to break the shackles of comfort, you'll never know what really makes you happy.'

Was that true? Was I living in a comfort zone? In a sadistic, masochistic cocoon that only I thought made me happy when everyone around me knew it was toxic to my life? What was the alternative? Another man? Another relationship? Was there a parallel relationship out there that was better than this? Would it not have the same hardships? Maybe I should stop looking for a 10 on 10 relationship and be happy with a 6 or a 7. Maybe we should accept the flaws of a person since they live with ours as well.

I took a cab back to my empty apartment and realized that Love indeed was a bitch.

Nineteen

The next few days, I thought harder about what Aditi had said. But a calamity at work shook me so hard that my viewpoint was completely reversed on the subject. I got fired or the equivalent of it. I was told by the Italian Embassy that I had bungled the brochure they had asked me to do and my work had become substandard. They never wanted to work with me again. I was shattered. I had thought I had done everything for them, but apparently, I had made a crucial mistake in their brochures, one that would cost them a lot of money to fix. They reprimanded me for my negligence. I was devastated. Even though there were plenty more offers I could have taken up, I had taken up this job and worked on it for four months. So I immediately called Arjun and told him I had been fired. He took off from work and came right over to meet me.

He postponed his meeting and was there at my doorstep within the next thirty minutes. Even pizza has not been delivered this fast! I started howling as soon as I saw him. And he held me till I cried the pain away. I kept trying to talk in between my sobs of, 'I'm an awful interpreter.' And, 'I really screwed up.'

He nodded and said, 'No, you're not, darling. They are all assholes. Everyone makes mistakes. It's all right.' And I cried some more. And then he asked if he could make coffee for us. I nodded. He knew me and my desire for coffee when things became too stressful. So he got up and walked to my small, airy kitchen with white marble tops and dark wooden cupboards on top and bottom. Interspersing the white tiles, between the cupboards, there were little tiles with paintings of fruits and vegetables. It was a pretty kitchen and it overlooked the sea. Okay, if you craned your neck out of the window really hard to the right, you could see the sea, but most of the time I drew the bright yellow and green curtains to block out the harsh sun and the peeping neighbours from a building away. The kitchen had seen some fun times with Arjun and me. But today he just put the kettle on the stove and took out the colourful red mugs to make me some coffee.

'Look,' he said from the kitchen after some time, 'I don't even know why you're working with these stupid people.' He brought out the two red mugs—a steaming hot and frothy cappuccino for me and a black coffee for himself. 'I mean translating is not even a real profession. It's a hobby. And you're getting paid for it so great, but is this what you want to do for the rest of your life?'

'I don't know,' I said, taking the cup from him. 'Cookies?'

He went back into the kitchen to get the glucose biscuits I truly loved. He kept talking while walking back and forth, 'I mean, how long do you want to be just a translator? Where will it take you anyway?'

I was going to say an international interpreter at the United Nations, living in Switzerland and travelling across Europe whenever I liked. It was a quiet existence, but it would give me two of my favourite things in the world, art and travel. I would have been an interpreter for art galleries, maybe working at the Louvre or discovering new forms of art and language. That was my dream. That was what I had wanted when I took up this profession. But I kept quiet. I was so under his spell and so morose from being fired that what he said had started making sense.

'Here's an opportunity for you to truly discover who you are. Don't think of it as a setback. Think of it as a blessing in disguise.'

I started feeling slightly better. 'Do you really think so?' I asked, still unsure of myself.

'Absolutely, baby. And I'm right here for you. I'll always be here whenever you need me, like I told you.'

He was right. He had proved it today. Arjun stayed over, and stuck by my side. I was truly, deeply in love with him.

Aditi's words had faded from my memory already.

A few days later though, a strange thing happened. I should have taken it as an omen right then, but I decided on an alternative course post it. Arjun and I had gone out for dinner to a beautiful new place. I had asked him to bring back romance into our relationship—one of the 'needs' I had. So we went on a Tuesday, a relatively light day for people to venture out. It had been raining that day and the air was damp and sultry. I had an ominous feeling about the whole thing. For starters that day, I had another confrontation with my maid early in the morning.

'Baby,' she had said very abruptly when I was in the kitchen trying to make myself a soy milkshake, 'what should I do with these underclothes?' she asked, as she held out Arjun's underwear in my face. They were clean since I had already done the laundry. She had folded all my clothes and kept them on my bed to put away into the cupboard. I didn't know why she was having a problem since she always folded his shirts and kept them on the bed for me to put away.

'Just leave them on the bed, Martha,' I said, drinking my shake and walking to the living room to watch TV. I don't know at which point in my life I had become more of a TV addict and less of a reader. But I guess when you have another person making decisions about your time, you begin to accommodate your tastes to get into his good books. Martha followed me into the living room and threw the garment on the couch.

'I am *your* maid. Not everyone else's,' she said with a pout.

'Now where did that come from? I thought you liked Master D'Souza?' I inquired.

She stayed quiet and I prodded her further, 'What is going on? Is he not nice to you?'

Losing My Virginity and Other Dumb Ideas

'No, no, he is very nice. It's just that I get this feeling . . . that he is married,' she said suddenly. And then for a moment I went pale. How had she guessed? But I kept cool and asked, 'Why do you say that?' She shrugged her shoulders and said, 'When you're not here and he's at home, I've seen him talking to someone very quietly, like someone would with a girl. And I know it's not you. It's a different tone. And it's like he has known her for a long time, not a loving tone—not as if he's cheating on you with someone new, but with someone else. So I can only assume it would be his old girlfriend or his wife. Either way, it's not good for you to keep seeing him.'

I didn't know why I had given my maid so much leeway to speak so many things. I suppose since she had been with me for eight years, she and I figured that she was the closest thing to a guardian I had in Mumbai and she felt she needed to look out for me. It was now becoming a disturbing equation since I would have to start hiding things from her along with giving her explanations about my love life!

'Don't worry too much, Martha. Just do your job,' I said, trying to sound nonchalant. I left it at that.

In the evening when Arjun picked me up for our romantic date, I felt I needed to hide this fact from him as well. And later that evening, we were exposed.

While we were having dinner, Arjun looked up and saw a familiar face entering the restaurant. He immediately panicked and asked me to go along with his story.

'Hi, Arjun!' greeted a tall, burly man with a thick moustache and a British accent. Arjun got up to shake his hand, and the woman with him, who had a saccharine-sweet smile on her face giving away the fact that she suspected something was fishy.

'Hi, Nina,' Arjun greeted her and then completely ignored me while he asked them how they were and when they came back from London. Nina took out her palm and stretched it to me saying, 'I'm Nina. I'm sorry, I didn't catch your name?'

Arjun immediately butted in saying, 'Ayesha. I'm so sorry

guys. I completely forgot to introduce you. This is Ayesha. She runs a production house and we're trying to figure out what to say in our meeting tomorrow to get her project approved with the channel.'

I was stunned. He was lying through his teeth to people I had never heard about before. What was going on? He gave me a look that said I had better play along with his story and so all I did was shake hands and smile. I didn't trust my voice. I was too shaky and uncertain about what was going to come out. After he politely told them that he would catch up with them later, they went to another table and Arjun immediately asked for the check.

'What is going on?' I asked for the second time that day.

'They are my wife's sister and brother-in-law,' he said, gulping down his drink and putting his credit card in the bill folder.

'So?' I asked unsure. He just stayed quiet as he got up and expected me to follow. So I left my drink half way and walked out with him. As soon as we got out, the cool air from the sea hit my face along with a stench of dried fish. It seemed as if there was something fishy about this night. We got into his car and I asked him again, 'Arjun, *so what* if that was your wife's sister? I thought you said your marriage was on the rocks and you would tell her as soon as she got back?'

'Ya but I don't want her to figure out through the grapevine.' He spoke while driving, his face stony hard.

'How does it matter? You'll have to tell her the truth anyway.'

'The truth is overrated,' he said this with complete calmness and I couldn't believe it. The truth was the most important thing to me! For some people, the most important virtue was loyalty or fidelity, or even if you weren't loyal, at least that you were supportive and loving. But for me, dishonesty qualified as a deal breaker. That's why I had slept with Arjun in Goa for the first time. He had been honest with me. Completely up front. And I had taken that decision because I liked that quality about him.

If he was not planning to tell his wife about us, how would

there be an 'us'? She had to agree that he was in love with someone else and then give him a divorce. How else was he planning to separate? And then a most horrible thought entered my head that made me blink back the fear that came rushing into my heart . . . maybe he was not planning to divorce her at all. Maybe he was just using me! So I asked him, 'Arjun, how do you plan to divorce your wife?'

That's when I knew that something was wrong even though I did not admit it to myself. He took a long time to answer, 'I'll figure it out.' He dropped me back home stating that he was very tired and his mind was reeling with this development and he needed to figure out lots of things. He was even slightly annoyed with me for making a suggestion to go to that place or for asking for a romantic night out. But I let it slide. I didn't fight back and quietly went home.

Aditi's words were coming back to me, 'Married men do not get a divorce—it's an urban myth.'

Twenty

Instead of confronting Arjun about his plans and about us, I attributed that date as unfortunate and left it at that. I submerged myself in work. It had been approximately two weeks since that night when he dropped me off in stony silence and I wanted a proper date again and a proper explanation . . .

It was Saturday night. He said he would pick me up at seven. 'Let's make it a long night,' he had said. 'We'll go out drinking, dancing and then come back to your place.' I was excited. With work and my new boss at the Russian Embassy taking all the fun out of my life, I had been feeling like an old maid of late. And this was probably going to be our last night together for a long time since his wife was supposed to come back the following week. Arjun had planned to tell her about us. God knows where that would end! So here I was at 6.30 in the evening, trying to decide what to wear. I didn't want to really dress up and make it look like I had overdone it. Nor did I want to feel I was underdressed in case he took me to a nice place. I felt like it was a first date even though we had been living together and he had seen me naked!

I pulled out a nice pair of jeans that didn't make me look too fat. I had managed to find a really good pair at Fendi after searching all the top brands. I chose a dark purple sleeveless top with a little bling on the collar, a pair of silver hoops and some silver bangles to match. I slipped my feet through nice, long heels to lift my butt and make my legs look longer than the 5 feet 4 inches I was. Okay, I was 5 feet 3 and a half, but that really didn't go well with my personality so I've stuck to saying five-four. A little kajal, some lip gloss like the magazines said, and I was ready. I switched on the TV and waited, flipping through the channels for a while. Same old reruns and I started getting a little impatient.

7.21

He still hadn't come. I SMSed him. 'Where are you?'
No reply.

7.33

I sent another SMS 'Hey. Beginning to get worried. Where are you? I'm at home.'
No reply.
Then I got really worried. What if he has been in an accident? What if someone has stolen his mobile and he was at the police station filing an FIR. What if . . .
My phone beeped. An SMS.
'Wife came back early. She fell. Took her to hospital. Call you tomorrow.' I read it a few times. Okay, so he had not been in an accident. That was the good news. The terrible news was that he was with his wife. But she was supposed to come back a week later. I was hurt and angry. His wife had taken away a beautiful night that we had planned, not to mention an entire week of togetherness. And why did he just have to be with her? Couldn't he have called her best friend or some other relative to look after her? But logic said it was obvious. He had to be with her. She was hurt and it was no fault of hers that she fell. Or was it? Did she get to know he was going out and purposely fall so he didn't have to go? Was it a ploy?
'No' my mind said. How could she know? He had been discreet. But the answer was right there in front of me. He was married. He was being discreet so as not to hurt his wife. His

wife. Someone he made a commitment to long time back. And no matter what he said about how he didn't love her now, he had loved her once. Otherwise why would he be in the hospital room with her now? God, why was I sitting here, fully dressed, making excuses for him? He had just dumped me. After making a plan for two weeks and rescheduling my work, his travel, and especially with his wife's return, I needed a night with my man. But was he even *my man*?

I got up and started taking my accessories off. I went into the bedroom, where I had strewed all my clothes and shoes and jewellery. My lovely king-size bed in the middle of the room, with side tables of dark mahogany, was completely covered with stuff. I had done up my place really well, I thought. I was an independent, successful woman who bought lovely, white bed sheets and colourful throw cushions from Zeba. A bed that showed how independent and aesthetic I was before I was in a relationship. And here was a bed that was covered with doubt, anticipation, and an entire wardrobe.

What had I turned into?

I didn't feel like crying. I could have, but I didn't. What came instead were the voices in my head.

'Why doesn't he leave his wife for you?'

'Do you *really* want him to?'

'Isn't the point of all relationships a commitment that will end in marriage?'

'For God's sake, woman! He is already married. And he has never mentioned marrying you ...'

'But suppose he was to get a divorce, get rid of his wife, and then marry you!' Isn't that what his wife had also thought?

'What if he does the same thing to me that he did to his wife? Find someone else after five years of marriage.'

'Don't be silly. He is in love with you. He has waited all his life to be with a person like you. He cherishes you and wants to be with you. Why would he cheat on you?'

It's true. My voice had reason. He would not cheat on me.

He loves me. And it was unfortunate that his wife had tripped and fallen. He was being a good 'man' rather than just a good husband by taking her to the doctor. And now he will tell his wife he loves me and get that divorce. It's a good thing she came back early. Things for a commitment will now speed up.

I was trying to convince myself. It sounded feeble but the dialogue with the voice in my head had changed my mood from dispirited to reassured.

My heart lifted. Slightly. I got into my bright yellow pyjamas and got the take-away menu folder from my side drawer. I called for a Subway sandwich and an iced tea. Yes, I wanted a brownie with that. I think I deserved a little treat That's what love does to you, I thought, it makes you more mature, more tolerant, more caring. I was happy with my new avatar. I started feeling a little bad for his wife. Poor thing was hurt, in a hospital room, and didn't even know that her life was about to change.

Looking back at it, I would always remember this night as when I truly lost myself.

Twenty-one

I was wrong. Her life wasn't about to change. Mine was.

He didn't SMS till the next afternoon. I had seriously started thinking the worst. But the worst was yet to come, when we met that night. He took me to a lounge where we could see the sea and listen to some nice jazz music, and the atmosphere was lovely. But the tension between us was unsettling.

I was wearing my Fendi jeans again, and a nice sleeveless white top with some long beads. My diamond studs in place, I felt I looked fresh enough for him not to even think about his wife anymore and cool enough for me not to be bothered even if he did mention her.

He looked great too with his two-day-old stubble and his casual chic grey pants and a striped black shirt.

As soon as we ordered drinks and starters, he started, 'Babe, I'm so sorry about yesterday.'

'Don't worry about it,' I said, trying to act cool and mature. 'I'm perfectly okay, so let's plan another night. I mean, we should, na?'

He paused for a second. 'Of course, we can. I want to. I want to actually plan a holiday with you.' This came out of the blue. I would have thought he would have the courage to explain why he had dumped me yesterday and why he hadn't called all morning. But instead of sounding like a colossal crib-oid, I just went all giggly and teenager on him. 'A holiday? Really? That would be great. Where should we go?' I said straying from the topic.

'Anywhere you want.' The bearer came and gave us our drinks and we toasted to 'Greece in the summer!' The wife matter was like an elephant under the table that neither of us was willing to notice.

I was dying to ask the question, but since I didn't want to bring up the 'wife' topic I said instead, 'For how long should we go?' I know our conversation was veering towards the absurd, but I didn't care what we spoke about as long as it wasn't his marriage.

'We can go for four–five days. I mean, with both our work and all, I don't think we'll get more time than a few days off including the weekend, and with Maria at home in . . .' he trailed off.

I stopped drinking. There it was. A slip of the tongue or intentional I would not know, but finally it was out. Something was not right. He seemed unsure and yet eager to please. This was not like him. The man I knew was supremely confident, took charge, and would tell me if we were going on a holiday, where we were going, when, and for how long. He would have made bookings and paid up and let me just pack my clothes. He wouldn't be hesitating and pausing. So I kept quiet. The waiter brought our order of food. I picked it up and offered it to him. He picked up a fork and a knife and gently cut it into four pieces and then offered the fork back to me. His manners were impeccable. Something that proved that he was nervous since he was generally a klutz. It was also a sign that he was playing for time. I waited for him to say something while I sipped my drink.

He had said her name. It was only right that I waited for him to elaborate or apologize. We had made a pact that we wouldn't say her name. We would only use 'her', 'she' or 'Mrs'. So it had slipped out.

'Kaveri, I need to tell you something.' I kept chewing.

'I want you to know that I love you,' he said with great conviction, though I could see he was holding his breath.

I felt better. Marginally. That was a nice thought. He loved me. I loved him. Whatever it was then, could be fixed.

'Maria is pregnant,' he blurted out.

At first I thought I hadn't heard right, so I wanted to say 'what?', but then I knew I had and didn't want to hear the name or that forbidden word in a sentence again, so I kept quiet.

I stopped eating. I couldn't swallow. I couldn't move. I wanted to scream. I wanted to hit him. But what I really felt was a wave of sadness pouring over me. I still wanted to act cool.

'I need a cigarette,' I said finally looking around. 'People in such situations feel better when they smoke.'

'But you don't smoke,' he interjected.

'So?' I retorted. I knew he was against smoking and secretly felt happy that I was going against his ideology. A rebellious act which seemed absurd compared to his. Yes. That's what I thought, I'll make him cringe like he had just made me cringe with his announcement. The comparison was stupid but it felt right at the time.

He remained quiet for some time till the bearer brought us a pack of cigarettes. I took one and the bearer lit it and left.

Arjun started speaking all at once, as if he was in a debate and was given only two minutes, after which the bell would go off ending his turn.

'This happened five months ago. She didn't tell me and she herself didn't know. It was on our trip to Paris, our last trip together where we decided that our relationship was not working—our last night together, for old times' sake. And I promise you I haven't slept with her since then. I have been faithful to you for these last four and a half months. When we came back, she left for her parents' place and I thought she would come back to take her things and say it's finally over. She never once mentioned this even on the phone . . .' He trailed off.

I didn't know what to say so I kept quiet.

He looked at me and took my hand. I recoiled immediately. I didn't want to be touched. I just wanted a plan, now that my dreams had been shattered.

'Baby,' he started, 'I love you . . .'

'I don't see how,' I interrupted softly.
'Don't say that. I didn't know.'
'Is that why you cancelled on me yesterday?' I asked trying to make sense of this new development.
'Well, she came back early and I realized she was pregnant . . .'
'Obviously,' I said sarcastically. My maid's words came back to me. She had warned me that he was talking to his wife. Obviously he must have known or suspected something but didn't say anything to me.

He continued in the background while my mind was racing towards where my life would be headed now. 'Then when I was leaving, she tripped and cut her lip on the kitchen counter. I took her to the hospital and while the doc was asking her some questions as to what meds to give, she confirmed that she was pregnant for about five . . .' he trailed off again.

'Please stop saying it,' I said quietly. I wish I could have raved and ranted. Or at least thrown the drink on his face and walked out. That would have been what Aditi would have done. But I wasn't her. And I didn't know how to react. All I wanted was the pounding in my head to stop and for him to take back his words.

'Okay, I'm sorry.' He stopped talking for a while and we sat there in silence. Then he cleared his throat and leaned over to speak, 'But I have a plan. So please hear me out.'

I started stuffing my mouth with food so I wouldn't start sobbing.

'I didn't know about this. She tricked me. I have been completely yours since we've met. I want to have you in my life because I can't see myself without you. So please tell me what you want after hearing me out okay?'

I desperately wanted to say okay and hear him out, but I couldn't. 'I don't know,' I heard myself saying. I could have just left. This man was going to have a child with another woman, his wife, in fact. Where did I fit into any of this anyway? Wasn't having a family a deal breaker in relationships?

The little voice in my head started again: who made these rules anyway? What does your heart say?

Should I ask him to leave her and be with me? A moral voice in my head said it was wrong. He was the Father. He had to do the Right Thing. Would his parents help her? Maybe, maybe not. How could I do this to her? What kind of an unscrupulous human being would I be?

But I knew I could not be with him either. Well, that's what I thought for now. 'I think we should break up,' I said. Though my heart was breaking just saying it.

'Please Kaveri. Please don't do that. We can work this out together.'

'How?' I said, almost in tears now.

'Please give me some time before I can be with you. Right now, I suppose I'll be around when she needs me and once the baby is three or four months and she is more settled I'll find her a place of her own, get her a good maid who can look after the baby, set the infrastructure up, and then I can be with you.'

It was logical. And less heartless.

'But wouldn't you want to be part of the baby's life? Her life?' I asked trying to blink away my tears and my shattered dreams.

'I don't feel a part of this baby. It was one night in Paris where she tricked me to save this marriage. I had specifically told her that it was the last time, as a goodbye and thank you for spending so many years together. I didn't know this was going to happen. Hell, she even said it was the "safe" time.'

He began to make sense in some odd way. Or had I completely lost my sense of self worth?

'And since five months are already up, it's only a matter of a few more. I'll be free of her and be yours completely. Kaveri, you have to believe me, I've never felt this way about anyone. After all, it has only been four months since we've known each other and I'm already "committed" to you. I was with her for twelve years and there was never anyone after her. Until I met you.' He pleaded. He was almost begging me not to leave. I had never seen a guy like this before.

I did love him. He was the first man I had slept with. The only man I ever wanted to be with. If he was genuine about what he was saying, I could have a future with him.

He saw a ray of hope in my eyes and continued, 'Please trust me. I want to do the right thing for all of us.'

He was a good man. Maybe I could wait. After all, what were a few more months? It was just a little more than half a year. And half a year slips by so quickly that even gym memberships would get over before you could actually attend the gym. My head was swimming in a sea of confusion and pain.

'I don't know, Arjun. I really don't know. I need time to think. I need to be alone right now,' saying that, I got up and left the place. He tried to run after me. But I was too far gone. I had got into a cab and left. I needed to breathe. I needed to cry. I needed to call Aditi and tell her that she had been right.

And I had been so wrong.

Twenty-two

That evening, I went home and tried to sort out my head. There were too many voices telling me what to do. I took off my clothes, got into my pyjamas and ordered a pizza and a brownie. I was depressed and hungry. I lay on my lovely bed and thought I should tell Aditi to come over. But before I could do that, my phone buzzed. I looked at it. It was a text from Arjun.

'Please don't take this the wrong way. I'm madly in love with you. I beg you. Don't break my heart.'

I refused to reply. I put on the TV and tried to distract myself. My phone buzzed again. It was Arjun. Man, he was persistent!

'I promise to make us work, if you let me.'

I had more ego than love right now. I wasn't going to SMS back. He could keep texting me the whole night, I thought. Let him *really* be hurt.

But the messages stopped. That was it. No more. And that pissed me further.

Shouldn't he be more remorseful? Doesn't he want me back?

The food came. I realized that this relationship was making me fat. I wasn't one of those women who didn't feel like eating when she was stressed. I was one of those who needed to eat more after a heartbreak. I thought food would be comforting, but halfway through stuffing my face with calorie-laden food, I started crying. I left the pizza on the floor of the living room and went to my room and slept.

Arjun didn't SMS after that. I kept getting up at night to

check if he had. Secretly, I hoped for many more repentant SMSes. But none came. I felt even more devastated. And when I woke up, I decided to delete him from my life. The next few days, there was so much work that I could not meet Aditi. I had to translate articles of senior delegates for a brochure for a conference to be held the following weekend. I plunged myself into work so I wouldn't think about my sorrow, that I would forget the loneliness. But caught in the crevasses of time, not being able to face the disconcerting feeling of being alone, I made another dumb mistake.

I started SMSing Arjun again.

And Arjun would SMS on and off and our relationship went back to the comfortable friendship that it used to be. This is what I loved about him, his ability to make me feel alive and special, the ability to make me laugh about my work and take it easy. His naughty SMS followed by my cribbing about work led us to being friends who would 'figure things out'. And that, I suppose, seemed good enough for now as compared to the depressed and lonely feeling I had been having for some time.

But I needed to tell Aditi. I needed female companionship. I met up with her the following Sunday evening. I was wearing my lovely new black skirt and an old, beige, silk top and some earrings and was feeling quite optimistic. Aditi smashed my positive attitude in seconds!

'He's what?' she gaped, in mid sentence at the Brouhaha Lounge, as soon as we'd ordered.

'Ya. He's having a baby with his wife.'

'What is wrong with you? And you're still talking to him?' I nodded my head.

Aditi was appalled, 'I can keep telling you what a scum bag he is, but until you feel it's over, it really won't be.' She elucidated every word in her usual manner. 'You are clinging to a man who is giving you less than you deserve. How much more *understanding* do you want to be? Till he uses you as a doormat and throws you away in a few years when he finds someone he can truly respect?'

I was upset. 'That's harsh,' I said.

But she continued, 'There's a saying—for every minute you're unhappy, you've lost 60 seconds of happiness. How many seconds have you already lost from your life by being with him?'

I reflected on that. She was right. Reality was that he was going to have a child! Someone who would be part of his life forever. And if I was with him, the child might be a part of mine as well. From mistress to stepmom—in the blink of an eye! Was reality so difficult for me to see?

I wanted to focus on what was good about us, what he was giving to me. So I said something that sounded logical only in my head, 'I can't base my entire love on him being physically present for me constantly.'

Aditi took a long sip of her drink and held out a cigarette. A waiter came to light it. She smoked occasionally and I profusely objected to it most times. But tonight I needed one as well. That was one too many, too soon, but I forgave myself.

She finally said, 'I told you to treat this as a fling. But you went and fell in love with him. Whereas he still treats this as a fling.'

Hmmm. That made sense. I should start thinking about Arjun as someone who gives me that momentary happiness. And use him for that. After all, maybe I was the one who read the signs all wrong. Or maybe, I was just fooling myself again.

'You're delusional,' Aditi commented. I looked at her with a wry smile.

Aditi continued, 'Alright. I know you're not going to give him up. So I give up. I won't even lecture you about it anymore.'

I smiled at her and looked away. We surveyed the room. It was filled with young career oriented people ranging in the age group of twenty-five to thirty. Most of them were couples, sitting on the white sofas against the glittering gold walls whispering to each other as the music became louder. They looked happy and in love. Not confused and in misery.

'Maybe he has stopped loving you because you've turned into his wife!' Aditi said suddenly, still looking at the couple who were toasting to each other now.

'Who says he's stopped loving me?' I asked indignantly.

'Well, maybe not stopped loving, but he's definitely not head over heels about you.' Before I could object she continued, 'If he was really in love with you, my dear, he would be here right now instead of me. He would be taking you out!'

I mused over that again and she took the opportunity to continue advising, 'Okay. So here's the way to go with this. Be the diva he fell in love with. Don't be the empty glass, be the colourful alcoholic drink he desires,' here she raised her glass which was already half empty and drank the rest in one gulp. She continued, 'Be out of love. Use him for sex! My original theory. But be on the lookout for someone new.'

It wasn't so easy to be out of love, I thought. How could you go from being in love to thinking the relationship was a fling? Really, 'Love' sometimes needs a manual! This was the exact reason why I had not been involved with a man till I turned thirty. In hindsight, maybe I should have waited a few more years.

'The best way to get over a man is to get under another one!' she exclaimed.

Aditi rambled on in the background about how love and sex needed to be different. How she had warned me about the dangers of being in love with a married man and how I should listen to her about the ways of getting out of this relationship. But I loved Arjun. I didn't know the exact reasons why, but I did. He knew me better than anyone. Even Aditi. He understood me better than my parents. I excused myself to go to the loo.

I looked in the mirror and saw a woman very much in love. He wasn't just having a fling. She believed in him.

And again, I did a dumb thing.

I took out my phone and sent him an SMS—'I believe in us. I believe this love can't be fake. I believe that God wouldn't have brought us together if He didn't believe we deserve this love. You are everything I've wanted in a man. I don't need to search anymore. This is not the end. We will get through this together. I will never let you go.'

He immediately replied with 'Thank you, baby, for keeping the faith.'

Okay, so it was snappy and curt. But it made me feel better. It made me feel *real*. I went back to Aditi with a better outlook and enjoyed the evening, even though she kept giving me gyan throughout the night.

Twenty-three

There comes a time in one's life when you really wonder what you were thinking. Because when you look back at your life, you know that obviously you weren't thinking straight. For some people, it can be about the way they dress. For some, it's about their decision to take up a job they hated. And for some it's about the marriage decision they've made. For me, it was the decision to stay with Arjun, even after he told me he was having a baby with his wife. I knew then what the term 'hopelessly in love' meant. It meant that you're hopeless to even think straight when you're in love.

Arjun and I continued meeting after his wife returned from her parents' place. But this time, things had changed. He was not available in the evenings or on weekends. I had to maintain a distance, so I couldn't call or SMS when he was at home. He didn't want to upset his wife and cause any danger to her pregnancy since she was already in a delicate state. At times, I was frustrated and really angry, but then he would take a day off every week to see me, and once, we even went away for the weekend to Alibaugh and I was back in love with him. This cycle repeated itself and it seemed good enough for me. As soon as I would get upset with the situation, he would pacify me by taking me to a fancy restaurant or coming over to make love. And as usual, our sex was so amazing that it made me forget all the bad things that were happening. But one thing I could not forget was the loneliness that had come creeping into my life.

And this aloneness translated into depression. Where I was earlier confused about why I was depressed, I now knew the exact reason behind the raging illness. It was because I was 'hopelessly in love'. Everyone has one friend in his or her lifetime who is supportive, encouraging and who loves you unconditionally and tells you exactly what you want to hear, even if it means being brutal. Aditi was my best friend. When I had any problem, I would go to her.

Today I was feeling low. I was having a tussle between my head and heart.

My heart was saying that I loved him and he loved me. My head was saying I deserved better. So I called Aditi and she immediately came over. We sat on my bed with the AC on, and a hot cup of tea. The opposites in my life were blaring!

'I'm feeling so mad at myself,' I started off. 'I'm feeling like such a loser.'

'Kavu,' Aditi interrupted.

'No, let me finish . . . I have a feeling that I shouldn't have given myself to this at all! I should have listened to you. I'm completely useless in matters of love.'

'Listen Kavu, please stop being so harsh on yourself. It's okay if you want to break up with him today, it's okay if you want to get back with him tomorrow and it's okay if you don't decide and let things be. I'm not going to judge you and more importantly, please don't judge yourself. You are a strong, intelligent, independent woman who deserves to feel like a queen. If you are unfulfilled and unhappy, then you need to take a call. Always be happy.'

This was a new side to Aditi I had never seen before. But instead of talking to her about her life and her goals, I went back to being self-absorbed. And after pondering on her comment for some time I replied, 'I'm not happy. With life.'

'So what can you do?' she asked softly, sincerely.

'I don't know.'

'It's okay, babe, not to know. You are a gentle soul. A really caring person.'

'Ya and look where's that led me,' I said, extremely dejected and angry.

'Shut up. Don't keep badgering yourself.'

I started crying and, between my sobs, I said, 'I can't let go of him. I tried to make him jealous, but he's still not responding ... I tried to call him, but he's busy ... I've tried to steel my heart against him, but I want ...'

Aditi waited for me to finish sobbing and I continued, 'I want him on my terms. I want him to be there for me when I need him. I don't want him to be there when it's convenient, or when he's not too tired, or when his wife doesn't need him. I want him to make me feel special.'

Aditi nodded understandingly, not talking, just letting me be. None of her usual gyan hurled at me. She had turned into a patient, understanding, mature friend and I could not even see it then.

'It's just so hard getting out of bed and doing anything ... I want to curl up and go back to sleep every morning I wake up!' I sobbed as I continued to rant. 'I get into autos and start crying half way through the journey. And I can't stop ... because it's just too painful! I can't push myself to exercise because my body feels like lead. I can't work because all I can think of is why is this happening to me?'

'Welcome to the world of a heartbreak, babe,' Aditi said jokingly and smiled. 'I want you to know that I will be there for you no matter what you do. I will always have your back.' And then after a pause, she added more firmly, 'But I seriously hope you do the right thing.'

'I don't know how to let go, Aditi,' I said with grave importance.

'Think how you will be affected long-term and make your decision. But just be happy. And be at peace with yourself ...' And then after a long pause, she added, 'And Kavu, being alone is not such a bad thing. Because if the alternative is compromising on your values, your happiness, your integrity, loneliness is just a minor aberration . . . you need to know you will find someone who will care for you. The way you want. And there will be a person out there. Maybe not today, maybe not in a year, but one day. And he will come. You need to hold on to who you are. Only then can you survive this game of love.'

'It's a game?' I asked incredulously.

'Yes, darling. It's a game.'

'I don't want to play games. I'm not good at games.'

'No one wants to. But you'll learn. And it won't be tough. And when you really fall in love, it won't be a game anymore.'

'When will that be?'

'One day, babe. One day . . .'

I sighed, feeling better already. And then a thought occurred to me. I asked her, 'What if I'm too old and too judgemental to see the Love? I mean, isn't it supposed to have happened by now?'

She shook her head like a wise sage and replied, 'Love is not about the *rest of your life*.'

'Then?' I asked.

'Sometimes it's just about having a great cup of coffee together.'

And I remembered that. And I knew I would think of her when that happened.

Twenty-four

One day after I had finished work and Aditi had finished a shoot schedule, we were lazing around in my apartment watching TV and drinking hot coffee from a new filter she had bought. We weren't making conversation. Aditi had said all she needed to about Arjun, how she felt about him, what he was doing to me, where it was 'not' going, everything. And I had made it clear that I loved him and I was willing to wait for him to come back to me, even if it meant being a stepmom to his child. So there was nothing left for Aditi and me to say to each other and we switched channels till we found something that numbed my pain and her exhaustion. One channel was showing the best bakeries in the world.

Both responded with a deep, 'Yummm . . .!'

And then she said, 'Remember when we went to Pune and sat at German Bakery the whole day having eggs and chocolate cake and . . .'

'. . . apple pie and coffee!' I finished.

'Hmm.' We said in unison again. Then we went back to watching the programme till it was lunchtime and we were starving. As usual, we wanted to eat out and didn't know where to go. So Aditi said something that sounded amazingly smart at that time, 'Why don't we go to Pune and sit and eat eggs and apple pie?'

I laughed, lying further back on the pillows that we had strewn on the floor, 'Are you mad?'

'So?' she said, picking up our coffee cups and taking them to the kitchen. And then I thought, why not? We both needed to get away from Mumbai and a change would do me good. The depression would melt away as soon as I covered it with some hot apple cinnamon crumble with cold sweet vanilla ice cream!

'Okay,' I said suddenly, 'let's go.'

And that was yet another very dumb idea.

So we went into my room, took out a bag from the top of my wooden cupboard and stuffed it with a few shirts and underclothes, grabbed some money from the safe in the locked drawer where I kept some for emergency. Then we locked my apartment, got into her car, and drove to Pune where we had an amazing lunch. Now that would have been a perfect story. But what happened instead was not. In hindsight, I wish I had said, 'Let's just order from Subway!'

What really happened was, we had lunch and pondered about going to Pune in any case. But being less than spontaneous and a lot more tired than usual, we decided to leave later that evening, once the sun had set. We thought we would be there partying at night and return the next day after having eggs and apple pie at our favourite bakery. This way we wouldn't have to check into a hotel and waste money.

So Aditi went home and collected her stuff and I went to the ATM from where I withdrew the little money I had. I contemplated calling Arjun to tell him that I was going away but decided against it. It was the weekend and he had said not to call, in case his wife picked up the phone. The thought made me sadder and more resolved to take some time out. I even considered spending a week in Pune, doing some retail therapy and letting Arjun miss me enough to stop him controlling my life.

My life. When did I lose it? In the span of half a year, I had gone from being a confident woman advising Aditi on her love life to a woman who needed advice on her own. On a whim, I decided to call my mom.

Thankfully, she was at home and not doing anything, so she could speak to me for some time. After some small talk about the weather and work, she asked me, 'Why are you sounding so low?' Mom had never asked me that before. I was amazed how she could gauge my state of mind.

'I'm not low. In fact, I'm quite the opposite. Aditi and I have decided to go to Pune in the evening and will be back after a few days,' I said, trying to sound cheerful so as to stop her from asking further inquisitive questions.

'When are you going? Who will you be staying with? When are you coming back?' Mom barraged me with the questions all in one breath.

I gave her some random answers. 'Okay,' she answered, 'but call me as soon as you get there and call when you're leaving.'

'Okay, Mom!' I said with exasperation. Seriously! Even when your parents are hundreds of miles away, you'll still have to be accountable to them for your life, no matter how old you are. Little did I know then that that call to my mother would save my life. But more on that later.

Aditi had packed enough for an entire month. 'Why do you need so many clothes?' I asked, stuffing my small duffel bag into the boot of her car.

She rolled her eyes at me and said, 'Because each outfit needs to have a matching handbag and shoes. And I never mismatch, or what do they call it nowadays . . . ya, cross coordinate outfits.'

'Whateva! Let's go!' I said, suddenly all excited and happy.

And we took off towards Pune at about six in the evening with loud Punjabi music playing on the stereo. I was finally looking forward to something new in my life.

Twenty-five

We almost didn't make it to Pune, or not in the state we had hoped. And that phone call I made to my mother two hours earlier, was the last time I would speak to her for the next twenty-four hours. But a call was made to my mother. From my phone. By a policeman who informed her that I was in a hospital in Pune.

Here's what happened as far as I can remember and with pieces put together later by Aditi and the policemen.

Aditi and I were listening to loud music and thoroughly enjoying ourselves as we prepared to party the night away in Pune. We had listed all the names of pubs we knew in alphabetical order and thought we should have opened up a pub ourselves. This was the conversation we were having when suddenly, there was a freak cloudburst. As people who have travelled to Pune would know, when there is rain on those uphill, curving roads, there's not much you can do but drive slowly and hope for the rain to pass.

What we had not anticipated was that there would be a truck that would slip on the road and push our car, that was trying to overtake it, on to the side of the mountain, leaving both Aditi and me compressed between the truck and a rock, with her car completely smashed.

The doctors told us later that we were lucky to have survived. But I had lost my voice due to shock and also because I had screamed so loudly that it took all my strength and sanity away.

I had also injured my right arm. Aditi had broken her left leg and had a mild concussion that kept her semi unconscious for twenty-four hours. It was an extremely scary situation. Although it was Aditi's suggestion to go to Pune, I felt terribly guilty for playing along with her impromptu plan. And all because I wanted to get away from a bad relationship.

The police officer said that since the call to my mother had been the last dialled number on the phone, it was easy to tell them where I was, and that they had informed Aditi's parents.

Aditi and I had woken up in a strange Pune hospital with anxious parents at our bedside. As soon as my mom heard that I was going to survive with no real damage, she burst into tears and started giving me the shouting of a lifetime. It wasn't a lecture. It was shouting. I couldn't even protest since my voice had gone!

She refused to speak to Aditi and warned me that if I ever did, I would be in serious jeopardy of losing the inheritance of jewellery she had kept for me. It was the most absurd thing I had ever heard and made me smile in spite of my aches. And immediately I had to tell someone.

But I wasn't thinking about Aditi. I was thinking about Arjun. I needed to tell him. I didn't know how. I couldn't call him because I had no voice and I couldn't SMS since my right hand was in pain. So I had to tell Aditi to call and let him know about our situation. But Aditi was in another room in a plaster with her leg up with her parents giving her the same lowdown that my parents had been giving me. So I called the nurse and gestured to her to give me a pen and paper to write. My mother was getting more agitated by the minute, 'What do you want to write now? You've been told to sleep and take it easy till they discharge you the day after tomorrow. And we're taking you right back to Bangalore. No more staying in Mumbai all by yourself. No, don't shake your head. I don't want to hear your stupid arguments anymore about how great that city is.'

My mother even insisted that she would write the note to

Aditi, but I told them I needed to sleep and they left me for a while. Then I told the nurse to write my note and give it to Aditi. The note said, 'Call Arjun and tell him where I am'. The nurse took the note and my mobile to Aditi in the adjacent room. I should have asked after Aditi. But my mind was possessed by thoughts of Arjun.

Then the antibiotics took over and I went to sleep for a few hours. I knew he would come and make it all better. He would take me home and look after me and save me from going back with my mother and living a life where I would be asked about my plans for the future everyday.

But he didn't come. He wasn't there when I woke up fourteen hours later. So I thought that maybe Aditi hadn't told him. I got up from my bed despite many protests from my parents and went to Aditi's room. She was lying in bed alone. I went and sat near her. She smiled at me and said, 'Hey, you. How are you?'

I nodded and mouthed the words, 'I'm okay.'

'I'm really sorry, babe,' she said squeezing my hand, 'I should have seen that truck . . .'

I cut her off by gently slapping her wrist and shaking my head. Then I kissed her forehead. We sat there holding each other for some time. Aditi was my best friend. And I was hers. We could have lost each other. And that revelation was hitting us at that point. After a few tears, I had to ask her what was foremost on my mind. I spoke softly, 'Did you call him?' and she said, 'I sent a text, Kaveri. From your phone. I told him that we were in an accident and we were both in the hospital.'

'And?' I asked, hopeful.

'And he wrote back,' she then picked up my phone and gave it to me to read.

By the look on her face I guessed what it be. But I needed to read it anyway: 'Thank God you're alive. Next time be careful.' That was it.

There was no long message about how he was planning to

come and get me or questions about when I would be home. Nothing. I looked up at Aditi, waiting for her to tell me she had 'told me so' about the guy. But instead she defended him.

'Maybe he is too scared and frightened by what happened. Maybe he didn't know what to say or how to react. Give me the mobile, let me send another message.' I kept quiet. Somehow I didn't believe that, but I gave her my mobile and let her send another text message. 'I'm shocked. And in pain.'

After what seemed like an eternity, but was only a few minutes, the phone buzzed. It was a similar message. 'It's natural to be traumatized. Hope your parents are looking after you. Will see you once you're back.'

What did he mean by that? Didn't he want to come and see me *now*? I could not believe it. I took my mobile from Aditi. She was now a witness to my relationship disintegrating. With great pain, I wrote back with hope one last time, 'Rescue me from my parents. They are threatening to take me back to Bangalore. And I don't want to go.'

And he replied, 'Smile. Maybe that would be a good option for you right now.'

What? I thought. Is this how well he knew my feelings?

Either he didn't understand the sarcasm in my text or he didn't want to come. Any which way, right then I realized that I could not depend on Arjun D'Souza anymore. And my relationship was finally over.

I ran to another floor where no one could find me and dissolved into tears.

Twenty-six

When I was released from the hospital, my parents wanted to take me back to Bangalore with them immediately. But I told them I needed to collect my things from my house and check if everything was okay. After many arguments and protests, my parents flew back to Bangalore and I flew to Mumbai with Aditi and her parents. I was still under the false hope that Arjun might come and apologize and offer to look after me.

I went back to my apartment alone from the airport with a sling on my right arm and a hoarse voice. It had been five days since we had headed out on a whim to Pune to have a fun day.

There are a lot of people who will say destiny controls you and there are a few who will say you need to control destiny. Most often you wish for the first, because it's the easier way out. You know how I know that's true? Because I thought I was waiting for destiny to make my life better and was riding with the wave, but the signal I got from destiny shouted out loud that it was time for me to take life in my own hands.

As soon as I got into my apartment, I called Arjun. He picked up and spoke in a soft tone, 'Hello.'

I started crying. I hadn't heard his voice in a week. Plus, I had all these questions to ask him.

'Hey,' I said, hoarsely.

'You sound terrible, baby.' I didn't say anything. He continued, 'I missed you, baby.'

And I cried some more and asked, 'Then why didn't you come to see me?'

'Baby. I'm so sorry. It was just that Maria started bleeding and the doctor said we needed to put a stitch in and we were in the hospital for the last five days. Can you believe that? What are the chances of two tragedies happening at the same time to both the women in my life?' he tried to laugh it off.

I wasn't convinced.

'But why didn't you SMS or call?'

'Because Aditi told me your voice was out and you couldn't call and I presumed your phone was with your mom and you know how I am about people finding out before the time is right. So I didn't want to get caught. Baby, we've discussed this. No parents involved at any time.'

'Arjun,' I said softly. 'My mother was asking why there was no one in my life who could look after me. She was hinting at the fact that there should be *someone* who can look after me if they die.'

He tried to interrupt, 'But . . .'

I cut him off, 'But I know they're not going to die right now. But I suppose all parents want their kids to settle down and be married so as not to worry about them in their old age. Things like, if my kid gets into an accident and I'm too old to look after her, will there be someone who will?'

He was quiet.

I tried to elicit some response and continued, 'I want to know whether you'll be there for me?'

He was still quiet. I realized that relationships don't get more intense with time, they get more casual. If there was a certain nonchalance right now, I knew I could not expect it to become intense later. This was as intense as I needed it and he couldn't step up to the challenge.

'Well?' I asked, with my voice raised.

He said, 'Kaveri, I want to be there for you. But I can't make a promise right now. I need to see Maria and the baby settled. I promise I will be with you. Just give me time. It is *my* baby, after all. You do understand that, don't you?'

I wanted to scream. I could not believe this! Here I was, giving him an opportunity to make it up to me and all he could talk about was his wife and baby. Yes, I understood it. I understood it very clearly.

'Arjun,' I said, now having made up my mind, 'I think we should break up.'

He tried to protest feebly, but I continued, 'Arjun. You need to be a husband and a father right now. And I need to be with someone who can be with me no matter what. I'm not blaming you. I'm not even angry. But I think we need to release each other from these promises. So that we can live a life that we truly deserve.'

'Kaveri, don't . . .' he pleaded.

I didn't know how to exist in a world without Arjun D'Souza, but with each word I spoke, I knew it was the right thing to do, 'Arjun. I wish you all the best with the baby and I hope you will remember me fondly. I know I will always remember you. Goodbye.' I hung up, truly feeling the weight of what I had just done. And then I cried for many hours. And this time I didn't order food or call Aditi or speak to Mom. I cried because I knew I had done the right thing.

Sometimes liberation and emancipation are words that make you feel strong and powerful. But when it comes the hard way, like breaking up a relationship that was The Great Love of your life, it hurts like hell. And so I let it all out. Till I could cry no more. Arjun sent me many text messages telling me to stop behaving like a child and try and understand where he was coming from. But from that moment onwards I knew I had to delete him and his messages from my life. And so I did. And then, I truly turned my life around.

I rightly stopped behaving like a child. And finally became a woman.

Twenty-seven

The thing with goodbyes is that it really isn't truly over till you can block that person from your head. Because even if you block him from your chats, your email, your Facebook, he isn't gone until you can lock him out of your head. And the only way to do that is to let every thought of him come in.

So I decided that I would let all thoughts of Arjun come into my head. Whether it was good or bad, I wanted to experience all of them so that I could purge myself of him, one thought at a time.

At first, I knew I was in trouble because he would write emails to me or try to send a message on Facebook or Twitter or try and chat up with me. It could have been so easy to go back to him. But this time I didn't. I had this image of him and his wife with a child and it really made me feel disgusted with myself for being 'the other woman'. I know I had not felt like this earlier because he loved me and I felt our love was pure enough to bear the burden of this anomaly. But now I felt I should have known better. I felt I shouldn't have let myself go through all that and given up such a huge part of me.

Then again, a little voice in my head said that if I hadn't given up so much of myself, I would never have experienced 'The Great Love' that I had felt. And then it hit me.

'My Great Love' had died.

I had killed it.

I knew *he* was still there, but I knew I just could not have the little he was offering. I wanted more. I wanted to have pure love that could carry on forever. I wanted to be in a trustworthy, reliable, mature relationship. I wanted to be able to have the freedom to have a dinner in public without him constantly looking over his shoulder or pretending I was his colleague.

I didn't need him. I wanted him. There was a difference. I didn't need him to be able to provide for me, get me a house, pay my bills, and change a flat tyre. I had wanted him for the way I felt in my head about us. I had seen a future. Even if it meant hurting my parents and tossing my head against society. I wanted an honest explanation, whether he would marry me or not.

And I never got one.

Aditi had told me once, 'Men don't want to give the truth. They can't face the fact that they're assholes.'

But I realized that women can't face the truth because often *they* are really naive. Really. If a woman had so much intuition, wouldn't she know that the guy was just not that into her? Wouldn't she realize after her friends told her so? Wouldn't she comprehend by listening to herself crib about him continuously? Why do so many women ask for the truth when truth is staring at them right in the face? It's probably because women need to hear it. From him. The man that she has given her heart to.

That's the real reason. She needs to hear him say the words, 'I don't love you. We can never have a future.' And how many men have actually said that? None. Because they always want to leave the window of 'opportunity' open for a 'what if'. And that's why women will be shattered over a break-up for a far longer time than men. Men don't need explanations. They think, 'It wasn't meant to be.' And have another glass of beer and go back to working on their Excel sheets in the morning.

I knew that I was questioning myself over this entire episode. And I knew immediately it was the wrong thing to feel. So I quickly decided to go to Coffee De to enjoy a good hot cup of cappuccino and indulge in a chocolate lava pie.

As soon as I got out of my apartment and started walking, it began to rain. A sudden shower from the heavens and I instinctively sprinted towards the coffee shop. But then I stopped and realized I loved the rains. I always had. It was one of the reasons I wanted to live in Mumbai. I thought it was romantic and I loved the way it made me feel. Carefree, excited, creative. Arjun had ruined that for me. He was the one always complaining about floods, blocked drains and traffic jams. He was the one who cribbed about the clothes never drying or the walls being damp or the slush in his shoes. I, however, had always loved it. But soon, seeing him so grouchy, I began to change my view. He was right as usual, I had thought. My feelings had all been intangible. After all, there is nothing exciting and romantic about traffic jams.

So I stood right there and took the rain in. It soaked my clothes and made my hair drip. But it made me feel alive again. A part of me came back. And I knew that I would have to let every thought of Arjun D'Souza come in, for me to push him out.

And I knew finally I could now handle his absence.

Twenty-eight

I didn't leave for Bangalore. I had never meant to leave Mumbai. I needed to face my demons right here and so I decided to cleanse my apartment of everything that reminded me of Arjun. I wanted to take charge of my life again. Something that Arjun had done for me for many months. And now I wanted the control back.

But saying that I was going to get my life back and actually doing it were two different things. I didn't know what people do when their hearts are broken. It was happening to me for the first time. I had actually thought that I would fall in love, get married and remain so, till I die. That's what my parents had done and I figured I would follow. But this entire year had been such a new experience. First, I had decided to sleep with just anybody to rid myself of my virginity, then I had actually fallen in love and instead of getting married to that man and living happily ever after, I ended up broken hearted after I had slept with him! That was a lot for a woman to go through in just one year. Especially, one who had never experienced love or sex before.

A heartbreak, I now knew, actually hurt. Physically hurt. And all along, I had thought it was an intangible feeling because, come on, how could you feel your heart falling apart, right? I mean, does the aorta burst or what? But those who have gone through this will know it feels like a dull ache in your back with cramped shoulders and heavy legs, as if you've just come out of a long spin cycle from your washing machine. A lethargy that incapacitates you from even thinking straight. And it takes all the strength inside you to be able to smile at that aunty downstairs or that colleague through the day when all you want to do is curl up like a ball and cry for days in your bed. ALONE. But I had made up my mind.

I was not going to take Arjun D'Souza back. And even though I had been upset with him many times before and had gone back to him, I decided that I would erase his number from my phone so as never to be tempted to scroll down and even send him an SMS. And SMS he did. Many times after our call.

He pleaded, sent angry messages, even tried to ignore me for several hours so I would relent as I had in the past and go back to him. But I didn't give in. I remained strong. And I cleaned. I cleaned my entire house like I'd never done before. I had always thought that cleaning was a domestic chore and I was above it. But when I started, I realized that it was actually quite therapeutic.

I started with my room, where we had spent several hours together. I removed all the clothes from my cupboard and everything from the drawers of my side tables and bookshelves and dumped them on the floor. Then I removed everything that reminded me of him. I kept them aside. I was going to give them back to him or donate them to charity. My maid looked on in wonder at what I was doing and helped me without a word of complain. Perhaps she had guessed that the man I was in love with and whom she had gotten used to, was now gone. Many a time, I saw her looking at me wanting to say something to console me, but my hardened expression and determination to clean kept her shut .

But I wasn't done cleaning. I cleaned my living room and kitchen too. I put away the red coffee cups that he used to serve me coffee in. I cleaned till I could clean no more. And then one day, I was finally done. Then I sat down at my door and looked at my clean and purged house. There was not a trace of Arjun.

And instead of feeling relieved like I thought I would, I felt tired. And I cried. I wept copiously. I knew that it would not be the only time, but the healing had begun. I knew that to be strong again, I needed to let go of him and find myself.

And then, just when I went into the kitchen to make myself a cup of tea, I found it. Lying on top of a heap of discarded junk mail was the visting card I had put away all those months ago. The TV and film director that I had met at the parlour when I was getting a makeover—Deepa Malhotra.

I came out to the living room with the card and sat down on the large comfortable cushion. I thought this was the sign. This was what I had to do. Arjun had always told me that my job was like a hobby. It gave me money but I couldn't do it forever. And I had thought I would. But here was an opportunity to not only clean out my house, but to clean my entire life. I could start afresh with a new career, meet new people, and have a new life. And only then would I be able to completely rid my thoughts and my heart of him. I knew I needed to step out of my box. If there was one thing I felt I could take from the relationship, it was Arjun's advice to do things that were not in my comfort zone. If you don't take this chance, Kaveri, I thought, you could just go to Bangalore and wallow in self-pity, with your parents nagging you to tell them what's wrong.

I decided to call the lady the very next day and see if I could find a new path in my life after all. I finally went to sleep peacefully for the first time in many weeks. My house was rid of everything that reminded me of Arjun. And now I was going to cleanse my mind too, one step at a time, one day at a time.

Twenty-nine

The next day, I called Ms Deepa Malhotra, the TV and film director, and asked if we could meet. At first, I thought she wouldn't remember me since our brief encounter at the beauty parlour many months ago. But obviously I had made some impression because she told me to come see her on Friday. I was anxious, to say the least. What was I going to say to her? I didn't know whether I wanted to act or help make tea on the sets. But reminding myself about my new resolution to try everything once, I decided to be excited and go.

Two days later, I reached her office at eleven in the morning and waited for Deepa to come. She was about forty-five minutes late with no apologies. A cool, calm, collected woman in her mid-forties, she was dressed in jeans and a flowing, floral designer kurta that covered her heavy hips. Since I saw her last, she had cut her hair again to a really short Victoria Beckham style that made her look fierce and dynamic—a well thought-out look. She nodded her head at me while talking into her BlackBerry and simultaneously taking out a large envelope from her huge Gucci bag and giving it to the receptionist, who was now waiting for instructions.

'Mail this out immediately,' she told the receptionist in a low tone, while still on the phone. The receptionist sent me in after another ten minutes of waiting. Deepa's office was grey. Literally. There was a grey couch on one wall, with a small table in front and a lamp on the side. The two chairs in front of her office desk were grey. The wall behind her was grey. And everything else was black and white. Paintings, cushions, photographs, certificates, everything. It seemed as if I had stepped into a 1920s monochromatic film. Despite the cold look of the room, the director was surprisingly warm, especially compared to her earlier fierce demeanour.

'Kaveri darling!' she said as if she had known me for a lifetime, 'you haven't gone back to the parlour for a long time have you?' She seemed very forthright. While my jaw fell in shock, she continued laughing, 'Your colour has grown out, so I know.'

'Oh yes. I just haven't had the time or . . .' I trailed off.

'. . . The inclination?' she completed.

I smiled. She sat down behind her desk and I sat on the grey chair in front. I guess she wasn't as friendly to invite me on the sofa for a chitchat. She ordered coffee and then asked, 'So tell me why you called?'

I took a deep breath and said, 'Well, I want to do something new with my life and I want to be able to have new experiences. I feel I've been stuck in a rut for too long and I was hoping you could help me.'

She nodded and asked, 'How?'

Just then, the receptionist came in with cake and coffee and I got a few moments to think about a question I had been asking myself the entire day. 'Kaveri, you've lost it,' said a voice in my head. 'You've come to a powerful woman in the TV and film industry with not a clue in your head about what you want from her!'

But when she smiled at me warmly and after taking a sip of coffee, I decided to tell her the truth. And so I started, 'Ma'am, I've just come out of a bad relationship. And I need to do something that will distract me. I am willing to do anything. I need a new experience to completely rid my thoughts of this man and my current life.'

She smiled, nodded her head and said, 'I understand. We've all been in similar situations.' She took a deep pause and frowned. 'Are you willing to have a new man in your life?'

It came out of the blue. I hadn't thought of that. A new man? I was barely over the old man. But I *had* said 'anything' to her. So I shrugged my shoulders and said, 'I suppose. But it might be too soon to get into a relationship. I thought I was discussing work here . . .' I trailed off.

She shook her head while waving her hand majestically, 'No, no, darling, it's not like that. I'm talking about a reality show.'

I looked puzzled and she continued, 'I'm casting for a reality show where there is one man and there will be ten women vying for him!'

'Oh?' I said, a little puzzled and unsure.

Then the director became a little strict with me, 'Look, Kaveri. This is the only thing I have on board right now. The markets are bad and there are no shows getting commissioned. There are hundreds of women out there who want to be one of those ten women. TV gives them instant fame and they make money for every week they are on the show.'

My ears perked up. 'There is money?' I asked.

'Of course, otherwise how can people survive in this world? Women are coming in droves to give the screen test. I'm giving you a slot. Become one of those women if you want! Just come and give your screen test and I'll make sure you're on board.'

It was a tempting offer but I didn't want to get involved with another man. My heart had already broken once. I could not be vulnerable again. 'How long is the show?' I asked.

'Well it's ideally for seven weeks. But don't worry about details. My producers will get in touch with you and tell you all that stuff. You just decide if you want to do that.'

I didn't know. I was still angry and hurting from my relationship. If I went on national television, it would show Arjun that I was moving on and that I was truly independent without him, which is what I wanted him to believe. It might actually make him jealous and come running back to me. Either ways it looked like a win–win situation at that moment.

And so I took another dumb decision. I decided to take the role.

'Okay. I'll do it!' I said, needing to break out of my comfort mould.

She smiled and said, 'Great. But we still need your audition tape for the people on the board. So come in at two and give the audition. The producer will tell you all about the show, the money, whatever you need to know and we'll take it from there, okay?'

I nodded, 'Thank you so much for giving me this opportunity and meeting me. I'm truly grateful,' I blabbered. And then a thought came to me, so I asked, 'Um . . . ma'am . . . why are you being so nice to me?'

She looked keenly at me for a bit and then said, 'I liked your freshness when I had met you some months ago. You had a wonderful face that said you're willing to try anything. Now, of course, you have a sad face but that spark is still there. I want to see that. It's genuine. It's real. And unlike the women who are here only for the fame and money, you want to prove something. I get that.'

'Thank you,' I said quietly.

'Don't thank me yet,' she said on a happier note, 'when you become famous, then we'll talk,' she laughed, stood up and walked me to the door.

My new life had begun!

Thirty

The shooting started a few weeks later. It was the first week of December. By now, my hand had completely healed, even though my heart had not. I barely had enough time to grieve over Arjun before I was put away in a house with nine other women. I had spoken to Aditi just once and she was recuperating at home with her parents. I really didn't want to go meet her to give her a sob break-up story. So I just mentioned I was going to do this reality show for six weeks in a secluded house with no external communication.

She laughed her head off and told me I had made her day and that she would be glued to the TV when it was aired. That's where I left my best friend, advice expert and soulmate to go meet nine of the most different women I would ever meet. Apparently, I was the oldest in the group, but thankfully, not the fattest, the shortest or the tallest. But I was still a statistic that set me apart. We were all supposed to be vying for one man. Now for me, that was a near impossibility since I had decided that The Great Love of my life had come and gone. And nobody else could take his place. But since this show was paying me money and distracting my thoughts from Arjun, I decided to act like the man who would be the protagonist of our show was worth all my attention.

The man in question here was all of twenty-five years. I was a full five and a half years older than him. But that didn't matter. I didn't have to try too hard to like him. He was a pretty package for sore eyes—six feet tall, wheatish skin, dark brown eyes, short cropped hair, clean shaven and a body that was totally ripped under his red shirt and baggy blue jeans. I couldn't take my eyes off him when he entered the 'house'. And neither could the nine other women. The cameras were all over the place. The producers had made us sign a contract earlier that made them superlords of our privacy while we lived in that house. They could have cameras in innocuous places, like the kitchen and closets and more apparent ones that would have cameramen zooming into our zits. We were supposed to behave 'naturally', but were encouraged to be backbiting, ruthless bitches!

A known male TV celebrity who was hosting the show had been organizing us since morning. We had already picked out our rooms, unpacked our clothes and made small talk with the other girls before we were introduced to 'the man'. The girls ranged from eighteen years to the oldest being me. They were mostly in their twenties, looking for fame and a man to settle down with.

'Hi, girls,' said the man, with an impish smile, and the host Aniruddh introduced us to Karan.

'Karan is a doctor. He is an NRI looking for the perfect Indian "bahu" who should be a mixture of the traditional and contemporary and . . . he thinks that one of you . . . might be her!' Here the producers, who were standing away from the cameras that were pointed individually at our faces, motioned for us to smile. So we did.

Aniruddh continued, 'He is looking for the girl of his dreams, and we have decided to help him. We brought you girls here because we thought you were the most suited amongst the thousands who auditioned. But it won't be so easy to win his love,' the host paused and we all were suppose to look interested at this point. 'All of you will be assigned hard tasks every day and given points. The person with the maximum points gets to go on a date with Karan and the person with the minimum points gets . . . eliminated!' At this statement, the girls nodded their heads and looked around checking out the competition. Suddenly the camaraderie had turned into rivalry.

Aniruddh's finals words were, 'So the more he gets to know you, the better he can make a decision.'

Some of the girls were smiling seductively at him thinking they might not have to do the task if they showed ample cleavage and a seductive smile. I was not in their league. I didn't want to show cleavage or want fame or his love. I just needed to be there to distract myself.

Karan then left and Aniruddh announced to us, 'Today's challenge is easy. You all will be given fifteen minutes to make a romantic dinner for Karan. All of you will go to the kitchen and prepare dinner for him. The person who has made the best meal and the best presentation will win the chance to spend time with him tonight.'

After this, the producers broke us up into groups and took us to the kitchen. Most of the things there seemed too bright and inadequate to cook with. Like they had no pressure cooker or wooden spoons for stirring. We were given specific ingredients and asked what we would be making.

The Gujju woman immediately replied that she wanted to make an elaborate vegetarian thali for her man. The eighteen-year-old replied, 'Ya.' Pause, 'I can't cook.' One of the producers immediately said, 'Oh, that's great!' we all looked towards him, 'I'll assign making Maggi to her then,' he clarified.

So we started off making our respective dishes. We picked out our five ingredients from the list that we could choose from and started cooking in batches of two, with two stoves each and half of a kitchen sideboard to chop anything extra. I decided to make pasta. Arjun had taught me that really well.

And since I already got chopped onions, all I needed to do was throw everything into a pan and stir till everything looked just about done. My dish was done in fifteen minutes. Seeing that I had finished my task, my cooking partner turned to me and said, 'Are you done? Can I use your side of the kitchen?'

'Sure, be my guest,' I responded. She introduced herself as Anjana and promised to chat up once her food was cooked. I took my bowl of pasta to the dining table in the adjoining room. The dining table I saw was being decorated by the producers of the show. My God, how many people were working on this serial, I thought suddenly.

'Kaveri, put it next to your name there,' said a short plump girl with spectacles. I saw that there were names around the table with a dish coaster next to each.

Then I was asked to go to my room and dress up for the judgement in the evening. Since I had a few hours to kill, I decided to go for a walk instead, around the property. I sneaked out of the house and started walking.

The place was really lovely. It was close to the beach and I could see the blue sea once I climbed up the hillock surrounding the property. I would have loved to come here with Arjun for a day. Oh God! Here I was, supposed to be getting him out of my mind and his name kept cropping up wherever I looked. I took a deep breath. 'It'll take time, Kaveri,' I thought to myself. 'Take it easy. Just enjoy the moment and give yourself time.'

Soon I headed back to my room to change and prepare for the night. I didn't know that there were hidden cameras all over the property, taping me even when I thought I was alone. I would learn of it the hard way when my walk as well as other antics would be on national television!

That night, we were called downstairs and had to make a grand entry with cameras showing our walk and body language to a connected TV (that we did not know about), where Karan was watching and commenting on each one of us.

Karan entered the room where all of us were standing and Aniruddh announced, 'Well, girls, you've all prepared your best dishes and now the time has come for Karan to select which is his favourite.'

Then the producer told Karan to go around the table tasting each dish. So a camera followed him and the producer prompted him to talk about each dish as he wrote down a number on the respective nametag.

Aniruddh read out his lines from the teleprompter a few times and got them wrong. He was told to do a few more takes before he got it right.

'Now the time has come for Karan to decide whose dish he liked best. This person will be the first lucky girl to go on a date with Karan. And remember, you don't get a second chance to make a good first impression. So Karan,' Aniruddh turned to the man and asked, 'whose cooking impressed you the most?'

Karan stood there and said with élan, as if he had rehearsed his lines, 'Well, I'm a real foodie, Aniruddh. I love all types of cuisine. I could have eaten everything.'

But Aniruddh insisted that he make a decision, so Karan continued to make it seem longer, 'Well, I really liked the thepla that was made by Anjana and the mutton curry that was made by Perizaad.'

The girls smiled at him and there were a few claps all around.

Then Karan began with great flourish, 'My favourite dish, however, was . . .' Then he paused for effect. The cameras were glued to our faces. 'Shalini's biryani.'

Shalini squealed with delight and walked up to Karan. They hugged. Aniruddh then said, 'Okay Karan, but now you have to take another decision.'

And Karan looked at him, surprised. He was directed to act likewise for the audience who would be watching later. I could almost hear the percussions of a dramatic moment as if in an Ekta Kapoor serial.

'You need to eliminate someone.' There was another dramatic pause before he continued, 'And I have the result of the lowest score here.'

All the girls were now most worried. I was sure I would be eliminated for the awful pasta I had made. Why had I been in such a hurry? Oh god, I thought, please don't let it be me. I want to stay here for a few more weeks. And then a thought rushed to my head, which even surprised me—I wanted to please this man! I wanted him to at least have one date with me!

But Karan said, 'You know what, I have a surprise for all of you.' And we waited with bated breath. 'There will be no elimination tonight!' he said cheerfully. 'I will have a twenty-minute meeting with all of you before your next task, so there will be no elimination for this one.'

And we all had to cheer a few times because we didn't 'get it right' the first time according to the short plump woman who had become a sourpuss by now.

Aniruddh announced that the winner and Karan would go off on their date now and the rest of us could go back to bed. But the date didn't happen immediately. By the time the final shot of the day was taken, it was already three in the morning and we were all drained, including Karan, who was in no mood to go on a date or even talk to anyone. He walked off to his bungalow next door and we all went to our rooms to crash.

My first day with reality TV had left me completely exhausted and most satisfied.

Yes, the fun had begun.

Thirty-one

Over the next few days, we all got to meet Karan and spend more than twenty minutes with him. All this was taped and recorded, to be edited later for the show, but the girls being new to this, were trying to behave as unaffectedly as possible given the circumstances. The producers helped us choose our best outfits for the meetings and the 'naturalness' of the entire show became more staged, more scripted, more planned. What we were supposed to say and do was left to us, but 'how' was made very specific.

My meeting with Karan was fixed for the evening of the third day of our stay. By this time, he had met six of the women and gone on his official date with Shalini, which she had been talking about most high handedly to the rest of us. I wasn't too sure if she was actually a snob or was 'told' to be so.

Somewhere, I had begun to like the idea of being around new people. I even wanted Karan to like me. For my date with him, I wore a pair of jeans, the same Fendi ones that made my butt look small, and a lovely turquoise silk top with black beads and accessorized it with silver hoops. It was given the approval stamp by the producer who casually remarked, 'We don't have to worry about you. You have more experience than these twits.' I felt pleased that I was not being compared to the rest of the women till I understood she meant in age and not in sexual prowess!

I expected Karan to be a complete idiot. After all, who would volunteer to go on a show for six weeks and be away from his work in the US as a doctor. Also, he was so young that I didn't expect our conversation to last too long. What would I possible have in common with this *boy*? So, I was pleasantly surprised when our date went rather well even though we'd got off to a rocky start.

The producers had different plans for him with different women. Shalini went bowling and go-carting. With Anjana, the Gujju woman, he went to a movie and had veg snacks at the food court. And the eighteen-year-old and Karan went to a discotheque and danced till wee hours of the dawn. Since I was the oldest in the group, they must have thought they should plan something low-key, otherwise my blood pressure would shoot through the roof and I might just flip over and die! So they sent Karan and me to the best five star hotel for a nice, quiet, non-exciting dinner.

He picked me up in a black Fiat Linea, which also had cameras on the rear view mirror and inside the AC ducts. They presumed if anyone wanted to get naughty in the car, they could capture it for better ratings in their show. So our conversation was stilted and minimum till we reached the restaurant. Even though there was a camera on us for most part of the evening, it was at a distance so we could try and be more relaxed. But there were microphones kept on the table, which were hidden under the salt and pepper shakers for the producers to listen in on and guide us. Everything was up for reality TV. Once we ordered our starters and drinks, we began to talk naturally. 'You know, I'm some five years older than you,' I said, as the first thing to get the issue out of the way.

'Yes, I know,' he said, taking a sip of water. 'But I find that fascinating. I feel that I will have so much to learn from you.'

I think it was his tone, but I became a little conscious about my age then. But instead of being offended, I decided to play along. So I said in a voice that sounded like an old lady's while pointing my index finger at him, 'Yes. I've opened an academy to teach you boys the importance of good behaviour!'

But he didn't get it.

He took offence and said, 'I'm not a small boy you know. I'm a doctor!'

'Well, what is a doctor doing in a reality show? Got bored killing people?' I added with a smile.

'For your information, doctors are supposed to heal people!' he exclaimed loudly. Since he did not get sarcasm, I decided to go to the restroom to decide what to do with this night.

Just when I stood up and said, 'Excuse me, I'm . . .' He interrupted me and said, completely shocked, 'You're leaving? What the . . .' And I completed my sentence finally and said, 'I'm going to use the restroom.' And we both stopped and looked at each other to gauge what the other was thinking before we said anything stupid again.

Right then, a producer came running from the kitchen saying, 'Very good, Kaveri. I like the sexual tension. Karan, you need to be a little more suave.' And then she ran back into the kitchen.

I suddenly felt I was Truman in *The Truman Show*, the movie where he didn't know that everyone was watching his life as a TV serial.

Karan turned to me and said, 'That's so absurd! As if I can be turned off and on on cue!'

'I know!' I exclaimed, and then smiled at him and then we both burst into laughter.

'Did you see how upset she was?' he asked, in between snorts. I sat down and laughed while having some water and nodded.

Just then the waiter came over with starters and I remembered Arjun and my first date. The starters had got mixed up and not only had we shared a plate after that, we had shared our lives as well. It was in this brief interlude that Karan noticed I was distracted and asked me so. I shook my head and changed my distant look to an interested one, 'So, why have you left being a doctor to come join a reality TV show?' I asked genuinely with a smile.

'Well, I was on a student visa. I needed a green card to stay on and work, so I finished my internship and then I was told to get out of the US so they could process my visa.' I looked confused.

'The long and short of it is that I had three months to kill in India and I thought I should audition for this show and maybe meet some interesting women.' He seemed genuine and nice. It wasn't as if a bratty boy from firang land had come to give me gyan. But I was just not into him. He didn't do anything to my heart like Arjun had. And then I had to shake the thought out of my head again, and I think he noticed and took a long gulp of his drink and looked away.

We spoke on a variety of subjects and he surprised me in being quite aware about the topics I brought up. It wasn't as if it was a scintillating conversation that left me wanting more, but it was pleasant enough. It felt as if Aditi had set me on a blind date. But obviously I hadn't mentioned past relationships, the other women in the house, or sex. I didn't want a twenty-five-year-old to think I was a fool or worse, fixated with my ex. But the topic about past relationships did come up.

Karan spoke wisely while digging into a chocolate fondant we were sharing, 'In any case, love is not a permanent thing. It's the friendship that is permanent. That you shouldn't let go of.'

'Are you saying that we should be friends with our exes?' I asked, pointing my spoon at him.

'Sure. Why not? Once the messy stuff is outta the way, we can all just hang out, I say.' Spoken like a true twenty-five-year-old man who didn't understand the depth of relationships or the gravity of broken hearts. I realized that maybe I did need to teach him a thing or two. So all I said was, 'Life is a series of mishaps till you meet the right person. But if you don't kiss a lot of toads, you'll never find your Prince Charming!' Apparently, Karan liked that and so did the producers, who beamed away at a table nearby.

He licked his spoon and said, 'You know, you and I could be good friends.'

'Is that your closing line to all the women?' I smiled as I asked him. I'd put down my spoon to signal I was done with the chocolate fondant.

He laughed. He had a lovely raspy voice. And he had an amazing smile. I was drawn to this boy!

'You caught me,' he shrugged his shoulders and winked. Then he scooped out the last of the fondant with his spoon and offered it to me. I reached out and ate it and then he licked the spoon after me.

'I don't generally do that,' he said, with a twinkle in his eye and I mumbled, 'Tell me what else you don't do . . .'

Back in the car Karan and I chatted more than we had on the way to the hotel.

'Kaveri,' he said softly, 'age is just in our head. I don't think of you as being older to me.'

And astonishingly I agreed. 'I don't think of you as a young boy either.'

'I really like you. I connect with you. I want us to meet again.' Now, this would have sounded nice if we were on an actual date. But come on, we were on a reality show and we would *have* to meet. And this is exactly what I told him. But he looked away and said, 'You know, Kaveri, I might be here because of this show, but I'm not forced to say things I don't feel.' And then, after a pause, 'And I'm not *forced* to like the girls. And I just like you. That's the truth.'

That was a nice thing to say. I smiled, 'I like you too,' I replied. Then he saw me to the door of the bungalow and kissed my hand and walked away. I think I heard a producer yell, 'cut!' somewhere in the bushes but it didn't bother me too much. It had been a pleasant evening. I realized that not every man that you share a part of yourself with would be there forever. But if you don't share a part with every man you meet, you'll never know if there could have been a 'forever'.

When I went inside, as was the drill, the inmates grilled me to spill the beans about my date. I told them the relevant facts and left out the intimate details. After all, this was a competition. And I didn't want to lose so early!

The girls were an assorted bunch. They were all intelligent and educated. But that's where the similarities ended. There was a docile looking salwar kameez clad woman from Lucknow, a biker–engineer from Bangalore, the eighteen-year-old college girl, the shrewd Gujarati woman from Mumbai, the Bengali who was a theatre artiste, the Punjabi woman who was a model, the woman from Hyderabad who was a web designer, the costume designer for ad films from Mumbai, the Delhi girl who was in the hotel industry and me.

The girls were friendly to a point, but when we started discussing Karan, it became a little competitive. I could make out that some of them had actually fallen for the guy and wanted to win not just for the cash prize, the fifteen minutes of fame or the holiday getaway to Australia. They actually wanted the man! I felt a pang of jealousy, which went away quickly with a thought that he wasn't my 'Great Love'. But the fire in me had been lit. Not only to win the man over, but win the game.

Thirty-two

The next day we had to perform another task to win a longer date with Karan. This time there would definitely be an elimination. We left very early in the morning and went to a trekking site. Our task was to do a combination of rock climbing, swimming and trekking for a short distance. It had absolutely nothing to do with 'how to win a man', but apparently it was good for the show. We were given a choice of costumes for the triathlon: a spaghetti top or full sleeve shirt with a jacket, capri track pants or tiny shorts, and a swimming suit or a bikini.

All the girls with great figures wore tiny shorts and bikinis. The rest were dressed more modestly but still showed skin. I doubt if any of them really wanted to win the task as much as to look good for camera.

The sequence was to first rock climb a little to get to the top of the hill, then trek down to reach a lake and then swim across the lake to the finishing mark. I decided to save time in changing clothes and wore my swimming costume under my track pants. I slathered some sun block, tied my hair in a ponytail and was ready to give these girls a run for their money. I'd show them who was old! I just hoped that I wouldn't break any bones while doing so!

I could hear the truck full of executive producers of the television show yelling at each other and shouting instructions at us when we reached our destination.

'Has everyone brought their swimming suits?' asked one producer. One girl said 'no', so the producer shouted at her but had to go back to get it for her.

'Where is Aniruddh? No one remembered to bring the host?' asked another producer sarcastically.

'Where are the snacks that have to be served at the top of the mountain?' yelled another to no one in particular, but wanting to seem very busy; she was on the mobile with someone who refused to pick up at such an early hour.

'Karan has come in his car. Where do you want him, Deepa?' shouted yet another and then I turned around and saw Deepa standing there. She was, as usual, in her cool, collected, calm demeanour, wearing a full sleeved white peasant blouse and dark blue jeans. Her multi-coloured bangles were tinkling away merrily as she gesticulated animatedly to Karan to stand in the direct sunlight next to a bush at the foot of the hill we were supposed to climb. She saw me and waved. I waved back. Then everyone started huddling around her and she got busy. We were supposed to start at six in the morning but the actual shoot only took place at ten. By then, the sun had come out over the hill and was beating down our backs. Some of the girls started complaining. 'Oh God, yaar! I'm going to get so tanned,' said the south Indian lady who was already a shade of bitter chocolate. No disrespect to her skin colour, which I admired, but it was pretty ridiculous to see her tetchy. 'Is there Bisleri water? I only drink Bisleri water! Oh God, there's no Bisleri water!' said the girl from Lucknow who had probably had 'pani puris' from a roadside stall all her life.

'Does anyone have any sun block?' said the model standing next to Aniruddh. She was already in her bikini top. I think she'd forgotten if the prize was Karan or Aniruddh. Anyone would do, she must have thought. Aniruddh was actually flirting with her. When it was his time to give some shots, it required a few takes to get him to say the correct words without the teleprompter and I could hear the producers muttering behind me, 'What a loser dude! He can't even get two sentences right without the prompter!'

Then Karan came on the scene and the girls waved furiously at him. He smiled casually. He walked over to interact with all of us and I just stood at the back, drinking water from the bottle. He winked at me and walked to the spot where he was supposed to deliver his lines. All the girls looked at me and seemed extremely jealous. I appeared nonchalant on the surface but my heart was racing wildly.

He had winked! That must mean something.

When Karan shot the air gun, the race started. I didn't think about the camera after that. I just wanted to do my best. The instructions were easy and the safety precautions were all adhered to. So there was nothing to worry about. We just had to have fun. And I had a blast. I climbed that hill as if I was Spiderman, and got to the top pretty quickly. I couldn't believe myself. I was flexible and strong. Some of the other girls scraped their knees and started crying. They started whining that this wasn't written in their contracts.

'Meghna, stop complaining. We'll pull you up if you can't do it, but just take a few steps for the camera so they'll know you tried, yaar!' yelled one producer from the top on a conical loudspeaker. We were all given microphones so everything we said was recorded, to be mixed later in the editing studio. I think half of it would have to be deleted since the girls were saying the choicest of abuses to the show, producers, Karan and, each other all the way up the hill.

I was the first to reach the top. The producers almost fainted, 'How did you do that? You're so old . . .' said a young intern.

'Yes, darling, but I took my calcium in the morning and I used my walking stick for support,' I said sarcastically. She gave me a wry smile. I took off my jacket and started the second part of the triathlon, the trek downhill. One cameraman followed me for company for some part of the journey and then returned to the other girls, who had now climbed to the top and collected there to have a snack.

I was left alone in the jungle for a considerable distance. And I'd never felt better. I couldn't hear a thing except the sound of the wind and the rustling leaves of the trees. It was amazingly peaceful. I had finally got what I wanted. I was distracted from thinking about Arjun. I sat on a large rock for a bit. There was no one around to pester me. I hadn't spoken to my parents since I'd told them I would be under house arrest for six weeks without a cell phone. I hadn't spoken to Aditi and I had definitely not spoken to Arjun. I felt emancipated. And honestly, I was doing pretty well. I had met nine interesting women and one very interesting man.

Another man! I didn't want another man but there he was. 'To get over one man, you need to get under another,' was Aditi's famous line. And she would have been proud to know that I was moving along.

But I missed Arjun. He had given me so much laughter, fun and comfort. I only had myself to rely on now. For a moment, I thought I was being too harsh on him and I should just get out of this reality show and go back to him. But then, I got off my arse and started walking again. I was not supposed to be thinking about him!

The forest was not that dense and sun shone in through the spaces between the trees and shrubs. It felt as if I was walking on a checkerboard. And I was the Queen. And I thought, this is it, Kaveri. This is your checkmate. You need to do something more with your life. And during my walk to the stream, I kept thinking, why don't I give this Karan guy a shot. Why was I being so elusive with him? He did like me. And no one was asking me to marry him.

Here I had been given an opportunity to meet an interesting man and I was still pining away for a man who would be just talking about sonograms and diapers if we were still together.

Before I could think any further, I had reached the stream, where there was already a set of cameras and a producer waiting. They asked me a few questions. 'How did you get here so fast?'

'Who do you think is your biggest competition?' 'Was Karan the motivation for you to get so far?'

I replied with care and diplomacy and then I got out of my clothes and since I had my swimsuit underneath, I swam across the lake. The water was cold and I could see the other girls reach the lake. Then they all went into the changing room to get into their bikinis and slather on some waterproof sun block. One girl couldn't swim so there was a boat that was going to bring her across. Another girl started swimming and got a cramp and the same boat picked her up as well. By this time I had finished and was draped in a towel sitting on a rock across watching the antics of these women. The lake was very small. It couldn't have been more than the size of an Olympic pool but the women were already exhausted and were keen not to complete the last task since they knew I had already won.

Suddenly from behind me a voice rang out, 'You won!' It was Karan. I turned and smiled. He was cute. Why wasn't I a little more open to him? I could at least try.

'Hi. I guess so,' I said.

He sat down beside me and I moved slightly away. 'Still don't trust me, huh?' he asked. I didn't reply. He continued, 'So guess where my date with you for tonight will be?'

'Where?' I asked.

'On a ranch! We'll be cleaning horse shit to see if we can live together in the wilderness,' he said animatedly, as I groaned. Then he burst into laughter, the same way he had in the restaurant and I realized he was pulling my leg. I smiled. 'Stop teasing me. I need a massage.' I said, holding my neck.

He swivelled round and caught hold of my back. Then he started rubbing my back and gently put his fingers on my neck and massaged the sore points. It felt so good. He smelt fresh and wonderful. Davidoff. Cool Water. And he was. This cool guy who just wanted to chill in life and have fun.

I must have looked like a train wreck and smelt like one too.

'Should I tell the producers to get someone else to come with me? I'm sure any of the girls would be happy to take your place. That is, if you're too tired to go?' he asked sincerely.

I squinted my eyes and looked back at him and said, 'Are you threatening me?'

He shrugged his shoulders and said, 'I'm just saying, dude!'

So I played along, 'Actually, I would *love* to see you clean horse shit with the designer babe. That would definitely make my day.'

'Cool,' he said and removed his hands from my back and began to get up.

Then I felt kind of terrible. I had been joking. I had become a bitter woman. I didn't want that to happen. Did I mention he was cute? So I caught hold of his hands and said, 'Karan! I don't want anyone else taking my place! So tell me where we're really going.'

He smiled and kissed me on the nose, 'Wait and watch. And for the record, I'll never let anyone take your place,' he said quietly.

Jesus, he was such a *boy*! But I immediately straightened my wet hair and fixed my towel closer around myself. The cameras were capturing all this and the producers were having a field day. We immediately realized and our moment was broken. But it had been a 'moment'. And I was so pleased with myself.

I warned him before he left, 'But we'll always have cameras on us, so we can't do anything *naughty*.'

'Naughty? Huh?' he said, laughing and leaning in a little more towards me. He smelt great. What was it about a man's smell that made me go weak? First it was Acqua de Gio and now it was Davidoff. I liked!

And then he leaned in and kissed me. At first, it was a gentle hesitant kiss, but when he saw that I was reciprocating, he moved his body in. I reached out and held the back of his head and he pressed my chest closer to his body. He held me tightly and kissed me deeply. It was romantic and passionate. Gentle and strong. Soft and supple. Something I hadn't felt for a very long time. The warmth from his body permeated into my skin and I felt myself tingle. I could feel the longing in his body. We were lip locked for a few minutes when it dawned on us that we were on national television. He let go of me gently, still not caring whether the world was watching and I looked into his eyes and smiled, suddenly not caring either. If there was an art to a perfect kiss, Karan would have been the van Gogh of it! And then suddenly, I realized Aditi was right, the best way to get over a man, was to find another one. All along I had thought only Arjun kissed well, and now I knew I was wrong.

Karan made me realize I had lived my life by other people's rules for too long. It was time that I explored my sexuality on my own terms.

I looked at him with a twinkle in my eye and said, 'Yes Dr Karan Raparia. Naughty!' And then got up and walked away. I looked back at him and he was watching me walk. God, I hoped my arse didn't look big in the swimming costume. Still, I tossed my hair back and looked at him and I knew he was checking me out. I was a new woman!

Then the interviews started, which was the norm before, during and after every task. We had to answer questions and Karan was asked if he was happy to be going on this date with me. He looked right at me and said to the camera, 'Oh, I'm definitely looking forward to it.'

The girls were burning, but my body was already on fire.

Then Karan did something nice. When no one was looking, he went and wrote a note for me on a piece of paper and put it in my jacket pocket. On the way back to the House, in the bus with the girls, I found it. It read, 'I'm so glad you won. I wanted to see you again. I need to repeat our kiss.'

I was really looking forward to our date once again. Maybe Karan was my second chance with Love.

Thirty-three

Back in the House, the girls started fighting again over who was going to use the showers first. A few of them went into the three bathrooms while the rest of us sat around in the large drawing room sofas and chatted.

'My body is screaming in pain,' said Shalini, the girl from Lucknow, who just a few days ago was wearing a full sleeve salwar kameez, but had shed it for the tiny shorts today.

'I need a drink,' said Shweta, the biker chick from Bangalore. We all looked at her and she replied in a hushed whisper, 'I know we're not allowed, but I smuggled some in.'

And then we were all in it. We all wanted some of that alcohol.

'First, we need to cover all the cameras here. At least in this room,' I said, organizing the whole thing. So we all got up and walked to the respective cameras and threw our jackets over them. We muffled the microphones in a similar fashion with other pieces of clothing and cushions around. Then we sent Shweta to her room to get the alcohol out. She came back with a large bottle of vodka.

'See, it will never smell on us and we can all have a little bit,' she said in a conspiratorial whisper.

I wanted to throw my arms around her and hug her, but refrained—it might be taken as a lesbian act and I would be voted off, if nothing else!

We all sat down with a large peg and began to chat. The

tension just evaporated with this common factor called Smirnoff, as we bonded against the producers and opened up to each other.

'So, Kaveri,' started Pooja, the web designer from Hyderabad, 'where are you supposed to be going on that date with Karan?'

Before I could reply, another woman intervened and asked me, 'How did you finish the task so quickly, yaar? How did you rig it?'

'I didn't rig it. And I have no idea,' I replied. 'I guess I've always loved nature and I used to go trekking with my dad when I was young. I hadn't done that in a long time and I just got into a rhythm . . . it was fun and I kept going,' I shrugged my shoulders.

'So Karan likes you,' added Ramneek, the girl from Delhi who was working in the hospitality industry.

'I don't really care,' I said, acting indifferent. But I knew I did. It was a nice thing to hear that a man preferred you over nine other women!

'Are you crazy? Why don't you care? We're all supposed to be competing for the love of this man,' spoke Meher, the costume designer from Mumbai.

'You know what? I don't care too much either. He's kinda stupid,' spoke Anandita, the Bengali woman who was a theatre artiste.

Then the women who had gone for their showers came out and joined us. But none of us wanted to move. 'Hey! What are you guys having?' asked eighteen-year-old Namrata who walked in first. 'I also want!' she spoke in a high nasal tone. I could just imagine her being a total brat in a rich household, having got everything she wanted from her rich daddy, including the spot in this show.

'You're not legally allowed to, darling,' said Pooja sarcastically, and who had probably just turned legal enough to drink.

'Oh ya?' said Namrata. 'Then I won't share my smokes with you!' and she went and got a packet of cigarettes and lit up extremely seductively in front of the others. Shweta got up and snatched the packet from her while handing her a glass, 'Stop being such a bitch. Here. Baby!' Then turning to me she asked, 'So what do you really want from Karan, Kaveri? Sex? Marriage? A baby to take home?' Everyone laughed at her joke. She lit up a cigarette and held it while plonking herself back on the sofa.

I just smiled. 'No, babe,' I said casually, 'I don't want any of that stuff. I'm here to meet interesting people. And I have.' And then I raised my glass to the lot of them.

'So you don't care if you get eliminated tomorrow?'

I shook my head and said nonchalantly, 'Not at all!' I didn't want to give away my secret.

Misri, the Punjabi girl who was half Parsi and a model, lit a cigarette as well and said, 'I want to just make this a platform to go on to TV serials, you know.'

'Me too,' said the reticent Anandita, 'I've been doing theatre for far too long and I'm not going anywhere. I need to make money. I can't live on roles for the soul.'

Shweta laughed, 'That's what they call it? What a loser you are!'

'I'm here to get married,' said Ramneek, the Delhi hotel girl, suddenly. Shalini, the woman from Lucknow, stared at her. I could sense she also felt the same way, but she didn't want to say it out loud to give away her feelings. So she got up and muttered she was going to take a shower.

Ramneek continued, 'I've been single for too long. I've gone through the matrimonial ads, the Internet and the friends of friends' thing. But nothing has worked out. The men I've met have been mostly losers. Not to mention ugly.' She took a long sip of her drink and continued, 'I'm ready to settle down. And Karan seems like a nice guy. He's intelligent, caring, NRI, doctor, rich! What more could a girl ask for?'

'Are you serious?' asked Meher, the costume designer and continued without a response, 'There are so many better men out there than Karan. I mean, you don't know anything about his parents, his background, if he has a girlfriend stashed away in the US.' I could make out that Meher also wanted to marry Karan, but was dissuading Ramneek from doing so.

Namrata butted in here, 'Oh, he had a girlfriend. A steady one.' We all looked at her. This eighteen-year-old was giving the rest of us information! 'Ya he told me on our meeting. But he said it was over some time back. And oh ya, I forgot to mention, he kissed me!' We were all in shock. She seemed smug and content.

I could see that some of the women were taken aback and would take up the issue with Karan the next time they met. I didn't know how to feel. I had begun to feel this fondness for him, but if he was just being a Casanova, then maybe I would have to back off and treat this like it really was. Just a show. Before the girls could grill Namrata further, one of the producers came in and gave orders for us to get ready for the elimination round. He also brought in some dresses for us that were sponsored by a leading brand store. We all had to shower, get into make-up and these gowns and head downstairs in half an hour. So we all rushed and forgot about the camaraderie that the alcohol had induced a while ago. But I could hear Ramneek crying in the bathroom later. This show was teaching us a thing or two. It had made me even more confused. If all these girls wanted Karan as their husband, who was I to have a fling with him and ruin the whole equation. And Karan was a fling. He could never be a husband for me. And suddenly I felt guilty. How could I not distinguish between Love and Lust? It was time I grew up.

Half an hour later we were on the steps of the House for the elimination. Karan and the producers were also present. Aniruddh walked in from the side entrance and said his lines to the camera, 'Well, the winner of today's task was . . . Kaveri!' a little applause and I was called down to stand next to Karan. Aniruddh continued, 'But while we get to Kaveri and Karan's date later, Karan, you need to make a decision right now. There will be an elimination. But we also have a twist.' Here, there was a dramatic pause for effect. 'Not one girl, but two, will be eliminated tonight!'

The girls wore a shocked expression. They hadn't expected this. Aniruddh continued, 'The girl with the lowest score on both tasks will be eliminated first. Now this is not Karan's decision. It is based on a point system. The girl I will call out must immediately pack her bags and leave the House. And the first girl to go is . . .' Here again, there was another pause and everyone waited with bated breath, 'Meher.' My God. I was shocked as were the rest of the inmates. She was the most classy dresser, and voted amongst the top three probables. But she was the first to go. Apparently, she had burnt her food and she had come last in the task today. She hugged a few girls, blew Karan a kiss and walked up towards her room to pack her bags. A camera followed her while the rest of us looked on surprised.

'Now the time has come for Karan to pick the person he is most incompatible with. So Karan, after meeting everyone, who do you think should leave the House.'

Karan looked sheepish and smiled, 'Well, I think all the girls are superb. They're so unique in their own way.'

Aniruddh now insisted, as was the norm, on elongating the process, 'But we need to know one name, Karan.'

Karan took a deep breath. I could hear the 'tension music track' playing in the background. Then he looked straight at the girl who had caused havoc a few hours earlier and said, 'Namrata.'

Namrata looked shocked. She must have thought that after her make-out session with this man, she would have definitely survived this elimination. She stood there with her eyes wide open and jaw dropped. Then, instead of hugging anyone, she took out her middle finger and showed it to Karan and stormed off into her room. I almost burst out laughing, but the producers looked stern and so I just pursed my lips and looked down.

Aniruddh announced that the rest of us could relax till the

next task, while Karan and I were sent off for the date. But when the producer yelled, 'Cut!' I was told to go rest and that the date would happen the next day. I would have to wear the same clothes and be ready by 7 p.m. Karan left without saying a word to anyone and we all went upstairs. I realized that he was also affected by the elimination process. He was getting close to the girls. And I was just one of them. I went to my room to crash for the night. But I could hear the girls sitting in their room discussing the elimination and analysing it in great detail. The game had begun, but now I wanted something else. I wanted to get out.

Thirty-four

Karan picked me up at seven in the evening and instead of going for a quiet dinner, we went to a New Year's Eve party that had been arranged by the channel. It was a red carpet event with a host of television stars, models, the press and photographers. Most of the producers were huddling around Deepa who was waving her hand and a few went off to get her something. There were cameras on Karan and me as well. Karan behaved like a movie star as soon as he stepped out of the car that had been sent to pick us up. This was a side to him I had not seen before. I was shy and nervous. I followed him, pleading with my eyes to not be left behind. I felt awkward and out of place. But I knew I was looking pretty. The gown and the make-up that had been applied earlier in the evening, along with the jewels given by Gitanjali, made me feel like a princess. At least people were taking my photograph along with Karan's. I didn't feel like an old cow as was mentioned by the producers and girls yesterday.

The rest of the girls were also there. But I was Karan's official date. We went to the party and the cameras followed us around as we met people and gave out bytes. We met TV stars from a variety of shows and were introduced to a few models who had gone from the ramp to TV and then to the silver screen. They towered over me and were wearing tiny clothes that showed off a lot of cleavage, legs, back or other body parts in ample amounts. I knew if Aditi were here, she would have fit right in. But I had always felt shy in public places and that side was emerging again. I needed to get a drink to feel at ease. I told Karan I needed a drink and he went off to get me one.

In the meantime, a reporter came up to me and asked, 'Hey, you're the chick who's on the date with Karan, right?'

I nodded.

She continued, 'So how does it feel to fall in love with a man who's loved by nine other women?'

Suddenly I got my confidence back. I knew what I had to do. I turned around and said, 'Love, sex and romance are all different things, dear. Don't ever get them confused!' And I threw my head back and laughed. She giggled nervously for a bit and said, 'Great! I'll see you around.' With that she went off.

Karan made me dance, which the cameras captured, along with our every move. But after that, the cameras left us alone and we could be natural. Or at least that's what we thought. I realized later that the hidden cameras captured our conversation and played it on national television which made the episode the highest rated on that channel for the show.

'Finally!' he said and came and sat next to me on the bench. It was a starlit night. The crescent moon shone brightly and we watched the traffic go by. He then turned and kissed me.

'It's about time!' I said naughtily. 'What took you so long?'

'I didn't know if I was allowed,' he winked.

'Oh honey, of course you're allowed,' I said seductively. And then he turned and put his hand behind my head and pulled me towards him and gave me a slow, deep kiss. His tongue touched mine so softly, as if it was asking permission. I turned towards him and mumbled 'mmm'.

We stopped after a few minutes and looked at each other. Then I turned and took a sip of my drink and said very indifferently, 'You know you have to eliminate me.'

His look showed he was completely baffled with my statement.

I then asked, very casually, 'Tell me, Karan, which of these girls do you really like?'

He looked at me and said, 'Besides you?' And here he smiled

and continued, 'Um . . . Ramneek's interesting. My mom will be happy with her . . . Shalini is so diametrically different . . . Pooja is intelligent and would be able to continue her career in USA . . .' he was talking as if the girls needed to adjust to his life and he would never adjust to theirs.

'See, darling, you're confused. You came here to get married. To find a correct bahu, according to what Aniruddh told us on the first day. And you know I'm not that. So why are you wasting your time with me?' I asked, matter of fact.

He tried to defend himself, 'But I like you!'

'Yes, but that's not enough and we both know that,' and after a thought, I added, 'Why did you eliminate Namrata?'

He swerved around and looked at me, 'I'm not supposed to explain to the girls why I eliminate them.'

I kept quiet. Then I said with affirmation, 'Karan . . . seriously, how about you eliminate me and save yourself some pain later?'

'Kaveri, I don't know what to say,' he felt dejected. I had hurt his ego. Here was a twenty-five-year-old man who had come onto a show looking for some fun and to pass time. He had not expected to get emotionally involved with the women or that a woman would be rejecting him!

'I thought we had something special,' he said.

'I'll tell you what,' I said, mischievously, 'Why don't we do something very special before we go our separate ways?'

He looked up at me. I raised my eyebrow and smiled. He looked around and pointed to the party where the journalists were and said, 'With the reporters here?'

Just then, we saw a hot air balloon on the lawns at the back with a man standing near it. We both thought of it at the same time. We went down the stairs and to the man there. The signage said, 'See Mumbai by night' and it charged a ridiculously high price, which was why no one was going for it. But we told the man that it was for our reality show and that the producers would pay for it. So he agreed. After showing us the safety measures, he sent us off on the balloon! I couldn't believe it. It was quite an escapade. We told each other stories, laughed out loud, pointing to places that were our favourite haunts and what we'd done there.

'Oh my God, see that house? That was my first girlfriend's house.'

'I didn't know you've lived here?'

'Oh yes, till I was five.'

'You had a girlfriend at five? Wow, you started early!'

'How early did you start?' he winked at me. I didn't want to tell him that it'd barely been a few months ago! And then I did it again. I surprised myself. I pulled him closer to me and kissed him. Sensuously. Passionately. Hungrily. And this time it was longer, deeper and sweeter. When he started putting his hands under my gown, I didn't stop him. I took off his jacket and kissed his neck. We slowly undressed each other, our eyes taking in each other's bodies, and lay on the floor of the balloon. It began to shake and we felt a little nervous, but the thrill prodded us along. He slid his hand under my gown and started caressing my breasts. I moaned softly into his ear and flicked my tongue around his ear lobe. He shuddered in delight. I picked up my gown and straddled myself across his legs. He ran his fingers down my back slowly unzipping my gown. I unbuckled his belt, all the while kissing him. He was no longer surprised. He wanted me then. Pure wanton lust in his eyes. I ran my nails down his chest. He had a smooth body and firm pecs. My heart started racing. This was the second man I would have sex with, and I wasn't even in love with him. But as soon as he sucked on my nipples, I grabbed his hand and lead him to another erogenous zone. My hand slipped into his pants and he wiggled out of them. He was ready. Hard. Firm to the touch. A slight gasp escaped from his mouth. I stroked him slowly and felt him shudder.

'Are you ready?' he asked.

'Are you?' I asked back defiantly.

'Yes. Oh, yes,' he pleaded. And then I sat myself down on

him as gently as I could. He fit into me perfectly. Our hips sealed together. We immediately went into a routine, breathing in patterns and touching each other all over our naked bodies. It was new, fresh and completely what I needed. We kept kissing each other as he stared into my eyes muttering, 'God, I want you.' I groaned in delight as he pulled me closer and I bit him on his neck to stop myself from screaming. I felt so ecstatic. Let the girls see the bite and feel jealous that their man had already been 'taken'!

The experience was completely different from my first time with Arjun. Karan was lovely. He was the toy boy I needed to be under to get over Arjun. He had a body that didn't tickle when I touched it in parts, and he moaned loudly without a care about whether the whole of Mumbai heard. And this time I was surer. I felt confident. Because I had lost my virginity to Arjun, I was always a little hesitant and wanted him to take charge most of the time. But with Karan, I took the initiative. I did everything as if it was the last time I was doing it. And he enjoyed it thoroughly and I commanded him like he was the schoolboy I needed to punish! It was the ride of a lifetime. And the ride lasted as long as we both wanted. Then we descended.

That having sex on a hot air balloon was risqué made this experience a truly memorable one.

We quickly wore our clothes and just as we were about to land, he asked, 'Are you sure you want to be eliminated.'

I replied, 'I've made up my mind!'

What a way to bring in the new year!

Thirty-five

A few days later, once I had got out of the House and got my apartment arranged again, and paid off pending bills, I called Aditi to check how she was doing.

'Yo, gurl! Wacha up to?' I asked.

'What is wrong with you? What is that accent? Did one of those women teach you that?' she asked, all surprised.

'No Adu. I was just teasing you,' I laughed confidently.

'Okay, so I need to meet you. I need to hear all about this guy. And, by the way, I'm only up to the second episode, so what happened? How did you get eliminated? Tell me all!' She had been following the show on TV and had become a mini celebrity in her colony because she knew me. And I had become a major celebrity once I got out of the House, since my photo was on posters all across town. It felt good.

'I will. I'll come over soon.'

Later when I went to her house to meet her, her cast was gone and her glow was back. There was something different about her. I was going to find out soon enough.

'You've recovered well,' she mentioned, as soon as we let go of our long hug.

'So have you,' I replied happily.

'Of course! I have parents who are looking after me day and night.'

That was the difference between Aditi and me. While she might complain about her parents, she actually loved them and needed them around. Whereas I loved my parents, but I definitely couldn't have them around for too long since they caused more stress than good.

After I gossiped about each of the girls, the headless-chicken producers and the dishy host Aniruddh, I started on Karan. By the time we had had two cups of tea and binged on some homemade hot, crisp samosas, I was feeling completely relaxed, as if we were back in our old days of living together where we would chat through the night.

'Karan,' I said, biting into another samosa, 'was the antidote for Arjun.'

'Oh, are we talking about him now? Can we? I mean are we allowed to say his name?' she asked, with mock seriousness.

I laughed, 'Yes, darling. Arjun! There. It doesn't hurt that much anymore.'

'But it still hurts a little?' she asked, knowing me fully well.

'It always will.'

'Do you want him back?'

I thought about that and said honestly, 'Yes. But on my terms.'

She nodded her head somberly but smiled in a moment and asked, 'Okay, so tell me about Karan! He looks gorgeous on TV.'

We talked about Karan, my date with him, what the girls thought about him and then we came to the last night together.

'You what?'

I nodded, 'I had sex with him in a hot air balloon!'

She was aghast. 'How could you? I thought you could only have sex with your soulmate?' and she used air quotes for the word soulmate and rolled her eyes.

'Ha ha,' I mocked, as I crossed my legs and made myself comfortable on her bed. 'But seriously, I had some connection with Karan, even though he was only twenty-five.'

Aditi didn't believe me. But I knew I had. I wouldn't have been able to do what I did if I did not feel something for the guy. Karan made me realize that what I thought about myself was more important than what a man thought about me. And all along I had wanted to please Arjun. I only felt good when he thought I was looking good or when he was in a happy mood. But with Karan I always felt good. He had thought I was sexy, hot and intelligent even when I had brushed him off. He had *wanted* to go out with me. With a room full of gorgeous women, he had spent the last few minutes of the past year with me instead.

That ... was a connection.

I walked over to the window and looked down at the greenery below. It was late in the night. Aditi's parents were away for a few days and there was no one at home. I missed this. I missed spending time with her, having someone to come home to, someone who had a full time servant who could make hot samosas. Then I asked what she had been up to for these past few weeks.

'Well, I've got some news too. I got a proposal for marriage.'

'What?' I asked, completely astonished. The imperial bad girl was going domestic? I couldn't believe it.

She told me that her parents had been asking her for a long time to find someone. She had been looking for the 'right' person the last couple of years but they had all turned out to be just great one nighters instead of great companions. So she told her parents to choose someone and knowing how obedient she was, she agreed to the guy they'd selected for her. He was from a good, middle class, Maharastrian family, with a decent government job which not only ensured a small house and a small car, but also a steady income.

'Aditi,' I said, finding it a little difficult to believe, 'you're going to get bored of your life. I mean I'm already bored hearing about your life from you before you have begun it!'

'Shut up!' she said, pushing me away playfully. 'I've realized something, Kavu ... there is no such thing as the perfect husband. There is no such thing as the perfect marriage. And there is no such thing as the perfect wife. So I plan to do the one thing that is perfect. Make my parents happy.'

'Aw, come on!' I said exasperated. I couldn't believe this was coming from her.

'Your parents will die in about twenty years and then you'll be bored and unhappy. God, you might be bored and unhappy in two months of this marriage, but will you stick with him for your parents?' I couldn't believe this. She had been the one to tell me to go after Love. And here she was giving up on it so easily.

She tried to rationalize, 'There is no such thing as unhappiness or happiness in a marriage. It is how you make it to be. Romance is you taking the initiative for being so. Sex is when you pull down his pants and demand it. And conversation happens when you talk and ask for a response. It's all when you want it. And if *you* want it.'

I couldn't believe her, so I asked, 'And what happens when you get bored? And you find another man . . . more attractive? And then you have the urge to go with this other man who excites you or is better looking or flirts with you in a bar?'

Aditi thought about this and said, 'You know everyone wants change continuously. But honestly, I've had so much change that it will be nice to have something permanent. When your expectations are not met, you want a change. But what if you change your expectations? Then you just might be happy!'

I took some time to think about that. Then I had another thought. Why was I trying to convince her to not be married? If she claimed she had been unhappy for a long time with so many men, maybe this was a good thing for her. And then there was me. I had believed in finding the Great Love, a soul mate, who I would get married to. But she saw that that had led me to be alone and single as well. I suppose she had wanted to believe that my theory was the one that worked. But it had not. Not one of our theories had worked. According to her, the next logical step was to get into an arranged marriage. The roles had changed. So I stopped arguing and decided to be happy for her, albeit a little sceptically.

'My God, Adu, you'll get married and go away. What will I do without you?' I said suddenly, with wide eyes.

She hugged me and said, 'I'll move down the road, stupid. Everyone lives in Planet Lokhandwala!'

We chatted till late that day and I spent the night at her place in her room. It was as if we were back to being roommates, chatting till dawn. Aditi had decided her course of life. She might never be the famous director she set out to be, but I knew she would be the perfect wife.

Thirty-six

After my stint in television, I decided I had gained enough confidence to deal with more people in larger groups. I started putting my connections to good use. I went on the Internet and became a part of an organization that helped tourists from different countries plan out their activities. So pretty soon, I was helping groups coming to Mumbai, telling them where to stay and taking them around the city, as well as fixing them up for sight seeing of neighbouring towns. I became a tour operator with a difference. Instead of a regular travel agent who just did the bookings, I became a friend to these people.

It was actually very challenging. I realized there are a lot of people who want to visit India but they were scared of being mugged, having communication problems, or scared of being put up in an awful hotel by tour operators out to swindle them. Here, I was a real person with a profile picture who would be on Skype, chat with them telling them about their plans before they came. And then I would plan their holidays tailor-made to their needs. And everyone would have a blast. And I had a blast. And I made a lot of money. Because even if I wasn't in it for the money, the people loved me so much that they tipped me really well over and above my fees.

There were people who only had four days and there were people who had two weeks. I had to figure out what they should do within their budget, so that they could have a wonderful glimpse of India. There were honeymooning couples who wanted spas and beach days and there were families who wanted the historical sites to educate their kids and there were female travellers who wanted cheap shopping during the day and exciting clubs at night. It was a wonderful plan.

Until I met Aaron.

Aaron was born and brought up in San Francisco. Although his father was originally from India, Aaron had never visited India as a grown-up. His father had died when he was young and his mother, who was American, remarried one of her countrymen. So the need for him to return to his 'roots' never existed, because he was an out and out American. But he decided he wanted to explore a part of him that had felt empty for so long. And he made his way to India.

Aaron was the complete opposite of Arjun. Yes, I made the comparison somewhere between picking him up at the airport and kissing him at my house. But I'll come back to that later. Aaron came out of Mumbai airport looking like he should have been in the movies. He had light brown hair, white skin and blue eyes. Nothing about him gave away his Indian genes.

'Kaveri?' he asked, seeing me.

'Aaron!' I said, my voice a little too high pitched, 'Hi!'

'Hey, I'm so sorry you couldn't recognize me. That photo I sent was years old, taken on a trek and it was so small, obviously you couldn't see what I looked like.'

'No, no, no problem.' I offered to help him with his bags and he laughed and said that the backpack and duffel bag were all he was carrying. But soon, I would notice that even though he carried very few clothes, they were always branded and he had a terrific sense of mixing and matching.

As soon as we sat in the taxi I had hired for the day, I started telling him about the plans I had made, 'So since you didn't tell me how long you were going to be here and the things you wanted to do, I've taken the liberty of planning an itinerary for a single guy like you for a week and if you're not too happy with that and if your budget allows ...'

He interrupted me before I could finish, 'Kaveri, I'm sorry I couldn't talk to you more before I left. But it was sudden. I decided to come to India the day before yesterday and here I am.'

'No, no, I'm not blaming you,' I clarified.

'Let me finish. What I'm saying is that I really don't care what all we do, as long as we get to do it at a leisurely pace. I'm here till I find what I'm looking for.'

Then he became quiet and looked out of the window. I decided not to probe. I would tell him his plans later. We only spoke once we reached the hotel.

'I booked you into Taj, the nicest hotel in Bandra. But if it doesn't suit your budget . . .'

'Don't worry about money. It's nice,' he said, as we got off the car and walked into the lobby. While he was checking in, I sat on the plush sofas next to the flower arrangement and tried to gauge his body language. He was definitely wealthy. Which meant a good tip for me later. He looked tired, which was obviously because of his long flight. But other than that, he was cute. He was relaxed and unassuming. He had this aura that made people around him comfortable.

'I've checked in,' he said. I nodded and replied, 'So you go rest and when you're all freshened up, call me and we can discuss the plans for your trip.'

'See, I think I'm going to be jet lagged for a bit so I'll call you and maybe we can have dinner here or something if you like?'

Suddenly, I felt that maybe he had got the wrong idea. Maybe he felt that I was an escort service instead of a tour guide. So I tried explaining, 'Aaron, I'm here to take you to places that you would generally not see on a bus. I'm not the type of person who has dinners and . . . does . . .'

'Oh no!' he was immediately apologetic. 'I didn't imply that. I was saying since I'm not up for a whole lot of adventure right now, if you want, you can fill me in on the stuff you've planned over dinner. Otherwise, come tomorrow for breakfast or coffee at whatever time and we can figure out a plan. Okay?' With that, he tapped my arm and left.

'I'm glad I made that clear,' I muttered under my breath and left for home. But once I got home I started thinking. Maybe I shouldn't have been so stand-offish. Maybe I was too conscious about the impression I made on people. I had always been guarded, because I never knew what to say. But I was more sure now. I knew how to conduct myself and I had met many tourists who loved my company. So maybe I should not have been so curt. And he hadn't even said anything. I had just jumped to conclusions. I needed to ease off instead of reading into every tiny little sentence a man says. That's what Arjun had left in me. A sense of doubt, suspicion and weariness. I needed to change that so I could be open, friendly, and less suspicious, even with single men.

I went for dinner with Aaron and we discussed the plans I had. He was extremely cool and didn't come on to me at all. Over the next few days, we saw all the tourist spots of Mumbai: Gateway of India, Chor Bazaar, Haji Ali, Marine Drive. I went with him since he didn't understand Hindi at all. And we ate at the local places and he thoroughly enjoyed the food. He relished the ragda pattice at Churchgate and the bhelpuri at Elco Arcade and the pao bhaji at Juhu beach. It was such a wonderful experience talking to him about culture, values, families, etc. It felt like I was a teacher, for he would sit and listen to me for hours. I would ramble on trying to educate this foreigner about his own land and he would ask significant questions that would make me proud.

'Why is corruption so big here?' he asked, when we were sitting one day for lunch at a small Lonavala restaurant. We had driven down so he could see some green hills and another part of Maharashtra. Even though I had come with Arjun to Lonavala a few times, being with Aaron had made me feel completely at ease. Arjun came to my mind a few times on the drive to Lonavala. But the scintillating conversations I had with Aaron about India drove his thoughts away. Aaron's companionship, his viewpoint, my opinions and a general sense of camaraderie made me feel enriched.

'Well,' I thought out loud, 'there are a lot of people who feel they are not getting what they deserve. Be it economically, emotionally, or morally. And if they've felt that for a long time from their family, friends, at school, and then see other people being corrupt, they think that it is the only way to feel better about themselves. Money makes them feel they have compensated for their deficiencies in other areas.'

The food came and we continued our discussion. He pointed out the flaws in my argument and I tried to justify them. We ended up talking about families.

'Arjun, why . . . I'm sorry, Aaron, what made you come to India all of a sudden?' I thought I had covered the slip of tongue well. But he caught on though he didn't mention it.

'I was cleaning out my garage and I found an album of photos, my dad had taken on our first, and last trip, to India. The three of us had come together and we had explored Bombay and some other places.' He was pensive while talking and I didn't disrupt his thoughts till he continued again. 'I was seven then. Dad died of cancer two years later. He didn't have his parents or close family in India. When Mom remarried, she encouraged me to be Indian. But I couldn't. I was so angry with my dad for leaving me that I wanted to kill everything Indian about me. I know, I know, it wasn't his fault. But somehow I felt he had abandoned me when I needed him and hadn't fought the cancer hard enough.' Aaron looked vulnerable.

I had never seen a man cry and this was a new experience for me. But I let him continue.

'But all my life, I felt that there was something inside me that was so strong that I couldn't suppress it any longer . . . and I didn't know what it was. I could not put a finger to it. When I found this album, I felt that maybe Dad was telling me to explore my Indian roots to find out what that thing was.'

'And have you found it?' I asked gingerly. 'What you were looking for?'

He looked at me said, 'Not yet. But I'm getting close. I can feel it.' He smiled and I smiled back. He paid the bill and we left. While we were heading back, I was quiet. I was thinking about what he had said. But I was thinking about Arjun as well. I had suppressed my love for him for so long. Would it haunt me one day if we met suddenly?

Three hours later, I got off with my bag at my doorstep. He followed me to my door.

'Thanks, Kaveri. I know it's your job, but I think it's the best vacation I've been on in a long time,' he said.

And right then, I made up my mind. I said, 'Aaron, don't take this the wrong way, but would you like to spend the night at my place?'

He raised his eyebrow to ask if I was sure.

I nodded. I was sure.

Thirty-seven

I didn't sleep with Aaron that night. He crashed on the sofa. But the feeling that there was another man in my house after so long actually made me feel good. We continued our conversation the next day after my maid gave him some hot *aloo paratha*s and me a suspicious look. He thought it was the most awesome food he had ever had.

The next day, he checked out of the hotel and moved in with me. He said he would pay me the same as the hotel stay for as long as he was in India and I didn't say no. I wanted this to be a business arrangement, even though we had become friends.

Over the next few days we took day trips around Mumbai, stayed at home and read the papers, magazines and anything 'Indian' that needed analyzing. We went off to watch Gujarati plays that we both didn't understand, but laughed so hard at. It felt like being on a permanent vacation. But we didn't have sex. It felt like having a buddy over after a very long time and I wanted to enjoy that. There were moments when he would look at me and I could feel the chemistry between us and I stared back into his eyes for a long time. But he didn't do anything and I didn't initiate it either.

Maybe somewhere I felt that because I had kissed Arjun first, I had had to make the relationship work. And this time, I would not be the first person.

It was one such day when I caught a cold and was lying in bed feeling miserable that he decided to look after me.

'This is not what you're paying for, Aaron. I'll set you up to go to Ajanta and Ellora caves. You go for a few days and come back. Don't waste your time here with me,' I insisted.

'Don't be stupid. We'll go together when you're better,' he responded.

'But that could take a while. My colds last for a really long time and since it is a virus you might catch it too.'

'Cool. Want some soup?' he asked nonchalantly and then went off to the kitchen to make some Knorr packet soup that he had bought earlier. And that was when I realized it. Here was a complete stranger who had known me for only two weeks, but had decided to give up having a good time to look after me. He was ready to ruin the only ten days off he would have for the next one year to be at my bedside, nursing me with soup. I started crying.

Aaron came back and was appalled, 'Hey!' he came over and held me. 'What happened? Want me to get something for you? Want me to call the doctor? What? Tell me!'

I sobbed into his shirt and said, 'Thank you!'

'It's about Arjun, isn't it?' he asked softly, holding me.

I looked up and immediately dried my tears. Where had that come from, I questioned with my eyes.

'Is it too painful to talk about him?' he asked.

I kept quiet. He immediately changed the topic, 'Sorry. I shouldn't have asked. Did you know that they have the same ingredients in the tomato soup here as they have in leading brands in the USA?'

I sighed, 'Arjun was the love of my life. He will always be the love of my life. But I was not the love of his life. It's as simple as that. And as complicated.'

'All love stories are complicated, Kaveri. Every life has its own complications.'

'Are you defending him?' I asked, surprised.

'No. Not at all. I'm just saying. There must have been something extremely complicated about his life as well. Otherwise he would never have said no to a wonderful person like you.'

'Actually he didn't say no.' I said, as an afterthought.

Aaron looked at me questioningly.

I continued. 'But he didn't say yes either. So I decided to get out of the limbo.'

'And live in limbo still?' he asked, while feeding me the soup.

'Who says I'm in limbo now?' I asked morosely.

Aaron shrugged his shoulders, 'I'm just saying . . . figure out what you really want, Kaveri. Then it'll happen.'

I started sulking. The cold was getting to me. 'You don't know anything about my life either!'

He nodded, 'Okay, babe. Just have some soup. We need you to get okay soon.'

Aaron helped me become better. Not just by giving me soup every evening or taking a walk every time my maid came so she wouldn't think badly of me, or by bringing me back flowers every time he returned. He made me better by sticking with me through my illness. Something that I had wanted a man to do. Something that I needed to know that a man *would* do. And it gave me relief to know that there could be a man who would want to do that for me. Even if Aaron wasn't permanent.

After a few days I recovered. And after a few days, I understood what Aaron had meant. I always sent mixed signals to people. I was undecided about my life and it showed in my actions. And the next day, I stopped sending him mixed signals Which led to many more nights of unmixed signals from me. Here's what happened.

It was late at night. Aaron wasn't the type to watch television, so we were reading. I sat on a cushion while he read out chapters. After some time, I stopped hearing the words and just watched his mouth move. His eyes lit up when he read something that excited him. His hands came alive. He had no pretenses about being an intellectual or about having travelled the world. He was simple, straightforward and uncomplicated. And oh-so-very-good-looking. My mind wandered.

My eyes left his mouth and found other parts of his body. He wasn't perfect. But his imperfection was what was most attractive. He was real. I lingered on his arms. And smiled. I took in a deep breath. He smelt so good. Hugo Boss. Dependable. Trustworthy. Strong. Just like Aaron.

His eyes twinkled and suddenly he stopped talking. Our eyes locked. He saw me staring at him. We looked at each other for some time. Paused. Inviting.

Then I got up and walked over to his cushion and sat myself down on top of him, wrapping my legs around his waist. Inhale. Exhale.

'I'm not one of those women,' I said softly. He nodded in agreement, without saying a word.

'Generally,' I added, as an afterthought. He smiled. Hesitant.

And then I leaned in and kissed him. He held my face and pulled me closer to him. I was in control. I parted his mouth and let my tongue slip in softly. He waited for more. Nibbling. Searching. Breasts heaving against his body. Unsure. Surprised. Pleased. Very pleased.

'Wait. Let me show you,' I said reassuringly.

I got off him and led him to the bedroom. I switched on the Chinese lamps that gave the room a warm reddish glow. I hadn't used them for a long time. I stood close to him and kissed him again. Deeply. Lustfully. I took his shirt off slowly. Stroking. Cupping. Yearning.

'Don't be afraid,' I murmured into his ear. We took off each other's clothes. Taking the time to gaze at each other. Admire. Approve. Appreciate.

I wanted to jump in. I only knew one way. But he took it gradually. Prolonged kisses. Raw sexual energy. He made me sit on his lap and look into his eyes. Tenderly. We breathed in each other's smell, we breathed in each other's energies. Desire mounting. We kissed with our eyes open. We sat there naked. Longing. He ran his fingertips softly down my neck, lingering at my breasts and stopping at my thigh. His white skin against my olive nakedness. Intense. He made me lie down as he ran his fingertips across my body. I was ready. I wanted him, but he didn't relent.

'Find your centre,' he whispered, as his fingers moved down and gently across my genitals. A soothing touch that made my skin tingle.

I knew what he was talking about. Suddenly there was a power inside me that had never been there before. A warmth within my body that sought immediate pleasure. I swivelled around and put my hands across his chest. He lay on top of me and looked directly into my eyes. Passionate kissing. Nibbling. Sucking. Right there. Yes. I arched my back and he agreed.

He was divine. I inhaled as he took slow, strong strokes and murmured my name over and over again. I was captivated by his love-making. Enthralled by his intensity. Suddenly he stopped and slid down. Lower and lower. His tongue drawing a straight line. Down my navel. Lingering around the edges. Teasing. Tantalizing. Slowly, but surely, he slid his tongue into me. I was conscious. But this time it was his tongue that reassured me. He tickled. He teased. It didn't stop. Not even when I begged him to. And then I knew what he was doing.

This wasn't just ordinary sex. This was tantric. This was of the souls meeting.

He sat me up quickly and pressed against me. Powerful strokes. Our hands all over each other. Faster. Biting. Pause and withdrawal. The room swayed around us.

And it continued. On my back. Reversed. Raised. More heat. A new connection. Deeper bonding. The earth moved. I lost control. He was insatiable. Fervent desire. Again and again. And I finally knew the meaning of multiple orgasms. I was left breathless.

We finished several hours later. The room was a site. I had no words left. Pure happiness. He smiled as he held me close. And in the early morning light, just as dawn broke and the rays of sunlight filtered in, he went to sleep holding me in his arms.

I recognized that I had just had mad sex with a man who

could never be permanent in my life. And it wasn't just for the sake of Lust as it had been with Karan. It was new and transient and still something precious. And I was okay with that. I knew that men would come into my life and leave. If I would not allow that, I would never meet interesting people who would enrich my life. And heartbreak was inevitable. But that didn't mean I couldn't live completely, that I wouldn't give my heart again and again.

Because really, there was no other way to live.

Soon one month was over. And he had to get back to his life in the US. And the day came when he had finished packing and was set to leave for the airport.

'What time is your flight again?' I asked, for the hundredth time.

'3 a.m.,' he said, as he finished writing something on a piece of paper. 'Kaveri, come here.' I had finished making some tea for both of us and handed him a cup. 'Here's your cheque.'

I stood very silent. I'd never thought I would be paid for my 'services'.

'I'd told you I would pay you for letting me stay at your place. And a promise is a promise.'

'Aaron, after all that we've been through, I can't . . .'

He came over and held me. He took the cup from my hand and put it down. 'Kaveri, this last one month has been amazing. I found what I was looking for. I found a reason. I might look American, but I'm an Indian at heart. That's what my dad was trying to tell me. And this trip will not be my last one to this country. And it's not just because of the place I fell in love with. It's the person. It's you. So I want to thank you for not only doing your job by showing me around, but by giving me a piece of myself that I had forgotten many years ago. Don't think this cheque is for any other purpose, Kaveri. It's purely for you to sit and think about what you want to do next. It'll sustain your lifestyle, I think, from what I've gathered of you in the last month. And if I'm wrong, please call me in Frisco and I'll send you more. Because what you've done for me, no other woman, or person for that matter, has.' Then he kissed me this really long kiss and I missed him already.

But I knew that Aaron was not the Great Love of my life. He was yet another man who had shown me that there could be beautiful experiences if I opened my heart to them.

And like the fleeting love that leaves you happy and depressed at the same time, he was gone.

Thirty-eight

Aaron had left two days before my birthday and I decided that instead of making any more resolutions at thirty-one, I was going to give thanks for the year that had gone by. And I would do it with the people I had taken for granted. So without further delay, I booked myself on a flight to Bangalore to surprise my parents.

My parents are a species from the planet of Culture Vultures. They do not believe in 'doing nothing'. They would never just 'be' or 'zone out' or 'take a chill pill'. All phrases I tried to teach them, mellow them, phrases that were never understood and that backfired most of the time. My parents had been together for thirt-five years. They'd met in college and got married when they were in the Academy. Both were in the Foreign Service and eventually my mom decided to quit and just stay with my dad. I've always thought it was regressive that a woman needs to give up on her career, but she said education gives us choices to be happier in life. And she wasn't happy in her career, away from Dad.

But even when Mom stayed at home, she decided to excel in everything she did. She was the topper of her batch and made sure we were reminded of it everyday for the last three decades. But whatever she decided to pursue turned to profit and, with her vast knowledge and many interests, her home businesses did very well.

My parents nagged me to do something constantly. It was a

huge pressure to keep on excelling. I learnt seven languages and studied all the time not because I truly wanted to, but because my parents needed me to do something *more*. Hence coming from this cultural background, it had become impossible to talk to them on a sane and ordinary level. Where most children would talk about how they hated their boss and how their friends were doing, my parents would expect me to know about the tax system in Monaco as if I had just met the Ambassador of the place. It had been a pretty tall order to live up to their expectations.

But now I was here. In their home. And I wanted to be here more than anywhere else in the world.

'Kaveri! Good you've come now,' said my mom, opening the door and hugging me. My mom is a tall woman, with olive skin like mine and hips that had begun resembling her mother's. Gosh, this was going to be my legacy.

'Why?' I asked, putting my bags down in the living room, knowing that Raju, our help, would take it to my room. I could behave like that in my parents' house. I was wanted and pampered. It felt good! Sometimes I wondered why I ever moved out. And why do people ever move out of their parent's houses when parents always looked out for you, made your favourite meals, worried about you if you were staying out late, were concerned about your career choices, gave you money when you were broke, and were involved with your life. So the reason to move out for most Indian children at any age, really, didn't make sense. Except the fact that your parents also wanted you to lead a life *they* wanted, and space was non-negotiable. You didn't have any. If you lived under their roof, you were accountable for everything. And sooner or later, you would want your own life. And mine was in Mumbai.

But all that was secondary right now. I was happy to be home and eating my favourite meal, chatting with my mother about the things I had been up to. But I left out the part about a man. My mom, keen to know more about that aspect, tried to probe by saying, 'So you know . . . Pooja, your cousin who's in Dubai?' I nodded, knowing fully well where this was going. 'She's got engaged. To an American. The whole family was quite aghast wondering how he is going to fit into our culture, but I was the only one supporting it. I think we should mingle amongst all cultures. I would be perfectly okay if you wanted to . . .'

'Mom!' I said stopping her, 'I know where you're going with this. But I don't have anyone, white, brown, black, red, yellow, whatever skin man, in my life. And thank you for the assurance that I can look beyond India. I am happy Pooja has your vote of confidence!'

She smiled smugly and said, 'Okay!' If she could get metaphysical poetry and candle making, I didn't understand how she could not get 'sarcasm'. And then she stayed quiet and I felt bad. I had snapped again. I was too quick to judge her, condemn her and dismiss her. How was what she had done any less important than what I had done? Look where I was in my life. I didn't have a clear career or a husband or a pot of gold to take me through life. All she had done was try to make me like her. And she did it because she wanted me to be as happy as her.

'I'm sorry, Mom,' I said, not giving a hug or anything but just a smile to say I understood what she was doing. 'I'll go to Pooja's wedding.' She knew what I meant. And she gave me another spoon of the rich kheer she had made.

My parents and I went out for dinner on my birthday. Bangalore Club was a lovely, quiet place they went to regularly. My father was well known there and my mother was highly respected. They loved the place. I thought the food was awful and had always complained about it to them. But this time, I just let them do whatever made *them* happy. They ordered way too many starters and had way too many drinks and, by the time the night was half way through, we were already stuffed.

'So Kavu, here's a toast to you being thirty-one!' my dad raised his third glass of whiskey, slurring a little but beaming quite merrily.

'God, I feel old,' Mom cribbed. '*You* turning old is making *me* feel old!'

I raised my glass and said, 'Thank you. Thank you all around.' And then I started on my 'Oscar' speech, 'I'd like to thank Almighty God for what I have achieved in these last few years, my parents for always supporting me . . .' And as I said the words, I realized that they had. They had always supported me. And I had always shunned them, thinking their way of life was boring, or too old fashioned or oppressive.

I might have been a much more contented person had I sat back and enjoyed their way of life. I continued, 'I truly want to thank you for letting me spread my wings and fly. I want you to know that I appreciate all that you've done for me.' And I kissed both of them on the cheek and I could see both of them getting misty eyed. But I had meant it. And I enjoyed my dinner and we had many more laughs after that. It felt good to be with them. It felt good to take that huge chip off my shoulder and begin to realize just how much I loved my parents.

I finally felt what Aditi had felt for her parents. A sense of deep respect and love.

Thirty-nine

While I was trying to somehow manage a living, Aditi was trying to organize a wedding. And she was going mad doing it. Her parents were driving her crazy and her relatives' list was becoming larger than the population of Shanghai. By the time I went to her place after my Bangalore visit, the wedding was only two weeks away and she was fuming at me.

'Where have you been? I've been going insane doing all this by myself. You're supposed to be my best friend who's supposed to be helping me!' I felt guilty. It was true. I should have been around her for such an important occasion. But since I needed to get away from the past, I'd landed up alienating Aditi as well and distanced her during my Aaron venture and my birthday.

'Don't worry. Everything will be all right. We can fix this.' I said with great authority, as if I had been a wedding planner all my life. 'Now,' I said, opening up a diary that was lying on her bedroom dressing table. 'Tell me what to do.'

She threw her hands in the air and said, 'I don't know what you should do, idiot,' she screamed, all flabbergasted. 'The cards haven't been sent out, the menu hasn't been fixed, the flowers haven't been chosen, the groom's clothes haven't been picked out, the songs for the sangeet haven't been selected, the DJ for the night hasn't been chosen . . .' Aditi rambled on and I listened patiently.

Then I got up and said, 'Okay then, I see that you've got most bases covered. I'll see you in two weeks, huh?' I pretended to leave and Aditi threw a pillow at me.

'Bitch! Get back here or I'll get you married to my dog!' she laughed.

'Aww. That's no way to call your fiancé,' I teased. She threw another cushion at me and we were back to being our old selves.

In the next few days, I dispatched all the cards and had thrown away a few that Aditi secretly didn't want to invite. If the people came, her parents would be glad and if they didn't, she would blame it on me and be secretly happy. We also picked out a DJ for the sangeet, since I knew one who was a family friend and would play for a very nominal fee. I bought a few magazines for Aditi while I took her to the parlour for a facial one day and we picked out the flowers and the groom's clothes. I realized in the middle of all this how, in just one year, our roles had reversed. Here I was, taking her to the parlour and making decisions about her life. Soon enough, most of the things that had plagued her about the wedding were sorted out. By the time the grand day arrived, everything was in place.

Aditi stood in her bridal finery in the hotel room allotted to us and said, 'I really thought you would get married before me, Kavu.' She was looking so happy. She had chosen someone finally and that person had chosen to be with her. It was a big step in her life.

I looked at her and smiled, 'I didn't.'

She gave me one of those looks like she knew what I had gone through. 'Aditi,' I explained, 'in my heart, I never wanted to get married. And you did.' Aditi gave me a strange look as if I had gone mad. And I knew I was not saying this to please her on her wedding day. I had thought about it a long time and I really believed this now. 'You went out with as many people as you could to see who you would be compatible with for life. I went out with one who was already married. I brought that upon myself. I get it now. So you know what? I'm happy you're getting married before me. It's okay.' I whispered softly.

She came over to hug me. We had a moment.

But before her mascara could run, I continued my thought,

'Ya'cos now, I'll be the one who'll be with all those men and you'll have to wake up to the same old, balding, fat man for life!'

'Shut up!' she laughed. And then said seriously, 'Thank you. For everything. For being my best friend. For being . . .'

'I know.' I interrupted, 'And thank you too, babe,' I said. 'Because you showed me *reason*. And I was running away from it for so long. I know you looked out for me. And I love you for it.'

She held me tight, 'I love you too.'

Just then, her cousins flooded the room and took her towards the mandap. So I let them and I stayed back in the hotel room to take a breather before I put on my smiley face in front of Aditi's relatives.

When Aditi and her cousins had left, I looked out of the window and saw the lights of Mumbai. It was beautiful. I loved this city. And I felt that even though I had loved and lost here, I had strength now to be something that I had been afraid of being earlier. I completed *me*. I didn't feel the need to be the person walking towards that mandap. I knew that if it had to happen, it would be a nice thing that I would cherish. But I had stopped believing in a forever. And it wasn't a cynical feeling. It was a practical, liberating, independent feeling. I realized that if I was never to get married, that would be okay too. Oh, I wasn't giving up on love. Or giving up on having a man in my life. It was just the opposite. I was opening up to love. I was opening up to having many special people in my life. At different stages. At different times. And I knew that each person I had, would be loved, even if I lost him later. That would not stop me from trying to love again, and I would not remain bitter at him or at the concept of 'love'.

And with that thought, I went to give my best friend away to wedded bliss.

Forty

It was about eleven at night. I was sitting at home checking my social networking sites to see what other people were up to. My voyeuristic pleasure seeking side emerged at night. Just then, I got a call from a woman who sounded American.

'Hi, I'm Susan from the Metropolitan Museum of Art,' she chirped.

'In New York?' I asked, disbelievingly.

'Yes. Have you got my mail?'

I quickly opened my email account and started reading the mail and before I could stifle a shriek, she continued, 'Kaveri, we have some very exciting news. We went through your application and we would like to give you a paid internship at the Metropolitan if you are ready to relocate to New York?'

'Of course!' I said too eagerly, 'Yes! Thank you. This is a huge. I mean . . . thank you.' She told me to go through my mail and call her if I had any queries and wanted me to start by next month. I told her I would be ready to do so. I would be studying and working at the museum around my favorite subject of all time, art. I was really psyched. I immediately thought of calling Arjun and telling him. We could still be friends and friends shared happy news! After all, he had been the one who had encouraged me to submit my application and the essay on Picasso. Before I could shun the thought, I dialled his number.

It rang. And rang. I hung up.

My excitement was truly lost. He didn't care anymore. Maybe

I was stupid for wanting to connect again. And he had truly moved on. Maybe exes could not be friends and I had made a terrible mistake. I didn't want my bubble to burst so easily, so I went for a walk by myself. I thought about calling my mother. But then, even though she would be happy for me, she would be a little melancholic that I would waste another six months doing something that was not organizing my wedding or finding a man to 'settle down' with. So I didn't want to hear her lecture or her wounded voice.

I thought of calling Aditi. But she was still on her honeymoon on an island where the connection was weak. But even then, I thought that our 'connection' might be weak from now on. She was married and needed to be a part of a new home. I couldn't be calling her in the middle of the night with exciting news or taking her out for coffee to Coffee De at seven in the morning.

Coffee De! That was it.

I headed straight towards it and sat down on my favorite red sofa with purple cushions and ordered myself a hazelnut café latte and a big chocolate brownie with whipped cream and nuts. I needed to celebrate myself.

Thankfully, at this time of the night on a weekday, there were no teenagers. I remembered that day, long time back. My God, it had been more than a year since when I decided to lose my virginity. I had changed so much. I could look back now and say, dude, what was I thinking? But I knew that if I hadn't made that decision that morning, I would never have opened up to the men that would follow in the last one year. There had been some incredible men. And I had formed some great friendships. Like the one who was walking in right now.

'Hi, Aniruddh,' I said. Aniruddh was the anchor in the reality show I had participated in.

For a second, he didn't recognize me. Till I said, 'From the reality show where I won the trekking contest? Remember?'

'Aah yes,' he said, standing near my couch hesitant.

'Wanna sit?' I asked.

'Are the tables reversed? Is this your casting couch?' he mocked.

I laughed, 'It could be!' What a serious change from what I was a year ago. I would never have thought of inviting a guy to sit with me. But the new me felt it was the right thing to do. He sat down.

'Hey, who won that show?' I asked.

'You didn't see it?'

I shook my head, 'I couldn't watch after I was eliminated.'

'Pooja. The web designer. From Hyderabad.'

'Oh ya. She was sweet.'

'Ya and Karan's mom, who came down for the second last episode, picked her from the final three.' Aniruddh laughed.

'What?' I asked, disbelievingly. 'The mother-in-law angle? He couldn't even pick his own bride?'

We both burst into giggles and I muttered, 'Thank God I was not there. I would have walked out on him and his mom.'

'But you made quite an impression on him and the girls,' he smirked.

My brownie came and he looked at me as if he had never seen a woman eating one all by herself. 'What? You've never seen a woman eating a brownie?' I asked.

'No, it's just that most women want to share a brownie or end up having a bite and saying they're full. Or they barf it out the next morning.'

'Ewww,' I said, with my mouth full of whipped cream. I handed him the spoon.

And he took a bite as well.

'Are we sharing?' he asked.

'No. I'm being gracious in offering you a bite since you were too *kanjoos* to order one for yourself!' I guffawed, and hit him lightly on the arm. Jesus! I was flirting. This was also a new thing in my life.

We laughed as we shared the brownie and we shared some more stories about the show and the girls in it. I told him the insider tale. I left out the part about the hot air balloon. It was fun to share nonsensical information about events in your life without having them analysed or judged.

'You read Mills and Boon?' he laughed again, feeling a little bit drunk after our fourth Irish coffee an hour and a half later.

'Oh, yes. I was a big closet fan. Amidst getting a graduate degree and being a topper, I would secretly read about men whisking the woman away into a faraway land!' I replied, a little tipsy myself. 'All the perfect romantic love seemed like a lot of work though. And very unrealistic!'

'Is "topper" a euphemism for the nefarious activities convent girls indulge in?' he winked, taking the conversation to another level.

'Shut up!' I laughed, feeling comfortable around him.

Suddenly I had another idea!

In my slightly drunken state, I leaned over to Aniruddh and whispered, 'Meet me in the bathroom in two minutes.'

He looked stunned. Elated. And then nodded in agreement.

I was unsure at first. And then I thought, 'Why not?' I didn't care anymore to take it to another level! I didn't need to prove anything to anyone.

I went into the bathroom and unlocked the door. Stood by the side of the wall. Two minutes later he entered. We stared at each other. Lust driven by danger. Promptly, he pounced on me, kissing me passionately. Wanting. Desiring. He unfastened the top two buttons of my shirt while I kissed him madly. He went down and sucked my nipples, cupping my breasts over my clothes. I scratched his back and he hoisted me up around his waist. Deep breathing. I liked dangerous sex. Oh God, how I loved it. I let my hands run across his tight ass. My thighs rested on his strong muscular legs. He lifted my skirt and stroked me tenderly at first, then built up the momentum. I felt my wetness building up. I moaned and he covered my mouth with his hands.

Our warm skin, throbbing with hot blood. Faint smell of Old

Spice. And sweat. He gasped as I ripped his shirt. Strong ripped body and hard, tight abs. He smiled. Not bothered. Fervent kissing. Necking. Sucking. Bodies burning with a hurried craze. Clothes half off. I stroked him softly. A gentle hesitancy creeping in. He nibbled on my ear and urged me on. I ran my fingers across his body, his hair, his hardness.

He sat down on the edge of the seat. I moved myself on top of him. Deliberate. Intoxicating. He held me tight against him. He was big, bigger than the others. Powerful. It felt like the first time. But better. Erotic. Assertive. Exceptional. He grunted as I entered him. Slowly at first and then faster. Harder. He cried out. He moved me. Short strokes. And then slow, longer ones. Silently. I felt invigorated. Sinuous. Warm juices mingling with each other. Raptures of delight. I began to feel a huge wave bubbling, bursting inside me. I sighed deeply. Breathless. Someone could hear us. He exhaled. And let go.

We finished and smiled. I quickly got off. Straightened my hair. Adjusted clothes. He left before me.

We had a smoke. Amused. Contented. 'That was refreshing!' he said, 'I've never done it in a public place before.'

I winked. Picked up my purse. Gave him a long kiss goodnight. And we both left. In separate directions.

Aniruddh was my first 'quickie'. And it felt good to see him go. I knew that we would be friends if we wanted to be, and more if we needed to be. But apart from that it felt good to be part of something that didn't need an explanation. I hadn't shared my life, my hopes and dreams or even the fact that I would be leaving for the US in a few weeks. I didn't need to. I didn't love him and he didn't love me. But we made love that I would remember forever.

Forty-one

Aaron had given me enough money for me to sit and do nothing for a whole month before I left for the States. That gave me just enough time after Aditi's wedding to decide if I wanted to start a new project or go back to being a translator. A part of me wanted to make some more money before I left, while another part wanted to enjoy my last few days in Mumbai.

My experience with reality TV had actually given me a boost in the entertainment industry. People had started calling me to do more shows but they were all in the same reality TV format or another one adapted from a Western formula. I wasn't interested. I had gone for a few casting auditions for ad films and had done a small campaign that gave me a little money. But I realized that wasn't really me. I wasn't interested in pursuing the limelight. I wanted to go for something far more interesting. I wanted to develop me.

Suddenly, one night while I was sitting and reading up on The Met, I remembered the dialogue I had with Arjun that night in Goa when he told me he was married. It was about tattoos. He had said it takes conviction more than courage to get one and that it wasn't about the pain. It was about if you believed in a permanent art symbol that described who you were. And till now, I didn't know who I was. I was a confused thirty-year-old virgin who went from believing in love to giving it up.

But now, I knew that I believed in *myself*. So I got up from the bed, wore my jeans and decided to walk down to the parlour and get myself a tattoo. It was as easy as that. I could hardly believe what I was doing. It was ten at night and my mind was telling me to wait till morning or figure out what I needed. But my heart, and I've always listened to my heart, said I needed to take a step that was bold and that defined me. And it had to be now, otherwise I would chicken out later.

I walked into 'Ink Station' which was always crowded, populated by teenagers. It was open till the late hours, probably expecting a half crazed woman to want something wild in the middle of the night. But tonight it was quiet. There was a woman and the owner who were sitting in a corner talking away and I suddenly felt as if I was intruding upon their private life. I quickly turned around, ready to leave, when the woman called out, 'Hey!'

I turned around and smiled, 'I'm sorry. I didn't want to intrude.' The woman got up and so did the man. The man moved towards the booth and the woman came up to me, 'Don't be funny. We run a business here!' she smiled. I smiled back. 'So how can I help you?'

'I wanted to get a tattoo, if it's not too much trouble.' She showed me a few designs from a book she had and then got me a cup of cappuccino and some cookies. We discussed what I should get. She started chatting with me about the man she was talking to and then got me to open up a little about my life. I told her I got the idea from an old boyfriend who had wanted a tattoo of Gaudi's sun a long time back.

And then I revealed myself to a total stranger. I told her who I was. Something no one ever knew and something I had kept hidden for a long time. I told her I was a woman who believed in Love. Not with one man. But with the concept that it existed, and that it was strong and powerful. I was a woman who believed in travelling the world and experiencing Love in its myriad ways. What I wanted from my life was a fusion of art, languages, men and the independence that defined Love. She got exactly what I was saying and gave me a tattoo on my wrist, a place where I could see it everyday and remember that I had come a long way. It was a painful experience that left me overjoyed and completely satisfied. Somewhat like my 'first time' with Arjun. Very symbolic and beautiful. I missed him and yet that night, I could happily let him go. I had changed. I had evolved. I knew that the tattoo symbolized *me*.

And that's how I landed myself with a tattoo that I thought I would never get. A piece of art that was truly me.

Forty-two

I was craving a hot cup of coffee again, like I had a year and a half ago. My God. I had really changed since that day.

I had been in New York for six months and had settled down in my new life really well. My job was keeping me busy and even though the pay was just enough to get me through, my research kept me alive. I had made friends and found new places to hang out in.

And then the connection that I had wanted for so long came. He emailed me to say he was in New York and he wanted to meet me. I had sat on my bed, in my studio apartment that overlooked a row of shops below. I had read the mail thrice. It said 'Hi. I'm in New York. I heard you are here too. Can we meet? I've missed you.' It was basic. I replied, and now was sitting at this coffee place instead of inviting him over to my place since I knew we weren't 'there'.

He was walking through the door of Bean, my favourite coffee joint in New York, right now. He looked just as bit handsome as when I had met him not so long ago, in that shack, with the sun against him and a bronzed body that made me know he would always be my 'Great Love'. I got up to kiss him on the cheek.

'Hi, Kaveri,' he said gently, as he kissed me and sat down. Arjun had matured. He had become a father and his gentle way showed. He seemed very different to me. Even though I had known this man better than anyone else, right now, I felt he was a complete stranger.

'Hi, Arjun. What can I order for you?' I asked, as I got up to go to the counter, suddenly all nervous and hesitant, as if I was a thirty-year-old virgin again!

'Nothing. Just sit. We'll order in a bit . . . How have you been?' he was being very tender. At that moment I felt my heart flood with emotions. There were so many memories that I choked. I had rehearsed for many months what I was going to say when we met, I had rewritten my speech about how he had let me down time and and how I had wasted so much of my time with him that my energy was sapped and I had to rebuild myself and that task at that time seemed impossible. I could really go on. But that speech was nowhere in my mind as he looked deep into my eyes as if he knew it all and was most apologetic. For several moments, there were no words between us. We both knew what our past was, and it was as if we were revisiting it looking at each other. As he held my hand over the table, I felt the same tingle return.

As I looked at him closely, I could see how he had greyed a little. His salt and pepper hair at the temples and a few wrinkles near his eyes made him more endearing. He had put on a few pounds around his waist, but he was still a Greek God to me.

'Let me show you something,' he said as he pulled up his sleeve and showed me his tattoo. Of a sun. Gaudi's Sun, which we had discussed on our date in Goa. 'I got it because it reminded me of you. I wanted something to remind me of you everyday, Kaveri.' Then he leaned forward and took my hand. 'I'm so sorry, Kaveri . . .'

I interrupted him because I didn't want our conversation to get emotional so fast, so I said, 'Arjun! Let's order coffee.' I motioned with my hand and my favourite waitress came to my table, even though it was a self-service. We ordered and she came back with steaming hot cappuccinos and muffins that Arjun had ordered. It was cold outside. Winter was harsh in this city. I could see outside the window that people were wearing their long black coats and designer boots while trying to brace themselves from the windchill factor. After living in this city for six months, I realized that most people in New York understood how to mesh fashion with comfort. They could run in six-inch heels while trying to catch a train with three shopping bags and a thin Chanel scarf to keep warm! Their basic colour was black and their basic dress size was 2. I soon learnt how to make myself a New Yorker so that I would fit right in. I had begun wearing heels, summer dresses and short skirts that were all a size 2. And now I was wearing a gorgeous white coat that I had newly purchased from Macy's. I stood up to take off my coat and Arjun noticed how thin I had become.

'You've lost weight!' he exclaimed, admiring my figure as I sat down in my dependable jaw-dropping black Herve Lager dress.

I smiled and said, 'Yes. Well actually, I've been craving home food and all this American junk doesn't suit my body.'

That wasn't the truth. Once I arrived in New York I had only eaten healthy and I had wanted to explore every bit of the city I could. So I walked everywhere. I would walk into streets that were lined with beautiful trees, lanes that lead to different neighbourhoods, stores that had never-ending floors, museums that were miles long and railway tracks that were artistically woven. I walked and walked till I got tired and would then sit in coffee shops that never closed. I would go back to my small studio apartment, that had the bare minimum furniture, just to take a hot shower and crash till I went walking again. And in between, I did my research and worked and learnt about art, people and cultures. My dream had actually come true. And in the midst of all this, was the man I had wanted back so long ago.

'I made a mistake, Kaveri. I made a terrible mistake,' he said after a long pause. I kept quiet. 'It wasn't working. It really never had been. I was too torn to do the right thing. I mean, I didn't want to hurt anyone and, in the process, I hurt everyone.'

I listened patiently. And he continued.

'Kaveri, I'm all done with the past now. And I'm sorry that

it took me so long. But it took this long for me to end everything. And I didn't want to come to you with half my life. I wanted to come to you to give my whole life. And I'm willing to do whatever you want.' He stopped to look at me in anticipation.

'What do you really want from me?' I asked gently, not knowing how I would react to my Great Love if he proposed.

'I really want you to come back with me.' He saw the question in my raised eyebrow and tried to explain. 'Kaveri, I made a terrible mistake by letting you go.' He paused and bit his lip. 'I made a mistake by marrying Maria. And a mistake in sleeping with her that night in Paris. But I don't regret having a child because I absolutely adore Anisha.' His face went soft when he spoke about his child. And I knew he wanted to bring her up since he took out his wallet to show me a picture of his child.

His daughter. He had a daughter. Some rational thoughts began to take over my suspended grey matter.

He continued, 'That's her name. Our daughter's,' he continued, since I wasn't speaking, 'I realized that I wasn't in love with my wife even before I met you. I had told you that . . . And it took this long for her to realize as well. I couldn't do it, Kaveri. I couldn't be a husband. I'm not the husband type. And that's why I guess when you asked me to leave my wife and think about marrying you, all the commitment talk made me run away.' He paused here and said, 'I want to be committed to you now, Kaveri. Even if it means I need to marry you, I'm okay about that now. But I can't lose you again. I only have one condition. That we have to live in Mumbai. My child is there and I can't be away from her. That's my only thing. And I'm begging you. Please just come back. You can do whatever you want. If you want, you can sit at home, or if you want, you can do research, or work at that agency. I can get you a job with my influence. And we'll stay wherever you want and you can do up the place whichever way you want. I'll give you all the money to live a luxurious life. We could start something new together.' He rambled on in the end and I let him. Then he took a deep breath and waited for me to speak. He had said his part.

That was it. My mind couldn't really grasp it though. Was that a proposal? Somehow I had kind of pictured it differently.

I looked at the muffin in front of me. It was gooey, hot, chocolatey with macadamia nuts. Just the type I liked. And I was so tempted to just pick up the fork and dig in. Stress had always made me eat. In moments of confusion and distress I had turned to chocolate. But in the last six months I had not been stressed. Even when I was out of money to buy food or when I had got lost wandering and it had become dark, or when my computer had crashed and parts of my research were lost. I had not felt anxious enough to reach for a muffin, or a brownie or a cupcake. I had finally got hold of my emotions long enough to separate stress from hunger. And that's how I had lost all this weight and was feeling great about myself. So why was I suddenly stressed and craving for this muffin in front of me?

I looked at him and said flatly, 'I don't get it.'

'What don't you get?' he said, now trying to convince me from another angle, 'We belong together. That's it. Remember how good we were together? Remember our weekend trips to Lonavala and Goa? That was who we were. And we'll have that back again.'

I remembered. They were nice until he had to make calls every morning and after dinner and text message during the day from everywhere, the beach, outside our hotel room, outside the disco.

'That could be us forever. We could be on a permanent vacation. WE would be living our dream of being together whenever we want, having mind-blowing sex . . .' Oh that was it. He had not been having sex. Or maybe not as good. 'Look. You complete me. I can't live without you. I need you to help me sort out my life, my house and my friends. You know everything better than I do. And we're great together. We have fun. Please say yes.' He finished. That was the end of his speech. And then he finished his latte and looked up at Becky to order another one. I sipped on mine.

I was playing back his words in my head and a host of visuals side by side of our past. And it all came rushing back. The evenings we had gone out to new places and the weekend trips we had taken out of town, the bike rides we had . . . From the hotel rooms across the Eastern Express highway to the dhabas dotted along Maharashtra, from the endless nights on Bandra Sea link to early mornings in the Sahayadris. We had had a good time. But it was in the past. And really I hadn't heard a thing about what I wanted. It was all about him. That I could fulfill his life, he would have this, and he would get that and that I complete 'him'.

And then it hit me. This was what I had wanted for a long time. But I did not want it anymore. All these images instead of being liberating, happy and loving were seeming claustrophobic, demanding and weary.

'Arjun, let me show you something.' I showed him my tattoo. The tattoo of Gaudi's Sun. Yes, that's what I had got. Gaudi's Sun. Alongside a heart and my name in Chinese, the one language I didn't know yet. It was a tattoo made like a bracelet around my wrist symbolizing art, language and passion, the three things that signified my life. As opposed to Love, Sex and Marriage that signified it two years earlier.

He looked at it completely shocked. But I continued to talk, 'I know what you're thinking. You're thinking where did I find the courage to get a tattoo.'

He interrupted me and said, 'No! I'm thinking we've got the same tattoo, Kaveri. It means we're connected. WE still love each other!'

I smiled and tried to exlplain, 'No, Arjun. It means that we were connected. You were the Great Love of my life. But Love is far more important than the person. Hence the heart. I got it because I would remember you not as a person but as a symbol of what love should be. I look at the tattoo and remember who *I* can be. I'm a person who loves art, who loves independence, who believes in breaking the rules of the game, just like Gaudi did. You showed me that. Before I lost myself. But finally, I've got it back.'

He looked surprised. He still didn't get it. So I had to explain. I took his hand very tenderly and tried hard to deliver my new speech. 'Arjun, you'll always be the love of my life. I'll always cherish what I had with you. And I'm so glad that I lost my virginity to you. Because that makes us even more special. But us being together does not make sense. For the simple reason that . . . I'm not in love with you anymore. That's not what I want anymore.'

'But Kaveri, the tattoos . . . we're connected . . . can't you see that?' he asked one last time.

'Yes, darling. I do see it. We'll always be connected. But we don't need to be married to be so.' I heard myself saying things that I would never have imagined. 'You might have changed to what I wanted a year ago. But I've changed from that to a whole new person.'

'But I can change to what you want now.' He desperately pleaded.

'Arjun, we're different people now. You have a life in Mumbai. I have a life in New York. And I love my life here. I don't want to compromise. And that might mean I sound like a bitch to you, but it's not that. I don't want that life that we spoke about anymore. I don't want to leave New York. For you or anyone.'

'But . . .' He was trying to hold on to a concept I had let go of. Once upon a time, I had told Aditi I wanted him back on my terms. And here he was, back on my terms, and I didn't want him. The irony of the situation wasn't lost on me. And I felt incredibly bad about asking the Universe to give him back to me when I knew I didn't want him at all.

'Listen. First of all, you don't listen! You have always taken charge and presumed what we should do. And I've let you because it felt nice to have someone lead the way. But I've thought about what I've wanted to do and have been doing it for so long now that I can't have someone else lead the way.' I paused to take a breath. Explaining things to a man was so difficult. Women would have got it so easily.

Arjun was flabbergasted. He was hurt, I could see. He had thought he would come and whisk me away to a life that I had wanted for so long.

'Kaveri, I promised you I would come back to you and now you're telling me you don't want me? That bloody sucks!' he said exasperated.

'I've moved on,' I said softly.

'Ya I heard that part,' he said, looking away in anger.

I wanted to say more, that what we had was nice but it was in the past. And it was over. And I didn't need him anymore. Emotionally, financially, physically, spiritually—I didn't need him anymore. But I heard myself saying, 'I hope you are able to find someone who does need you and, more importantly, I hope you are able to realize that you really don't need anyone to complete you. Our relationship never belonged in the real world . . . it belonged in the shadows of the soul. I want to thank you for all that you did for me . . .' I said with a pause, weighing every word so as not to offend him. 'I want you to know that I truly loved you. But I want you to *let go*. And be happy. For me. And for yourself.'

The fact was that I would always love Arjun. Yes I would. But I knew I could never live with him. I knew what I did not want. I did not want to be a stepmother. When I had to be maternal, it would have to be with my own child. And I didn't want to go back to Mumbai. I was done with that city for now. I wanted to be here, in a new city, exploring a new land, experiencing new seasons, living independently, even if it meant that I would be alone and, maybe, lonely. I wanted all that and more for myself. Because I was no longer scared. I believed in myself.

I heard myself say in conclusion, 'We will always be special for each other. Let me be a good memory for you. Let that tattoo inspire you to follow your heart always and not make any more terrible mistakes.' And then I said the words that I thought I would never say to Arjun, 'Goodbye, my love.' He was stunned.

Arjun and I parted sweetly that night. He was half expecting me to call him back to my place for a nightcap one last time. But I didn't. I didn't want a sleazy last image of my Great Love. And I knew that the different men in my life were all a little bit of my Great Love. I knew that no man could ever be just that. I wasn't disillusioned. I was just more confident about Love as a whole. Because I knew that a greater love lay in me.

But it took some time for Arjun to realize this. He emailed me a few times to try and convince me again. But I didn't reply. I had finished saying what I needed to and moved on. I understood myself now. I might be a nice person, but I might not necessarily do nice things. And that doesn't make me a rotten person. Just a vulnerable one looking out for myself.

Forty-three

It was my birthday again. I had turned thirty-two today. And I was holding a cup of coffee in my hand. Alone. And I wasn't at Coffee De. I was looking at Antoni Gaudi's Sun. I don't know how and why I needed to see it, but I did. And the culmination of all my research and my memories had led me to this point.

I had lost and found myself again in New York over the last year. If it was the city that never sleeps, *I* never slept as well. I lived in a noisy neighbourhood and, while it kept me awake most of the nights, it kept my mind active as well. I was a woman on a mission. I wanted to do as much as I could before my birthday. And I did.

I saw offbeat films at Greenwich Village. I went to art fairs, museums, photography exhibitions and comedy clubs. I went alone and I went with friends. I walked across the Brooklyn Bridge several times. From Chinatown to the Empire State Building, from Jewish Harlem to Ellis Island, from Union Square to Central Park, I walked everywhere and I saw everything. I even tried my luck at ice skating, heard baroque performances in parks, and a Mozart opera in a concert hall. I did it all. I spent a lot of time at Times Square, cafés, cathedrals, pubs, restaurants, parks, and the library. I researched my work and found out what I should do with my life. I went with a friend for a Julliard concert, a few Broadway plays and when no one would go with me, I went alone to the Guggenheim, walked on the shores of

Coney Island, sat at Union Square and tasted fresh fruit at sunrise at Green Market. I spent a day at the Brooklyn botanical garden and haggled at the Sixth Avenue antiques market. And when I finally did not want to see anymore, I knew what I had to do.

And that is why I was here, in Barcelona. Alone. On my birthday. I had come here two days before my birthday because this was what I wanted as the last stop before I went home. I needed to know that I could be anywhere in the world on my birthday and be happy with being just by myself. Not with a man, not with Aditi, not with my parents. Just alone. And I was. I really was. But a week ago I had begun to think of all my relationships. And, yes, I had a few more in New York. They were all friends 'with benefits'. I had begun to understand men finally. And I realized that of all the men I knew, the most significant one would always be Arjun. And I still loved him. It was hard for me to acknowledge it a week ago but I had. It wasn't as if I wanted him back or I was planning to ask for his forgiveness. I wasn't *in love* with him. I was just happy to know that I could still love someone who had hurt me so much. It was just a cathartic moment for me to realize that I could now have a real relationship. And it was because of that moment that I decided to fly to Barcelona and see, in person, Gaudi's Sun that Arjun had tattooed on his arm for me.

I fell in love with Barcelona the moment I stepped off the plane. The city completely charmed me with its rich culture, tradition and architecture. And I knew I could live here for another year exploring its rich wonders and being further enhanced in my research of art. But I knew that I could not research all my life. I had to get back. I had made a plan to combine art with technology and start a business back in Mumbai. I needed to get back to the life that I had been running away from.

My parents had been calling and chatting with me regularly, and were finally proud of what I was doing. It was educational and respectable! But they missed me and wanted me to be close by. And, as a single child, an only daughter, I felt it was my duty to do so. So I had booked my ticket back in a week's time. By that time, I would have explored as much of this city that would fill my heart and I could always come back again for it to fill my soul.

My coffee had gone cold. I had been sitting in Park Guell for many hours, not wanting to move, feeling a sense of relief, love and power all at once. It started becoming dark. Reluctantly I stood up and started walking towards the exit to go home. Suddenly, I saw this woman sitting in a corner with some eclectic objects next to her. It was a force deep within that drew me to her. I walked up to her and gestured to ask what she was doing. She replied, 'You are from India!'

I was taken aback. I hadn't been to India for almost a year and nowhere in my clothes or personal belongings did it say I was from India, so how did she know.

'How do you know?' I asked in Spanish.

'I read you face,' she said in broken English. I was intrigued. Not one to believe in the hocus-pocus that astrology, numerology, tarot, etc. claimed to be, I could not help wonder if she could predict my future. Why is it that even if you never want to know about this occult science, someone, somewhere, draws you in.

'I read your cards.' The woman said, now in Spanish. And I surrendered to the mysticism that was about to be unfolded. She looked like a gypsy. She had these extremely dog-eared, faded cards that looked nothing like the tarot cards from cool boxes sold in bookstores. She took them out and asked me to pick a few. She didn't ask for my name, my age, or anything. She just pondered over them for some time and spoke in halted sentences. 'You look for love.'

Well, yes, I thought, but so do most people.

'You found love once, but you lost him. He was not right. You will find love again.' Predictable, but promising.

'You will find love in Barcelona,' she continued to stare at my face while holding my hand.

I kept quiet. That did not make any sense at all! I was leaving in a week. And knowing my nature, I would never give my heart to someone so quickly. But I smiled and said, 'Will he be a prince, with lots of money?'

She dismissed my question and continued, 'You will marry him. And you will take him back to India. Because it is through you that he can go back home. And it is through him that you will find true love.'

'True Love?' I asked. 'What is that?' I asked, with great sincerity.

'It is something that blows your mind away. And lets your heart make all the wrong decisions!' she said prophetically and laughed knowingly.

'Oh!' I said with intent, 'Ya, I've already had that. Don't worry. I'll be aware of it the next time it happens.' I said with a wink.

She did not smile. She only said, 'Love never happens just once. It happens many times. The real relationship you will ever have . . . that is called true love . . . is the one you already have with yourself. The other love with men . . . that just makes you feel better in the day!' She explained in broken English.

That did not make sense. But I smiled and gave her the money she wanted and walked away. I would know what it meant very soon.

Forty-four

I knew I should not have listened to all that mumbo jumbo because, for the rest of the evening in my hotel, it was playing in my head. So I decided to take myself out for a birthday drink and landed up at Las Ramblas. I walked the street where there were street musicians, live mimes, cartoon sketch artists, florists, cafés, restaurants and a vibe that made me feel alive and happy suddenly. I stopped to hear a band play an old song, bought myself a single long red rose and headed to a pub that overlooked the waterfront. I felt completely kicked. I put my rose on the table and tied my hair into a ponytail. It was quite warm for an April night and I desperately needed a glass of wine. The waiter came up to me and I ordered a whole bottle for myself.

'Will the gentleman be joining you?' he asked. I looked confused.

'The one who has given you this beautiful flower?' he stated.

I laughed and said, 'No, no, I just got it for myself since it's my birthday and . . . uh, never mind!'

'Oh, then happy birthday,' he said, and went away in a hurry. I thought that was rude. But he quickly came back with a bottle of wine and said, 'On the house. Happy birthday!'

That made my day. Here was a total stranger who didn't owe me anything, and he just made me feel that I was special. Later on, after a few hours had passed and I had almost finished my bottle of wine and the restaurant seemed more deserted, the waiter came to me and asked, 'Another bottle, senora?'

'Senorita,' I corrected, very tipsy, cheery, 'I'm still unmarried. And according to a woman in a park, I should be with a prince!'

'Well, that makes me even more happy,' he flirted.

'No more wine, thank you, just the bill,' I said, and looked away towards the road where there were a bunch of college kids singing and teasing each other as they passed the window. He went away and got me a small slice of cake.

'Oh, thank you so much!' I exclaimed, with sheer delight. 'That was very sweet of you.'

'I am also from India,' he said to my surprise.

I looked flabbergasted, 'How did you know I was from India?'

'It is the colour of your eyes,' he explained. 'They say a lot. They say that you belong to an exotic country and it can only be India. And also, you have the most beautiful laugh I've ever heard in a woman.'

Then suddenly, I became a little defensive. After all, I was drunk. And I was alone in this new country and this man seemed to know too many things about me. 'Look,' I said a little abruptly, 'I'm not interested . . . I just wanted to have dinner. So I'm sorry if I gave you the wrong impression or anything.' I started trying to give him an explanation while finding money in my wallet.

'Senorita, please don't be offended. I will go away right now and never bother you again if you say so.' And then he looked at me with wide eyes and said, 'But please don't say so!' and laughed.

I smiled. He was so charming. He was a young boy who could not have been more than twenty-five years old. But he had shoulder length dark curly hair that he tied in a low ponytail and a trimmed French beard that made his blue eyes sparkle. As I noticed him with greater attention, I saw that he had a slim body that was not too muscular. Fit. Sinewy. Strong. His arm had some bruises that had healed and faded. He was unconventionally good looking. He wore distressed jeans and a white Armani shirt. And his smell? Polo. Ralph Lauren. Fresh. Attractive. Young. So desirable.

A little voice in my head said, 'It's okay if you want to be with someone. Stop judging people. And they won't judge you.'

'Well, what's your name?' I asked a little flirtatiously.

'Ray,' he said, while sitting down at the table next to me.

'Well Ray, do you flirt with all your customers or is it a promotional policy from the management?' I asked.

'Oh! Flirt? This is not flirting. This is just conversation. You should see me flirt!' he exclaimed with a smile.

I laughed as he poured some more wine into my glass.

'Okay, show me!' I said daringly. I had begun to like this boy. He then rose and went to the back of the restaurant from where he brought out a guitar. He came back and sat at my table and began to sing! This boy was serenading me in a restaurant with his deep, beautiful voice in a language that was as rich as the dark chocolate cake in front of me.

When he finished, a few people clapped along with me and he got up and bowed to the other tables. He turned to me and said, 'Well, does that impress you enough to go out with me?'

I shrug my shoulders and said, 'Eh, not too impressed!'

He then got down on one knee, and for a moment I was stunned. I had a déjà vu. I had once told Arjun that I wanted to be proposed to on bended knees, like the Mills and Boon stories I had read, in an exotic location in front of the whole world. And here I was, getting that from a complete stranger. So what if it wasn't for marriage. It meant something larger in my head.

Instantly, I panicked and got up. I mumbled an apology and ran from that restaurant. My head was filled with thoughts about how I didn't want to be led astray by another man and how I didn't want to give out any more vibes that I'm readily available again for marriage.

Forty-five

The next morning I woke up feeling guilty for my rudeness. So instead of walking around to explore more of Antoni Gaudí's works or the city itself, I found myself pulled back to that little restaurant. I wanted to see that waiter again. It wasn't because I was attracted to him, honestly we would have nothing in common, it was because I wanted to tell him I was sorry for my dismissive behaviour the previous night. But he was nowhere to be found.

I went up to the manager who was standing at the front of the restaurant writing something on a piece of paper and asked him, 'Excuse me.'

He looked up and said, 'Si?'

I had forgotten his name so I was struggling with the words, 'This might seem like a weird question ... but do you know where that waiter from last night is? He is skinny, dark hair, cute ...'

'Ahh Ray. Yes, he has gone to do his day job.'

'His day job?'

'Yes, he only works at nights here. Evening shift, you know.'

'Okay,' I tried to make sense of this and what was even more puzzling was why I wanted to pursue this.

'He is a tour guide for Barcelona buses.'

I wanted to apologize, so I went off to find the tour buses and say goodbye. When I got to the Barcelona tour bus origin, I could see he was hanging around with a few other bus operators smoking a cigarette. He didn't look that skinny today. He looked fresh, as if his face had been scrubbed and his hair caught the sunlight and shone. He didn't seem that old, but his self assurance could be seen in his confident body language. He saw me from a distance and started walking towards me. He flicked his cigarette into the waterfront as he approached me.

'Hola, Senorita,' he said smiling, but a little distant.

'Hola, Ray,' I said.

We stood there in silence. Obviously it was my turn to speak and I didn't know what to say.

'Why are you here?' he asked, before I could speak. I took a moment to answer. He tilted his head to one side and I could see how gorgeous he was. His mop of shiny hair left loose today and those piercing blue eyes made me feel inadequate and it was strange. I was an independent, strong woman.

'I wanted to apologize for my behaviour yesterday. I am generally not like that. I have become very guarded . . . Can we start over?' I trailed off, and then I put my hand out and said, 'I'm Kaveri.'

He kept quiet and then took his hand out and said, 'Hi, I'm Ray.'

'I know,' I said. 'You told me last night.'

'Yes. But I wanted to make a new impression. I wanted to start afresh, Kaveri.' He said my name with a roll in the 'r' and I liked it. So I smiled.

'You smile. Will you run away again? Because yesterday you were smiling and then you ran away. I didn't know I sang that badly!' he looked shocked and offended.

'No, no, Ray,' I said, and gently put my hand on his arm. 'You sing beautifully. In fact, you are the most beautiful singer I know.'

'In looks?' he teased. I blushed. What was happening to me?

'That too.' I said, and pulled my hand away from him.

He caught it and held it gently. We started walking towards the sea front. This was so new and yet felt so familiar to me.

This warm assurance. The soft hand. The comfortable silence. I forgot he was a stranger. I forgot he was younger. Way younger. I forgot he was a waiter and a bus driver. I forgot, because he seemed to be so much more. From so much planning in my life I had come upon this moment where, for the first time, I didn't know what would happen or how I would react. And then I thought about it. I suppressed my heart and thought about it.

I let go of those stupid notions in my head of an ideal man. The perfect love. So what if he wasn't an intellectual who could teach me art. So what if he wasn't brown skinned and from my motherland and who understood my customs. So what if he wasn't tall, dark and handsome like a model. So what if he was younger. These things did not seem to matter right now.

'Did I tell you I was named because my mother saw a ray of light the first thing she opened her eyes after she delivered me?' he said looking down at me. He was almost my height. But I rested my head on his shoulder and it seemed he was taller.

I had always gone with my heart instead of my head. I had loved Arjun with all my heart and had lost my head. And I had loved Karan and Aaron with my heart to blur out my head. But for the first time my head and my heart were telling me that this was the right thing. 'You know, Ray,' I said, feeling very romantic, 'I think I want to know more about you.'

'Whatever you want, my senorita,' he said, while kissing my hand and walking.

And somewhere right then, I knew that there was a prophecy that was beckoning, and a plane ticket I needed to reschedule.

But at the time, all I said was, 'Can I buy you a cup of coffee, Ray?'

Acknowledgements

I thought I'd be giving an Oscar speech one day and start by saying ,'I'd like to thank God and my parents . . . blah blah blah.' But since that hasn't happened so far and my parents have got tired of waiting, I thought I should add a note to them:

Thanks, Mom and Dad, for being my unending support (and ATM), way past my formative years. I love you both dearly.

And also . . .

Sunaman—Thanks for letting me take my time to write a book that I promised I would ten years ago and for letting me be who I am for the entire time together.

Dadu—Thanks for knowing I can write and encouraging me from far.

Ariaana—My sweetest treasure. You've given me a new way of looking at life. I love you the most in the whole world! I attempt to make you proud of me everyday and will do so till I die.

Ani—I know we've always dreamt of being famous together, but bro, I'm ahead of you! Love you always.

Parikshit—We don't need the words. I'm grateful to God for giving me that one studio where you walked into my life . . .

Bharati—Thanks for all the magical 'getaways' that helped me write this book. You inspire me to be a better writer, a stronger person and a greater human being. Without you, this book would not have taken shape. I'll love you always, with all my heart.

Vaishali—I'm so happy that my first manuscript landed in your lap. You're more than a great editor, you're a lovely friend.

My in-laws and Arindam—You're the best family a girl could have. The fact that you're so proud of me at all the Delhi parties gives a huge boost to my ego! Thank you.

Neha—You're the best sister in the world. Truly. Honestly.

To everyone who asked me the question, 'What are you doing with your life nowadays?' And to which I replied, 'I'm writing a book.' I'd like to say thanks for the knowing smile. It encouraged me further.